Twell and the Uprising
The Como Chronicles, Book 3

Kate O'Leary

F&I

Published by
Fire and Ice
A Young Adult Imprint of Melange Books, LLC
White Bear Lake, MN 55110
www.fireandiceya.com

ISBN: 978-1-68046-449-8

Cover Design by Caroline Andrus

To Jon, for loving me unconditionally and believing in me when I don't. You are my everything.

Why does the truth enrage them so?
They'd spill our blood so we'll never know.
Why must we fight for our own free will?
To protect their lies, they're so willing to kill.
When will the violence ever end?
Rage and revenge play over again.
How can I live if I just bend?
If I don't try, it will never end.
When will we ever truly be free?
I can't rest now...it's up to me.

Chapter One

They emerged from the dark of the room like ghosts, their glassy black eyes staring soullessly down at me before two of them seized my head in their thin, bony hands. My mind chugged sluggishly, paralysed with panic in an unfamiliar atmosphere. I could not focus, adrenalin crashing over me like a wave as my mind became saturated from the unfamiliar thickness of heavy humid air. A high and ragged gasping sound echoed around the room, and I knew whatever was coming could not be good. Realisation hit me like a wall of stone, terror making me tremble even before they inserted one of their weapons into the base of my skull.

Click

White-hot fire seared through my brain, jolting my bones against the cold hard metal of the table. A high-pitched scream ripped from my lungs as the stench of burning hair and flesh permeated the air, horror shocking every cell in my body as a deafening ringing filled my ears. My body arched and jolted, my head staying behind as their hands gripped my skull like iron claws. I twisted and thrashed, as I struggled to get away from the pressure building up in my brain. The ringing became a roar, pressing against my brain like a vice, as it swelled against my skull. The metallic smell of blood tinged the air as it trickled from my nose to my lips and filled my mouth, tangy and thick. Through murky vision I saw them smiling over me, their thin mouths splitting open to reveal sharp gleaming teeth. It was too much for my spirit to bear, and a final strangled cry emerged from my chest to fill the darkened room. Silence bore down on me; the isolating feeling of hopelessness crushing my soul before the darkness finally swooped over me, taking me to a blessed temporary escape.

I've experienced all types of pain in my one hundred and eighty-eight moons on Como. The pain that comes from a physical accident like a bruise, a cut, or scrape. Fleeting pain that heals with time. I've suffered more extreme pain, from another injuring me deliberately. Broken ribs and loss of blood, accompanied by the fear of dying.

I've known the hurt of unrequited feelings, and later, the agony of realizing my own people were against me and I against them. The feeling of isolation was a wound in itself.

But the most heartbreaking pain I've ever felt was the sensation of hurting the ones I love. The look on their faces, the betrayal in their eyes... pure agony stabbing through me like a blade, clutching at my stomach like iron hands. That hurt lingered on, seeping into my nightmares, and making me feel physically ill.

But still, I had not yet experienced the worst pain of all. The kind produced from being tortured physically and mentally until I could endure no more—until I truly wanted to die.

I woke slowly, like one does when they don't want to wake up. For a brief moment, I forgot what my reason was, in that tiny fraction of time when one is not fully aware, and feels no threat or fear of anything.

Then the comprehension of my situation hit me, the harsh blow of reality worse than the dull heavy ache at the base of my skull.

The room was hot, like nothing I'd ever experienced. Sweat plastered my clothes to my clammy skin, and my matted hair to my scalp. It cloyed in my chest, and I realised the rasping sound filling the small cell was the air squeezing in panicky short breaths from my lungs.

The metal of the table felt hard under my spine while thick hard cuffs pinioned my wrists and ankles firmly to its surface. Slowly, my bleary gaze travelled around the cell. The room was made of a dark grey substance I couldn't identify. It looked like rock, yet held the sheen of metal, or polished stone. The ceiling was of the same material, but I could faintly see the outline of large round lights, which were not currently in use. The air smelled stale, like it had been hanging around in this room for too long, and been used by too many prisoners before me.

Looking past my bare feet was a long window. Dark and yawning for now, I suspected it was hiding whoever was observing me from the other side.

Gingerly I flexed my fingers, and exhaled in relief as they uncurled at my command. My wrists were still cuffed to a short lead on each side of the bench upon which I lay. I raised my feet and found I was no longer strapped to the table by my ankles, as I had been when they shot the device into my brain.

Panic broke fresh sweat over my skin as I remembered there was something unknown inside me, and that it could definitely do something to me of which I wasn't yet aware. Raising my head an inch, it felt as though I was trying to drag it up through wet sand.

As I moaned with the effort, the lights above me snapped to life. The light illuminated the three Abwarzians looking down on me, and fell across my body, exposing me to their cold gaze. I froze, willing them not see me if I remained absolutely still. But my heart beat so audibly against my chest it gave me away.

"There is water, beside you," the Abwarzian in the middle said in perfect Comian.

I blinked in surprise. I hadn't expected them to know my language. Maybe that was naïve considering my guardian, Shay, was proficient in several world languages, but it was still a shock.

He was tall for an Abwarzian, taller than the others, and broader, as though he had trained for a long time to build such a physique. His face formed from hard angles, and his night black hair was slicked back in a way that emphasised the harshness of his features. Black eyes glimmered as they observed me coldly, with no white of the eye like I possessed around my dilated purple irises.

A raging thirst lit like a fire in my throat, burning with urgency as I tilted my head-on instinct. A dull heavy sensation throbbed at the base of my skull again, and I winced as I tried to raise my head higher. A thin metal vial perched on the table beside me. Water. I was so thirsty I could smell it. I yearned to reach for it, but I remained immobile. It had to be a trick. Or poison.

"It's only water." The man sneered as if he had probed into my thoughts. "It will not taste quite up to your Comian standards of course, but it will keep you alive…for now."

My eyes flicked back to his. I believed him on both counts yet I still didn't dare to move. If I did it would feel like I was complying, or obeying. I planned to do neither.

"If you don't drink, I will be forced to hydrate you by other means," the man said bluntly. "Do not make this worse for yourself by inconveniencing me."

I gulped, which was difficult given the scratchiness of my parched throat. There was something terrifying about the cultured yet undefinable control in his tone. The others, one female and another male, remained silent, observing me with keen dark eyes like I was a foreign specimen. Which I was. Perhaps they'd never seen a Comian before. Still, I didn't know what they were waiting for me to do…or what they would do to me.

"Drink," the man commanded, bringing my attention sharply back to the present.

Against my will, my desperation for water won out. The room tipped, waves of pain thudding against my brain as I slowly lifted myself up. I cried out as my vision swam, gripping the side of the table as I desperately sought gravity.

The cuffs on my wrists kept me from falling, pulling my arms slightly back as I regained my balance. My army uniform gone, I noticed I was wearing a pale grey smock, like a hospital garment that tied at the waist. My boots were gone too, and I felt uncomfortably underdressed and unarmed as my bare feet found the warm floor of the cell.

I remained still, staring at the ground while my heart clattered away in my chest. Once the floor stopped moving I raised my head to glare at the Abwarzians. The faces of the silent two were lit up with sadistic expectation, but the leader's expression remained impassive, giving nothing away.

I glanced at the vial. Water brimmed to the top, beckoning every cell in my body with the promise of relief. Unable to resist, I stretched my right hand toward the vial. It stopped short, a hair's space from the water, at the end of the lead. I strained my fingertips forward, my arm shaking with the effort, but I could not get closer. Just within my reach, yet entirely beyond my grasp.

In consternation, I switched my gaze back to the Abwarzians' leader.

"Go on." A cold smile twisted his mouth upwards. "Take the water."

The volume startled me, reverberating around the small bare room. I didn't know if it was fear shaking my limbs, or anger.

The man's lips pressed into a hard line while his eyes flashed in warning.

"Then you will learn to obey."

The threat in his tone was undeniable as he turned to the female Abwarzian, giving a curt nod of his head.

Smiling in response she turned back to look at me, her expression morphed to one of such eager anticipation it froze the blood in my veins.

Moving her hand over something unseen in front of her there was only a heart beats delay before I arced back on the bed, my head filling with agony so consuming I felt I'd explode. Clutching the base of my skull in terror my fingers scrabbled at my flesh, trying to discover the source of the agony. Yet I couldn't seem to relieve the sensation as it burned hotter through my brain. Losing all sense of myself I fought wildly against my restraints, but the blinding pain stabbed my brain with such intensity it knocked me back onto the table.

My desperate screams bounced off the walls of the cell as the pain burned hotter than fire, until I could bear no more. My body collapsed onto the table in defeat, shuddering involuntarily as my cries exhausted to a small pitiful wail. Just as quick as it had come on, the pain stopped.

In that moment, I felt such hatred toward them, any compassion I'd ever felt for their race died a quick and violent death.

My body exhausted of any strength left; it was all I could do to raise my eyes and glare at them.

The leader gazed back, his features twisting smugly. He'd won this round.

"Do you feel like a drink now?" he suggested as though I were a guest being offered refreshment, and not a prisoner he'd just tortured.

Traitorous tears ran warmly down my cheeks as my courage slunk off the table and slithered away into a shadowy corner of the room. The stupidity of the situation I'd put myself in hit me so hard it was a good thing I was lying down.

"Drink." The leader's eyes glinted with promise of more torture to come if I disobeyed again.

I didn't bother to sit up, I didn't have the energy to do that as well as muster my powers. Afraid they'd fried my brain and destroyed my abilities, I gasped with the effort of concentrating through my distress. But slowly, shakily, the vial lifted off the table at my will.

The side kick Abwarzians gasped, the first time they'd made a noise. Their eyes shone with excitement as they looked at me in a new way. Like I was the answer to a problem they hadn't been able to solve. Until now.

I refused to look at the leader as the vial wobbled uncertainly toward my mouth. Without even smelling it for poison, I tipped it against my mouth and drank greedily. Not sweet like Comian water, it tasted bitter, and slightly off somehow, not quite quenching my thirst.

"Unsatisfying, isn't it," the leader commented as I pulled a face. "A travesty your world has forced us to endure for decades of course." The resentment in his voice was palpable, and I raised my head just enough to give him a filthy look.

"Where's Shay," I rasped, wishing there was more water. My throat still burned.

"She is alive and, well…not so well." The man smirked as he watched me carefully.

My anger reviving me, I struggled to sit up. Leaning toward the spectators as far as my tethering would allow, I wondered how I must appear to them. My hair fell in thick sticky tangles around my face, and my skin was damp with my sweat. My aubergine-colored eyes brimmed with rage, and I probably looked as primitive as they believed we were.

"Take me to her and I'll show you what you want to see," I offered as I looked the leader in the eye.

"Trying to negotiate with us again, Comian?" His sharp teeth reappeared in a sickening grin. "Have you forgotten already what happens when you try to negotiate with us? Shall I remind you once more?"

Biting my lip hard to contain my hysteria, I tasted blood as my teeth pierced through the skin.

"If you want your guardian to live, you will do exactly as I tell you."

I noticed he didn't say 'If *you* want to live.' Although it was the price I'd been willing to pay when I allowed the soldiers to take me, his words still had a physical effect. Fear stung my heart as every muscle in my body tensed in dread.

"Silence!" he barked. "You may rest, for now."

One only needed rest in order to regain strength. I shivered, the implications of his words clear in this ice-cold tone.

The light switched off, plunging me back into darkness. I held my breath. Were they still watching? Waiting to see if I'd try and escape? Silence filled my ears but I sensed they were still there, watching me from behind the safety of the glass.

The door to my cell slid open, my heart lurching at the sound. Through the gloom, I peered at a small sallow old man, his expression wary as he entered. Right behind him was the young female officer who'd triggered the pain in my head. I fought the urge to shrink back, as they moved toward me, the urge to flee redundant while I was still chained to the bench.

The old man's eyes were watery with age, and fatigue was etched all over his papery skin. Yet his expression as his gaze met mine was inquisitive.

There was no fear in the woman's expression. Her eyes were bright, but not with health. They burned with such viciousness my stomach cramped in trepidation. I knew she was enjoying my fear as I squirmed under her callous gaze.

Roughly taking hold of my ankles she re-anchored them to the bench. I was too scared to even struggle as she pulled the restraints tight against my flesh.

The ceiling opened and I stared in horror as a machine of some sort dropped down, just above the level of the bench. Despite my exhaustion, fear rolled over me in fresh waves as the woman seized my arm and placed it inside a long tube in the middle of the device.

I felt a prick as something sharp inserted into my arm, followed by the cool sensation of liquid trickling into my veins. My heart thrummed in time to the machine, panic threatening to overtake me. But my arm held fast in the device, pinching the needle into my skin as I tried to pull my arm free.

The old man glanced nervously toward the window before he bent over me. "Only wa…ter…keep… alive," he muttered in soft, stumbling Comian.

My eyes met his with surprise. Did they all speak our language? His expression was almost apologetic as the woman turned on him with a face of fury. Her words were clipped and brittle as she gave him an angry push toward the door, and he staggered back, his own expression suddenly fearful.

When she turned back to me I saw in an instant she wasn't seeing me as another human, but as a threat that needed to be extinguished. Her narrowed eyes pierced mine with hatred, and although she only looked a few years older than me, she clearly believed the propaganda the Abwarzians were fed about our people.

Abruptly she turned and marched out of the room, the door closing firmly behind her.

I was alone again, the moan of the machine slightly overpowering the sound of my rapid breathing.

What had the young woman been taught to make her delight in my fear and pain? Knowing what they'd done to our people had made me want to go to war, but if I were in her position, with a prisoner at my mercy, would I be as capable of such hatred, or of physically hurting someone?

Of course you could, Twell. Remember Raze? A nasty little voice piped up in the back of my mind.

"That's different!" I protested. "I was protecting myself, not torturing anyone!"

And yet you took a life to save your own.

Self-defence! I argued weakly to myself.

Violence to end violence…

Even my conscience had turned on me in this room, and I'd never felt more alone. No one knew where I was. My craft had been brought here with me, and there was no reason for the Governing Body to assume I was still alive. Abwazians were not known to take prisoners.

What have I done?

My last moments before leaving Como flooded my memory with sickening clarity, playing over and over in my mind in a revolving montage of horror. Maza trying to bury me and my ideas alive, my friends coming to my rescue...kissing Avin. My heart squeezed accusingly inside of my ribs. I'd kissed him, and then I'd run. Or flown, to be literal. Flown as far away as I could possibly go in the universe. I'd hurt him, there was no doubt. But it was not his pain I had run from...it was from Jonaz's.

An image of Jonaz pressed upon my mind in a sudden assault. I yearned for the safety of his arms. I longed for the comfort of his touch. I knew he'd never want to touch me again after the way I'd left him. I thought about how he'd react when they told him I was dead. I wondered if he'd still care as much as he would have before I'd betrayed him.

The thought of his pain shattered the last of my courage into fragments, and a small lone sob escaped me. I wanted to wrap my arms around myself, curl into a ball and hide away from this nightmare. But the restraints kept me exposed and vulnerable, and there was nowhere to hide.

Too afraid to use my power in case they were watching, I remained trapped in every way. The excess of adrenaline had sapped every ounce of energy left in my body, and feeling utterly helpless and alone, I saw no way to save myself.

The cell was dark, but my soul was darker. And it consumed me.

Chapter Two

Light and sound jerked me awake as my captors entered the room. I blinked up at the old man again as he worked in silence, releasing the needle from my arm, and my arm from the machine. His touch through gloved hands, was firm but not rough. Yet he would not meet my gaze as he had before. Averting his gaze, he undid my bindings. Stooping slowly down, shackled my feet with new cuffs unattached to the bench.

My heart sank as the female soldier slid around him into view. Dismissing him with a jerk of her head, he hastened from the room, his head bowed in submission as he left me alone with her.

"Get up," she clipped out in perfect Comian, "And if you try anything, I will activate the chip in your head."

Glancing fearfully at the device she was pointing at me, I pushed myself to a sitting position, waiting a moment for my head to stop swimming.

"On your feet," she snapped. "Or I'll help you."

I stood on shaky legs, the room pitching alarmingly, the heat pressing in around me as my lungs constricted in protest. I stood still for a moment, taking deep, long breaths to calm myself before I turned to face her.

"Whatever they told you about us is a lie," I began. "Our people have done nothing to—"

"How dare you speak to me, alien," she snapped, her tone dripping with contempt. "I forbid you to speak to me." Shoving me hard toward the door, I struggled to retain my balance, the shackles hindered my steps. My stomach turned as I saw the stains of old blood on the floor beneath my bare feet. Fighting the urge to jump over it I turned to face her instead. "What is it they told you?" I persisted as sweat trickled

10

down my back. ''I want to know what you've been taught about us.''

"They taught us the truth," the soldier snarled. "How you let our people suffer for your greed, and how you murdered our soldiers in your prison camps. Also, how you want our entire race extinct. Now move, and stop talking."

"That's a lie!" I exclaimed. "We gave you all the water we could afford until you attacked us for more!"

The girl froze, her face screwing up in fury a moment before she hit the button. A sharp hot blade pierced through my brain, lightning streaking across my vision as I shrieked and sank to the floor.

"I told you not to speak to me," she leered as I clutched at my head. "Now get up and walk."

The pain cleared away as I staggered to my feet, glaring at her in a way that probably wasn't a good idea, considering she was currently controlling the thing in my head. Ignoring my filthy look, she indicated for me to move ahead of her. I shuffled awkwardly out of the room into a stark grey corridor where another guard waited. I recognised him as the other man who'd observed me through the glass, and my stomach tightened as he looked at me with the same lack of humanity as the woman. There would be no compassion on his watch or hers, only severe punishment if I stepped a toe out of line.

I walked in halting steps along the passageway while the two guards conversed in Abwarzian behind me. Their language sounded so abrupt and harsh to my ears, I couldn't help but wonder if that was how they talked to their loved ones. Did they always sound so aggressive, or was that a tone reserved for their enemies? Maybe they didn't harbour feelings for relatives or partners the way we did on Como. That would explain how they could use their children as bait in the war without remorse or shame. Maybe love didn't even exist in their world. Perhaps that was the reason they could fight and kill, and endlessly plunder...because it was only survival that mattered, life or death, and nothing else...

"Stop."

The girl switched back to Comian as she punched a code into the wall, and the wall slid apart, revealing a large circular room. I squinted against the harsh lights, slowly taking in the seating that ran around the circumference. On every inch of the seating sat the enemy, watching and waiting. Waiting for me. My legs shook as the girl pushed me toward the centre of the room. It looked exactly like an arena, and I knew with heavy certainty I was the entertainment once the girl stepped rapidly away from me, as though I was infectious. Dread filled me as I spun in an awkward circle. My stomach clenched harder as I took in the faces staring back at me. They were all in the identical grey uniforms, all part of the law and order of their world, the select of their people.

Most of them looked older than me by a few hundred moons or more. It struck me that they could easily be the same generations of my parents, the generation who had started the war against our people. They looked at me with open hostility, with the preformed hatred instilled throughout their lives toward my race.

Others looked closer to my age, and they stared with eager curiosity, or with fascination at seeing a rare creature for the first time. The exposure was mortifying, and not for the first time, I wished I were like Sazika, with the power of invisibility. I caught the gaze of a young man who looked a couple of hundred moons or so older than me. His expression was calm, but I was sure it was distaste I saw flicker briefly over his sharply angled features. His eyes burned darkly into mine as he observed me. I shivered in response, sure that if the hatred he felt for me could burn into my skin, it would be sizzling right now.

I turned away, my cheeks burning with the humiliation of being their specimen. The air was stuffy and uncomfortable, but it didn't seem to bother the Abwarzians. Their hair had not turned into a swamp serpent's nest like mine had. Their skin did not glisten with sweat like mine. Had they adapted? Because no matter how deeply I inhaled, it never felt satisfying to my lungs, and it left me panting before I'd even tried anything.

Completing my circle, I caught a different type of expression and it stopped me. Just near the entrance to the room sat the older Abwarzian who'd been in my cell. He gazed at me sadly, and then lowered his head, looking away. The look told me two things. The first was vaguely comforting. It said I am sorry for your situation. But the second was more deflating. But I cannot help you.

People murmured to each other in hushed voices as they stared.

Emotions crackled through the room as they judged and condemned me, and the hairs on my skin stood to attention as trepidation rolled over me in shuddering waves.

The entrance to the room slid open behind me, and my heartbeat broke into a gallop as I spun to see the leader striding into the room. Walking over to the seating, I watched as the others moved to make room for him. He sat down between the two familiar guards, as though equal in rank. But I could tell he was still the leader by the hush falling over the room, no matter the seating arrangement.

He spoke in his native tongue at first, and every eye in the room snapped to me as he rose to his feet.

"My name is Vaero," the alien said as he switched to Comian, "and you will answer my questions without delay." His black orbs fixed on mine, daring me to refuse him.

I nodded in response, my stomach tightening in nervous anticipation.

"What is your name?"

"Twell. Twell Anar."

"How old are you?"

"One hundred and eighty moons." I croaked. I figured the question was harmless enough, or as harmless as they could get.

Immediately the female guard began to speak and I realized she was interpreting my language for those who didn't speak Comian while he interrogated me. So they couldn't all speak Comian. Maybe it was just those who were highly ranked in their armies or Government.

"When did you commence combative instruction?"

"Sixteen moons ago."

Murmuring rippled around the room as my words were translated. The general consensus seemed to be disbelief.

"What a waste of resources." Vaero's lip curled in mock amusement as his gaze swept over the room. Other officers laughed in obedient unison, a few people shaking their heads and smirking in a patronising kind of way. Their response didn't surprise me. I knew Abwarzian children were trained in combat from a very young age, or used as decoys to trap the enemy. That was the difference between them and us. Quality of life wasn't even a consideration.

13

"And when are your people planning to attack ours?"

The mood sobered immediately, a tense silence stretching across the room as Vaero pinned me back in his narrow gaze.

"They're not." Good. We were getting to the point fast.

"You are a soldier, are you not?"

"Yes."

"And what are soldiers for, but to fight?"

"On Como, we do things differently. We are trained to defend."

"Lies." Vaero smiled. "Do not lie again."

"I'm not lying," I retorted. "We'll fight back if you don't leave us alone, if you leave us no choice. But we do not choose war, like you do."

The moment my words were translated the room's tempers flared. Adrenalin rushed through my veins as fury overtook their faces. They began to shout untranslated insults, their bodies leaning toward me with such malice it took every ounce of courage not to step back. Their anger at my words proved at least some of my education of their world was true. They were fueled with lies, and maybe some truths about what our people had done to them, or not done for them, and nothing I said would be believed. Or appreciated.

"Veastak!"

Immediately the spectators simmered down and resorted to glaring at me like I was a piece of moga poo instead. Woah. I guessed that word meant shut the heck up.

Vaero walked forward until he stood directly before me, only a Comian length away.

"Defend your own people?" Vaero arched a thin black eyebrow as an ominous smile stretched over his thin mouth. Standing up, he walked casually over to the opposite side of the room so that I was forced to turn my back to the crowd in order to face him. "Perhaps you can demonstrate how you would defend them right now." Vaero nodded toward one of the soldiers, and in the next instant a concealed door opened right behind him.

I gasped as two emaciated Comians staggered into the room. Their clothes were so bloody and torn, their faces so haunted with torture and starvation I could hardly bear to look at them. I searched their faces, taking in the fear mixed with fatigue in their eyes before registering that Shay was not among them. So they had taken others from Station Three after all. The G.B had never disclosed how many others had gone missing the day they attacked one of the intelligence stations orbiting Como. I hadn't had the time to decide if that was a relief or not before the room fell deadly quiet. As they shuffled to the centre of the room a static energy filled the air, and the hairs on my neck raised in warning as Vaero's sudden command boomed throughout the room.

"Protect them, Comian. Show us how you win a war!"

"What?" My words broke off abruptly as the soldiers turned on the prisoners, their eyes widening in fear the instant before the soldiers fired.

"No!" My legs melded to the floor, my brain frozen in horror as the laser beams sliced through their skin and bone so fluidly there was almost no sound. They never even screamed while they were dissected, the process too quick for their minds to comprehend. The light faded from their eyes the moment their heads severed from their necks. Hitting the ground, one prisoner's head bounced and rolled across the floor till it came to rest at my feet. Startled green eyes stared vacantly up at me, the horror of such a death frozen permanently in its glassy stare. I stood shaking all over, my hands pressed over my mouth to force back the rising scream in my throat.

"Oh dear." Vaero chuckled as I fought back the bile rising in my throat. "I'm afraid you have failed to demonstrate your beliefs to our people."

"You just murdered them to make a point!" I gasped, wheeling furiously toward him. "You didn't need to do that!"

"Just like your government didn't need to bomb your schools and hospitals, and say it was us in order to gain your full support to fight us."

"No!" I staggered back, my head shaking as much as my limbs.

"Come now," Vaero said as he shook his head at me, his smile mocking, "do you really think we could have penetrated your orbit without your intelligence seeing us coming? Light years away? Did you not wonder why your own people didn't warn you of our coming attack? Did you not question how it could have happened so easily, without any immediate counter attack from your government?"

"We were recovering, protecting the living, and healing the wounded!" My stomach flipped over in retaliation to my words, doubt smothering me like a dark cloak. Could there be any truth to his accusations? Uncertainty slithered coldly into my mind as anxiety pushed against my chest.

"Why would your army need time to recover? They were not harmed in the well-aimed attacks at your youngest civilians, or worse, the ill and disposable...surely there is no reason they could not have reacted immediately...if there was any real threat to react against?"

"I already told you. Our people don't want war," I stammered uncertainly. "We want peace."

"A civilization wanting peace, would not pull together as many soldiers into a new army as yours have been doing for the last several moons. Our satellites have not missed all the new army camps cropping up over your deserts, no matter how much sand you try to conceal them with. I think it's time you admit you're just a young and naïve pawn in an age-old game."

"And what game is that?" I hissed as anger simmered over my fear. I didn't know who I was angrier at, him for telling me what I didn't want to hear, or me for not wanting to hear what might be the horrifying truth.

"Why the game of war, of course." Vaero chuckled as his narrowed eyes glistened. "War is a game that is never fought fairly. Just look at your genetic advantages..." I saw him reach to his hip and withdraw a weapon from his holster. I recognized it as a laser gun, the ones they'd used to slice the prisoners into pieces. Raising it quickly he pointed it at my face, his finger on the trigger.

Fatigue forgotten, self-preservation awakened my defences as my mind buzzed in response. My powers shot out, wrapping my mind around the weapon and yanking it from his grasp. I yelped as the spot where they had chipped me immediately flared with pain. I focused harder, ignoring the stabbing pain as I lifted the weapon out of Vaero's reach. Before I could think my actions through, I pulled it through the air into my own hands.

Chaos erupted around me, yells of panic clogging the already stifling air as people scrambled to get clear. Soldiers sprang forward, forming a tight circle around me as the female soldier scrambled quickly for the device linked to my brain.

Pivoting back toward Vaero, I saw he was still smiling; calmly holding his ground while his soldiers closed in on me.

Without a word, I let go of the gun, boosting it into the space between the leader and myself. The sounds of terror ceased as everyone froze. Watching me in stunned silence, I sent the weapon back to its owner. I held his gaze determinedly, seeing the surprise flicker in his eyes as I nudged the weapon firmly into his hands. I saw his eyes darken with anger, instantly understanding he'd meant for me to retaliate, to prove his words true, and to justify showing off the chip they'd inserted in my brain. As displeasure flashed over his features, I knew without a doubt I'd be punished for showing him up.

A few gasps leaked into the silence, but the tension had morphed into a new sensation, one I had hoped for. Confusion. I'd just given up a chance to retaliate, and that just wasn't the Abwarzian way.

"Maybe I can't speak for my leaders, but I know my people do not want another war. We do not want any more death over a commodity that could be civilly negotiated."

The spectators broke into a mixture of responses, as those who understood Comian translated to those who didn't. The female officer remained mute, her expression stony as she refused to relay my words. Mistrust stretched across most of their faces, or open anger at my audacity. The youngest of them shook their heads, arguing animatedly amongst themselves as if I'd contradicted everything they'd been taught of our people. But there were a few who stared back at me with interest, and all of them were old enough to have experienced the first war, as old as my parents would have been. If they had lived.

The older man also seemed to measure the weight of my words seriously as his tired, dark eyes caught mine.

"How many of you have your ability?" Vaero's tone was deadly with warning, daring me to evade the answer.

"Very few. I'm a genetic abnormality." My pulse quickened as I carefully controlled my tone.

"More lies, I believe." Vaero's features hardened. "What other abilities has your race been hiding?"

"Only this, as far as I know." My heart pounded treacherously harder. "but they pulled me out of school into the army, in the hopes they could make something of my difference."

"Kiel. Kiel Iat Atche!"

I could only assume she was calling me a filthy little liar as the female officer spat out her native language with pure venom. Clutching the device in her hands she pushed down on the button. The spectators looked on in fascination as my brain exploded, dark daggers slicing through my vision as my screams reverberated around the room. I tried to push the sensation away with my powers, but the pain was stronger, burning through every cell with an intensity that made it impossible to focus.

Satisfaction smeared over the girl's face as I fell to the ground, clawing at the base of my skull. I thrashed helplessly against the burning pain, the room watching on in unbearable silence as I curled into a rocking ball of agony. I looked at the old man through streaming eyes, and I noted his features were arranged in careful indifference. But something more than regret gleamed in his eyes. Fear radiated from his being, freezing him in his seat. I understood that fear for his own life was the reason he could not help me. Or would not.

As my body arced in another spasm of agony, my head rolled back, my eyes falling on the younger soldier. I searched his face for the pleasure his people were meant to feel from my torture. But his expression remained impassive, only a slight twitch in his jaw indicating there was any human reaction at all.

Vaguely, a small part of my brain that wasn't on fire wondered if they were killing me now, just for their entertainment. It felt like I was dying, or at least that I would like to die if it went on much longer. My body convulsed against the hard stone floor while my fingernails raked so hard at my skull my hair ripped from my scalp. Heavy darkness pressed over my eyes, and a frightened scream built in my throat as my sanity threatened to leave me as well.

"Mietz. Mietz kalt!"

The floor shook beneath me, a sound like thunder rumbling down the passageway on the other side of the room. The hairs on my arms rose in warning just as Jonaz burst through the doors, and dozens of Comian soldiers streamed in behind him. The Army of Powers stormed the room, the army I'd deserted, now come to save me.

There were weapons secured to Jonaz's belt, but his hands were raised, outstretched and ready to inflict the pain he held within them.

The warmth I'd always known in his gaze was gone, replaced with cold mechanical determination as he focused on his enemies. He was not feeling, or even thinking, merely reacting as all his training snapped into place and he became the weapon he'd been trained to be.

His expression devoid of any humanity, he laid hands on the Abwarzian soldiers intercepting him, and then it was their time to suffer as he snapped their bones with the slightest touch, and tore open their flesh with the lightest of pressure.

I shivered as my captors screamed, suffering at the hands of my people as Jonaz worked his way toward me, enemy by enemy. As he brought them to the floor and incapacitated them, I knew he could kill them if he chose to, and I wondered if that was what I wanted. An eye for an eye, as the ancient texts from earth described revenge.

But revenge was not his goal. Reaching me was. My heart beat faster as I understood his plan, while the Army of Powers worked all around me. The air crackled with mingling powers as I rolled onto my knees, the skills of my peers unleashing around me. Comian soldiers with electrical abilities threw out lightning fast currents with a force that rendered the receiver unconscious. A cadet flew over my head as he crash tackled an officer behind me, and to my right another Comian moved so fast he was only a blur as he flashed from each armed Abwarzian to the next, seizing their weapons before they even knew what was happening. Disarmed and maimed, they were quickly overcome, more helpless than our race without their weapons. Again, I noted how my heart pumped faster with the thrill of victory at their screams, and satisfaction flooded my veins.

"Twell! Watch out!"

I froze, my heart skipping a beat as I recognised Avin's voice. Across the room, he met my gaze, his silver eyes flashing like lightning as I registered the Abwarzian leader bearing down on me. He raced toward me, ducking and weaving around the fighting, and leaping over the bodies of those who were flayed.

I leapt to my feet, the training taking over before my mind could think, or warn, or challenge my instincts. It was war now. And war was not murder. Or so they had assured us. But my body didn't seem to care about any of that. It only wanted to react, protect…and survive.

I harnessed my powers at the same moment Jonaz reached my side, but I did not focus on him as I reached for Vaero with my mind and yanked his body toward me. He tried to resist, but it was futile as I propelled him across the floor and threw him to my feet.

As Jonaz turned toward me I pulled the laser gun from his holster with my powers, pushing him aside as I simultaneously aimed the gun at the leader's head and pushed my powers against the trigger.

The laser burned through the centre of his face so perfectly I saw straight through his brain, like a porthole to the bodies lying on the ground behind him. He swayed on his knees a few seconds more before the rest of his face collapsed and his body slumped to the floor.

I stared down at him without remorse and wondered if I still had a heart, because I couldn't seem to feel anything. Then I looked up and saw both Jonaz and Avin before me. Jonaz's expression was hardened with death, his eyes burning into mine with accusations and anger. But it was sadness I saw etched over Avin's features, his hypnotic eyes swirling as I felt their pull. For a moment, I was captured in his gaze, feeling every ounce of his disappointment.

Nausea filled my insides, rising up into my throat. I wrenched my eyes away, feeling the hypnotic fog lifting as I whirled and stumbled away from him, slamming straight into Jonaz. Time stopped as I dared to lift my eyes to his. Jonaz stared back at me coldly. Worse than that, with total detachment. My heart clenched and stuttered in my chest as my eyes began to burn. I opened my mouth, wanting to say so much, wanting to say how sorry I was. But no words came, because there was nothing I could say that could ever redeem myself, or undo the damage I'd done.

Staggering back from him, my knees gave way and I sank to the floor. I knew with sickening clarity that neither of them had come for me, they had only come because it was their duty, and they were simply following orders.

I stared at them both in mute horror as they turned in unison and walked away from me without a backward glance.

Then I knew I still had a heart. Because it was breaking all over again.

Chapter Three

The sting of the needle sliding into my arm jolted me awake. I was back in the cell, tethered to the bed, and I felt like I'd just been tortured. Oh, that's right. I had.

"I take bl..ood f..for test."

Thirst burned my throat, while the now familiar dull ache pulled persistently at the base of my skull. Shifting slightly, I was rewarded with a stronger stab of pain that made me wonder how much damage they'd done when that moga of an officer pressed the button. In a panic, I counted to one hundred, ran through the alphabet, and tried to remember all the names of my school friends, pets, street names and so on until I was satisfied I hadn't lost any of the brain cells I truly needed. Then I focused on the figure standing over me and met the eyes of the old man.

"You... passed out... in th..ere," he muttered.

My heart contracted into itself as I realized I'd been dreaming. Or hallucinating. Jonaz had not come for me. Nor Avin. Nor any of my people. Not that I'd expected it. What with being a deserter and all...

"There is only... so much... the body can stand...each time."

A shiver rolled down my spine at the implication of his words. Each time? How many times? How many ways? I felt exhausted at the thought, and in no mood for a chat.

"You're not supposed to talk to me," I reminded him crankily. "Better not get yourself into trouble. They seem pretty big on the punishments around here."

"I give you fr...fresh water, if we have—" He shook his head ruefully. "But it hardly fresh...or...satisfy. But...be gr...grateful...get this way... don't have to taste."

22

"Gee, how thoughtful. Thanks ever so much."

The old man's chuckle caught me off guard, seemingly unperturbed by my snippiness. I had to give him points for translating both my language and my sarcasm.

"I remember taste… your water." He smiled as he stared across the room for a moment. "From good old days...when still civil to barter...it taste so pure...so life gi...giving.''

Looking up at his time worn features; I frowned at the wistfulness in his watery gaze. His crinkled expression seemed heavy with the burden of his knowledge, and I wondered what kind of things he had seen and done to appear so haunted and sad.

"What is it like, to live in your world?'' My interest was piqued despite my current situation. I'd been taught my world's version, but I now knew it was a black and white perspective, mixed with lies and secrets. I knew there had to be a reason they'd become so brutal, so focused on survival that war seemed the only answer.

The old man's eyes darted nervously to the window, before he bent his head lower, pretending to fuss over the machine. "From young as re...member, always struggle...enough water for people," he began as he looked away through the dark viewing pane to his past. "As child, I listen to parents...speak with...fr...friends. There was worry in voice... tension in con...versation. And al...ready strictest water rations... and...pen... penalties in place."

"Like what?" We also had water restrictions on Como, because it was such a precious bargaining resource. Even though we still hadn't discovered just how much water our new world held, we still had the fear of our pasts to remind us that the water could and would run out when it was misused and unprotected.

We'd desalinized on Earth, but in the end, global warming drove us to find the new world, Como. Determined not to make the same mistakes again, we adhered to allocations for household duties. Water was collected at every opportunity in every location. Gardens were made up of stone and water features, where the water flowed in continuous repetition through fountains, rather than be wasted by watering man made gardens. Timers were installed in our showers and controlled by the districts councils. A warm mist for a short period was hardly sufficient to wash hair as long and thick as mine, hence my constant hair dramas, but one thing we never worried about was having enough to drink. There was no cap on drinking water, and I'd never appreciated it more in my life than I did now.

"Even then, we restrict... only two small cups of water per person, a day," he mused, "and lots sickness...disease, all around. I was aware...very young, the concept of death. I could fe...feel fear in adults, in own parents. It feel like waiting game. Who next? Neighbour? Friend? One of our own? Eventually... all of those. I lost youn...ger sister, but it was so common... grieving kept sh...short as we pushed on, in stru...ggle to beat odds."

"Odds?"

"Sta...tistics. One in five die... because without enough wa..water, fatigue lead to low im...munity, which lead to illness and disease... countless de..deaths."

"One in five? I had no idea—they never taught us that."

"Of course, no." He smirked a little. "History put authors race in good light, al..always. Provide fact... might give sym...pathy to opposition... or cause de...depression in population. Never allowed."

"Perhaps..." But my heart sank at his words, because I already knew he was right. The night my friends and I hacked into secret government data to find out what our part played in the war, was the day my understanding of my own people changed forever. It was the night I realised my people were as capable of revenge and murder as our enemies.

It was also the night I realised I was in love with Jonaz Maven. A hugely significant night that had changed my mind and my heart forever...

"Have they t..t..told you, about our water, why so ter...rible?" He stared at me seriously, his smirk slipping away as his mouth tightened into a frown.

"Lack of nutrients?"

"Lack of right salt body needs to thrive... survive."

"Salt? But don't you desalinate the sea?"

"Is not right ty..type salt, but even if was, waters is full of po..ison, from our weaponry waste. We have to process and fi..lter water... with more chemical, to make sa..safe. By time okay drink…not only lack in mi..neral, but also, salt body need. Then we suffer, hyponatremia"

"Hypo what?"

"It begins, muscle cramp… vomit, dizzy…"

"And ends…"

"In… coma, then death."

"I had no idea…they didn't…"

"Of course… death is preferred to the de…deformities…last g..generation be born."

The old man sighed, looking away from me as his eyes misted over. I already knew about the deformities. Blindness, seizures, stunted growth, learning impairments… They'd really stuffed things up for themselves. But when their mistakes equaled the suffering of their offspring…well…it was nothing to gloat about…enemy or not.

"I'm sorry to know of it," I mumbled. "If only your world hadn't attacked ours, we might have kept on trading."

The old man looked at me sadly for a moment, regret etched deeply over his features. Clearly their history didn't cover the fact they'd attacked us first.

"What's your name?" I asked.

"Lanestiax-822,450,01."

"Huh?"

"Lanest…will do. Number just ID in pop…ulation."

If he'd been Comian, I would have pressed my hand to his cheek, but as my hand wouldn't get that far, and he was an alien, I reached out toward his hand instead.

He froze, fear flashing over his features before he jerked out of reach. I dropped my hand. Did he think I was toxic? Or worse, that I might hurt him? I studied his face as blood flooded his wrinkled old cheeks, and thought I understood. He was afraid of touch. For some reason the one thing that comforted me, frightened him. How did they raise a person to fear affection? What had happened in his lifetime to instill such a reaction? Was there truly no kindness at all in his world? *Let's see. You've been imprisoned and tortured since the moment you got here,* my conscience whispered rather snidely, the answer seemed pretty obvious.

The door swung open, several guards bursting into the room as though launching a surprise attack. At seeing the old man unaccompanied, the female guard burst into a loud diatribe of easily translatable accusation and threats. The old man's sallow cheeks flushed in mortification, his hands trembling as he held them up toward her in submission.

"Pa..rdon my er..ror, Officer Sevran." Although he deliberately spoke in Comian, he avoided eye contact with me as he scuttled for the door. His head was bowed as he moved past Sevran. She glared at him sharply, her mind ticking as to why he'd used my language.

"What? Did you miss me, Sevran?" I conjured a provoking grin that quickly achieved the desired results. Her head whipped back to me, and she stalked toward my bed as Lanest slipped safely away, a gleam in her eye like a predator honing in on its prey.

"No, I certainly did not." Her mouth twisted unattractively as she scowled down at me.

"Oh dear, don't you do sarcasm on your planet? That's a shame, some of my best work is lost on you.''

"I despise you and your people,'' she spat, proving me right. "You're a selfish, greedy nation who hoard your water and refuse to help other worlds. The decline of our populations is your peoples' fault, and I can't wait until I get to witness you receiving the justice all your people deserve.''

I stopped grinning, my flesh prickling as I imagined a thousand ways they might execute my death. "So who was it?" I asked her quietly as she glared down at me. "Your mother? Your brother...your partner...or perhaps it was your own child?"

Sevran jerked back, genuine shock streaking over her sallow features as she drew in her breath. Her eyes filled with agony and then worse, utter despair transforming her features. For a long moment, she lost her focus, her eyes shining with pain she had carefully concealed. The room seemed to grow colder as a mask of ice slid back over her features. Her eyes emptied of emotion until they were as hard as glittering slate. Her arctic gaze fixed back on mine, chilling me to the bone.

"I'm sterile, thanks to a defect caused by malnutrition as a child."

She seethed, "So it's not a wise move, attempting to pull on my heartstrings with the children I'll never have, thanks to you and your people."

"I didn't mean to offend you," I blurted, "I'm just trying to understand you."

"Understand this."

The moment she lifted her hand to strike me, my mind shot out, intercepting her just before her fist met my face. Coiling my powers around her wrist, I forced her back so hard she staggered, clutching at the side of the bed for support.

"You do realize I could make you punch yourself in the face if I wanted to? Heck, I could even make you pick your nose if I fancied it."

"How noble of you," Sevran spat, "Knowing the consequences would only be more severe."

"Look, can you just take me to wherever you've been directed to take me? Chop chop, we don't have all day."

"With pleasure." Her grin was sickening as she stepped back and let the other officer release my arm from the hydrator. Undoing my bindings, the soldier yanked me from the bench and pushed me in front of him until I was once again heading for the arena. I felt ill, the floors lurching under my step like I had a virus. Maybe I did, maybe they'd inserted one of their diseases in my brain. Gingerly I touched the back of my skull, then pulled away, wincing at the tenderness of the small but lethal wound.

When we reached the arena, the atmosphere felt different. The room was packed not just with army or law enforcement, but what appeared to be their regular citizens. Dressed in dark grey slacks and shapeless shirts, I found it initially difficult to discern male from female. The men wore their hair shorn close to the skull. The women wore the same clothes as the men, only their hair was grown a little longer, and cropped no longer than chin level. The hairstyle seemed to sharpen their pointy chins, while the dark grey emphasised the pallor of their dull greyish skin. There was no health or vitality in their form, and the soldiers seemed only marginally healthier. Maybe they were rationed a little more food and water than regular citizens, because I couldn't see how else they would find the energy to keep going.

Their reaction, when they saw me, was chilling. I'd expected hate, like their leaders, and revenge burning in their eyes. But there was no fervour, no excitement at seeing me captured, no smiles of victory. Instead carefully arranged faces surveyed me grimly, while black soulless eyes promised that only bad things lay ahead for me in this room. I shivered at those vacant yet controlled expressions, because it was obvious to me they were afraid to show any reaction at all. They were as afraid of their leaders as I was.

My insides knotted as I realized they were here to observe what was about to happen to me. Bile rose in my throat, my insides churning as I guessed they would be sent back into the community to report on what they saw. My heart crashed against my ribs as I pressed my knees together to try and stop shaking. I was probably not going to survive the example they would make of me.

A ring of ghostly, grey clad soldiers stationed themselves around the room, every few Comian lengths. Taking them in, I recognized one of them as the young man who'd observed me from the first session. As his eyes met mine, they seemed to widen slightly, almost like he was trying to warn me of something. Then, swallowing hard, he wrenched his gaze away, readopting his impersonation of a statue.

But I barely noticed, because I'd jerked to a stop in the centre of the arena, my eyes fixed on my guardian like she was the only other being in the room. They'd tied her to a post in the centre of the room, but her body was slumped, the ropes holding her upright.

"Shay!" At my cry my guardian's matted head lifted slightly, her greying hair ripped long free of its usual tidy bun. A hush fell over the room as the spectators observed our reunion.

Sweat beaded on my skin as I assessed her condition. It wasn't good. Her eyes were sunken and glazed, barely focused as they sought mine. Her skin was as gaunt and shadowed, and as grey as the Abwarzians. Small shallow breaths wheezed through dry cracked lips, and her eyes struggled to focus on me, like she was fighting consciousness. They had clearly withheld water from her long enough that she was dehydrated to the point of death. They were killing her. Slowly. And they wanted me to see it.

"Now, Twell, I think it's time you really showed us these skills your race has been breeding and hiding from us." Vaero had been standing beside Shay all along, but I hadn't noticed, so focused on whether or not she still had a pulse.

As I turned my attention to him, I noticed he was holding some sort of an intravenous bag in his hand. It looked like water, and I assumed if I submitted and went along with whatever they wanted, they might let her have it, if only to keep her alive for more torture. But then another officer stepped forward. Taking the bag from Vaero he hung it from a hook above Shays head, then taking the long tube attached, he inserted the sharp thick needle at the end straight into a vein in Shays neck. I gasped as she flinched, starting toward her in pure instinct, desperate to touch her.

"STOP!" Vaero commanded. "If you move another step I will squeeze this bag of salt water even faster into her blood stream, and you will be the cause of her rapid and uncomfortable death." Demonstrating, he squeezed the bag. Shay jerked, moaning weakly.

"Stop it!" I threw my hands up helplessly and snarled, "What do you want me to do? I'll do it!"

Shay twitched again, shaking her head very slightly. Even on the door of death, she would rather remain loyal to our Governing Body, the very ones who had failed to protect her, and had failed to rescue her. If they had even tried. But I had no choice. She had to understand. Her life was worth far more to me than my own.

"You will fight six of my soldiers, to the death. If you can take them all down before the fluid in this bag reaches the half way line, your guardian will probably live, although most likely with permanent organ damage and complications. If not, well…"

"If I die she dies?" I whispered to no one in particular. My mind chugged sluggishly. I couldn't think beyond my terror, or comprehend what was about to happen. It wasn't real. I didn't want it to be real.

"You Comians catch on quick," Vaero smirked. "And now you must educate us as to how you are so certain we are inferior."

"Twell…no…" Shay's rasping plea was lost in the roaring of blood in my ears.

Click.Click.Click.Click.Click.Click.

I spun in a wary circle, no time to plan my defence or tactics as the six soldiers aimed long, black, shiny tubes at me. The ends of the tubes flared into a wider disc with tiny little holes, just like the misting showerheads we had back on Como. But before I could even guess at what they did the first soldier stepped forward, his expression devoid of any emotion as he pointed his weapon at my head. The other soldiers raised their weapons one by one in response, falling into identical crouches. I mimicked their stance, my powers bursting from my mind, forcing through the pain and fatigue as the soldiers' fingers squeezed the triggers.

Jets of white powder sprayed out toward me as I took out two soldiers' guns in my first pulse of power. Pulling the weapons across the room toward me, I hit the floor at the same time as a fine white spray moved over my head. Some of it travelled down, settling on the bare skin of my arms as I threw them up to cover my face.

I screamed in agony as my flesh began to sizzle, bubbling into instant angry red blisters as I crawled out from under the cloud.

As the soldiers advanced, the pain jolted my senses, my temper igniting like a switch flicked inside me. My training took over, my mind reaching out to yank the weapons from two more soldiers while I rolled out of the way of another blast of acid. Forgetting who I was, or anything I'd ever believed, I seized a weapon in each hand and fired the white powder straight back into their faces. The effect was mesmerizing, their faces melting off before my eyes like hot wax; their exposed eyeballs staring at me in shock from bony sockets as blood curdling shrieks rose from their lungs. My own skin continued to cook, but there was no time to be horrified as I blocked out the pain and focused on the soldiers behind me. Casting my powers out, I dodged another stream of acid, lunging at a soldier while using my powers ahead of me to turn the weapon around in his hands. Shoving the barrel against his cheek I fired without hesitation. His features froze in a split second of shock before his face concaved inwards and his body sunk to the floor.

A burning white-hot pain licked my left hip like I'd fallen into a fire. I staggered back as incomprehensible agony followed. Tears blurred my eyes as I howled in rage, turning on the soldier responsible. Fury burned my insides as my powers evolved beyond my control, bursting out of me with new life as I seized the soldier and smashed his body into the ground. His body bounced and cracked against the floor, but I barely registered a fleeting sense of satisfaction before I turned to the next soldier.

Ducking under his fire, I seized his gun, yanking it into my hand as I wrapped my powers around him and propelled him across the room. As I dumped him at my feet he grabbed my legs, pulling me down on top of him as his hands reached for the weapon. But I was quicker, shoving the gun against his chest as I simultaneously pulled the trigger. The acid opening a chasm in his chest, melting straight through his heart while he screamed and bucked to a quick but painful death beneath me.

One soldier left. Scrambling to my feet I spun to meet him, knocking his weapon from his hand as I advanced on him. Raising the weapon still clutched in my own hand, I pressed it against his skull, meeting his eyes.

Chapter Four

It was the same young man whose dark eyes stared back at me, the one from the beginning, whose contempt I'd been sure of, now the last threat to dispose of. He sunk slowly to his knees, his features still holding the same expression he'd worn all along. Only now I understood it. His training and duty did not allow him to show any emotion, even in the face of death.

Time stretched out, silence pressing in on me as I searched deeper into the inky depths of his gaze. Deep down, where no one else but I could see, I saw something flicker. A small flame of spirit shone back at me, the essence of humanity. It was not hatred that burned back at me in those eyes, but courage…and deeper still…hope. My heart squeezed inside my chest in a vaguely familiar way. Deep down, beneath my instinct to survive, something shrieked at me to stop, stop, STOP.

Frozen in time, the room thickened with tension, until it was stifling. Still as silent as a grave; the soldiers who had not attacked remained stationed around the room, weapons trained on me, waiting for my next move. Or their next order.

"Do you know what mercy is?" I said. Slowly I turned my head, fixing my gaze on Vareo.

"Mercy is weakness, the downfall of weaker worlds," Vaero snarled in reply.

"No. It takes strength of character, and compassion; assets at the very core of the humanity you are lacking, and the reason to go on living." Stepping a few lengths back from the last soldier I stood in the centre of the room, the gun held slack at my side. Adrenalin kept me on my feet. Shock kept me from feeling any pain.

Twell and the Uprising

The final soldier remained on his knees, looking uncertainly at Vareo for direction. In answer, Vareo gave a single nod. My stomach clenched as the remaining soldiers swung their weapons toward him, ready to reduce him to a melting pile of flesh and bones. The thing that struck me as most horrifying was the continued eerie silence of the citizens. They had not cheered for my death, their enjoyment notably absent. But nor did they seem sorry for the demise of their own soldiers, or even plead for his mercy. They observed impassively, as though accepting his fate. Not a flicker of emotion. Not a shadow of regret. It scared me much more than the execution itself, because if failure equalled death on Abwarz, then I was the only person in the room who felt any regret. He would die because of me, just like the others had. Yet another life extinguished at my expense.

"No!" Spreading my arms protectively in front of him, I pushed out with the last of my dwindling energy. There was a collective gasp as their hands were forced down, their weapons pointing toward the ground as I strained against their resistance. Behind me, I heard the soldier inhale sharply, but my eyes were still focused on Vaero as anger stormed over his face.

"There is no honour in being saved by the enemy," Vaero barked. "You insult him."

"Insults are better than death in my world." Letting my arms fall I pressed my palms to my temples, trying to stop the room from spinning as I felt the soldier shift slightly behind me.

"Very well. But when the time comes for him to kill you, as he will now have to do to earn back his honour, you will know as you're dying because of the stupidity of showing mercy to our kind."

I glanced over my shoulder at the soldier. He could have attacked me from behind at any point of Vaero's speech to redeem himself. But his eyes were trained on the ground, no longer sharing any of his secrets.

"Aite vak Aza." Vaero spoke sharply. Climbing stiffly to his feet, the young man walked away from me without so much as a backward glance. By the time he'd re-joined the other soldiers, the mask of indifference had slipped back over his face, and he would not meet my gaze.

33

Numbly, I cast my gaze on Shay. She wasn't moving, and had thrown up on herself at some point. Lifting my eyes higher to the bag, I saw the liquid had run down to the marked line.

"Is she alive?" I croaked, forcing the words from my parched throat.

"Barely. Lucky you fought fast and clean. Very impressive."

Clean? I looked around at the mess of skin and bone around me, inhaling the stench of smoking flesh, and my own cooking skin. Sinking weakly to the floor, I began to retch, in front of a whole live audience.

"Please," I rasped as the room began to spin faster. "Please give her water …" Vareo's humourless chuckle floated coldly overhead as the room swam in and out of focus.

"You want me to show her mercy? Like your people showed ours in your prison camps?" Vaero's thin lips pressed into a cold smirk." Your instincts are no different than ours once you get a taste for revenge."

"No, we aren't like you." The words were forced out in a whisper, but they hung feebly in the air without strength because my heart lacked the conviction. I'd spared one life out of five, but just barely, my instinct to protect myself overpowering my conscience.

"Just look at the history of your ancestors," Vareo sneered, "war after war after war, until Earth was destroyed. Your descendant's track record of violence carried on in your DNA, and no matter what planet you move to, or new rules you make to try and hide it, you are still the same selfish race. At least our people don't pretend to be something we are not."

"We're striving to amend our ways so we can live at one with our new world and protect it," I argued tiredly. "We've learned from our mistakes. We are trained to defend, not to kill."

"Oh? Like you just demonstrated?" Vaero's chuckle was icy and forced, but it ignited my temper.

"We don't want to kill! You forced me!"

"Did I?" Vaero leered, "or did you choose murder in favour of self-preservation?"

"You left me no choice but to act on my instincts. "I glared up at him. "But it was not my will, and that's where our differences lie."

"But it's still the same result in the end, don't you agree?" Vaero smiled victoriously, "Learn from your instinct, and your past. Human nature does not change."

"It's your people who refuse to learn from your pasts, and who refuse to change. It's a choice. Yet rather than repair the damage you've done, you still think more bloodshed will solve the problem. Read your own history to see how that keeps working out, genius. At least my people are trying to evolve!" I know. I know. Sometimes I couldn't believe my big mouth either. But hey, what were they gunna do? Torture me?

"Do you think I need an ignorant alien reminding me of our misfortune?" Vareo's tone hardened as his smile melted into something more sinister. "It sounds like you are forgetting your guardian's predicament." I flinched, Vareo's warning snapping me out of it. I cared what they did to me, don't get me wrong, but I was more scared of what they would do next to Shay.

"You say misfortune, I say stupidity." Oops. It was like I wanted to get us both killed. But I couldn't help it, his screwed-up mentality was too depressing to bear, and if his mindset represented the populations, it was no wonder there was no hope for their world. No one likes a victim mentality, and as a nation, it was an epic sign of continued disaster.

"Stop talking." Vaero's tone was calm, but his intent was deadly as he casually lifted his hand to the bag at Shay's neck.

"I'm picking up what you're putting down," I snapped. "We're not going to agree or change each other's opinions anyway."

"Oh, but I can make you change yours." Vaero's mouth twisted into a grin that made my blood run cold, "Let's see how well those abilities of yours work with a little interference."

Things happened very quickly. In a heartbeat, Vaero squeezed the contents of the bag into Shay's vein, and her body snapped straight up, her eyes rolling back in distress as she began to shake uncontrollably. A low garbled wail of protest rose from her fluid-filled lungs.

I'd barely launched forward before instant agony exploded at the base of my skull, searing through my mind like blades of fire. Pressure built up behind my eyes, until they felt like they would pop, and I stopped, pushing my palms against them in horror as I felt something burst behind my right eye. Blood pooled over the lens, painting the room red as Shay was reduced to a shaking silhouette across the room. Desperate to keep focus, I squinted through my left eye as I staggered toward my guardian.

I knew what he was doing. Trying to prove we were all the same, no matter our race or world. They wanted the fighting to go on and on, in anger and revenge without a thought for where it would all end. They craved violence to solve violence. They did not want to change.

But I could. I had to. Or he was right. We were no better than they were, and then there was no point in fighting for my own people, or fighting for my own life. If we were all the same, there was nothing worth fighting for.

A long drawn out wail rose from Shay's fragile body, piercing straight into my heart. Clambering shakily to my feet I pulled the feeble remains of my energy together and faced Vaero as beads of sweat rolled down my blood-stained skin.

Click.Click.Click.Click.Click.

The remaining soldiers waited for Vaero's orders. But none came, only a silent grin that stretched across his face so wide it seemed ready to split in two.

"Enough!" Reliant on my remaining senses I threw my powers out and wrapped them around Shays bindings, snapping them like twigs. She fell forward, the tube yanking from her skin as she tumbled into my outstretched powers. I swayed, the pressure in my brain so unbearable a sob wrenched from my chest as I propelled her into my grasp and collapsed back onto the floor. Shay lay motionless in my arms, as white as a ghost, staring right through me with haunted eyes. I held my breath as my fingers scrambled to find a pulse in her neck, dread clutching at me until she moaned weakly. Watery blood oozed back out from the puncture site in her neck and my hand fluttered over the wound as I fought the urge to apply pressure. Her cells were overloaded, and I hoped it was better to let her bleed a little longer, to lower her blood pressure at least. Laying her down, I crouched over her; pushing through the screaming pain with the last of my energy, as I let my words become my final action.

"You can kill us," I gasped as the room pitched and lurched around me, "but it won't end with us. It will never end, until you learn that war never solves the problem. It only silences it for a while." The red murky clouds stretched over my vision entirely, as I struggled to stay conscious. "Change is the only answer to your survival, and if you listen before attacking for one moment, you will see the truth. So follow us, stop fighting us!'

Then I was done. Slumping over Shay, I let go of hideous reality, sliding gratefully into to the blessed relief of unconsciousness, and the only escape I knew I had left, apart from death.

* * * *

Bright lights pried at my left eye, trying to seep through my lid and pull me from the comfort of dark solace. Rolling my head away from the source, familiar pain bit at the base of my skull, pulling me back into the horror of consciousness.

My right eye was blind. A dark pressing veil seemed to have covered the pupil, and I fought to control my short panicky breaths as hysteria threatened. I didn't need my sight to sense I was back in my cell, chained to the same bench. I also knew someone was in the room, but I was too miserable to care.

"I have wa…water for you."

My throat burst into flames of longing as I tilted my head to find Lanest with my good eye. It didn't matter that I wanted to reject anything they offered me. My body had other ideas.

"Thought you would be d..de…dead by now."

"I think I'm supposed to be." I croaked. Everything hurt. Every cell of my being. Shifting slightly, I winced as the raw skin on my waist rubbed against my tattered clothes. A low moan formed in my throat, then died off with lack of moisture.

"They see u as valuable…or they kill you."

"How wonderful for me."

Lanest drew closer, his dark eyes darting furtively toward the window as he bought a vial up to my mouth. On instinct, I lifted my head to receive it.

"Owwww." My head flopped back on the bed, as the room pitched and reeled. Lanest pressed the vial gently to my lips, tipping it slightly so the cool fluid ran into my mouth, and down to soothe the flames in my throat.

Only it didn't. The itch was somewhat reduced as moisture restored some rehydration to my cells. But something was still lacking, some element required to quench one's thirst. It tasted incomplete, and I was left wanting.

"Disappointing, I know." Lanest sighed at my expression.

"Shay!" I croaked, as my sensibilities reassembled, "Is my guardian alive?"

"I do...don't know," Lanest replied, his dark eyes somber as they struggled to meet mine."

"Please. I have to know, Lanest... can you help me find out?"

"I'm so...orry, I only obey orders...not allowed to ask qu...estions."

"How can you stand it?" I flared up in frustration, "How can you live this way?"

"Because no oth...er way." The defeat on Lanest's face said it all, the bleakness in his tone conveying the hopelessness oppressing him.

"There is, if your leaders are defeated," I replied. "I saw the looks on your citizens' faces in that room. They looked like you do now. They looked like they would prefer another way, but they're too scared to work out how."

"Rebellion equals instant d...de...death on Abwarz." Lanest looked fearfully at the black window, as though they might be standing behind it, ready to pounce on him.

I fell silent, unable to argue against such certainty. I thought about the consequences on Como for rebelling. It wasn't as severe as the death penalty, but there were still penalties. They had locked me up for my beliefs, and punished me for opposing their laws on partnering. In my opinion, although no one was asking for it, it made both of our worlds wrong.

"How do you know Comian, Lanest?" I asked to change the subject.

"All Abwarz so...soldier and offi..cers are t..t..taught other wo..worlds la..nguage, for int...tell...igence, and int..te..terrogation."

"Wow. Impressive."

"Our pe..ople do everything im..pressively." Lanest smiled ruefully.

"Including torture and murder." Bitterness laced my tone as I observed my own tethered limbs.

"You think it our na…nature, but you wrong." Lanest shook his grey head, frowning at me. "We taught those wa..ays, they enforced. They th…reaten our youngest, that they will t…t..ake them away from us, if we re…rebel. Or ex…execute the elders. Our children live in f..f…fear. We want di..different but we have no control against leaders who k..ki..kill own p…people for even v…voicing their objections."

"So you understand why my people must stop them."

"Are your people c..ca…capable? Is it truly p…ossible?"

Finally meeting Lanest's tired watery gaze through my one blurry eye, I knew he wasn't asking because he was concerned for his own people. He was asking because he hoped we could.

"We have no choice now but to try."

"Yes. It must. St…stop," Lanest whispered, his face sagging with weariness.

"So help me get out of here."

Lanest trembled; fear etched over his wrinkled face.

'They will k..k..ill me."

"I'll protect you."

"They will ki, ki…kill. My family…my chi..children…my gr..grand children."

"They're already suffering. I know you don't want this life for them!"

"I ca..ca..can't"

"Please, Lanest!"

"Aitche iet geite!" Sevran stood at the entrance of the cell, fury rolling over her face like a perfect storm. The device connected to my brain was clutched so tightly in her fist her skin stretched almost translucent over the bones of her knuckles. Lanest leapt away from me, his face filling with terror as Sevran rushed at him, her black eyes glittering with fury. Lanest fell to his knees, covering his head with his hands. The old cowering before the young.

"Leave him alone!" Anger boiled up in my veins like lava as I strained against my bindings.

"How dare you converse with him," Sevran snarled, swinging toward me instead. "Do you think he has sympathy for you? He's merely keeping you alive until the tests reveal if you're usable."

"Usable? For what?" My muscles tensed instinctively as an ominous prickling crept over my skin.

"For breeding, of course," Sevran sneered. "You wouldn't be alive if we didn't think we might be able to breed your abilities into our people."

"You're using my blood?" I screeched in outrage. I felt the tingling at the back of my mind, tickling my mind as pain ebbed in my skull. Sevran stepped closer, fixing me with a look so inhuman my blood stilled in my veins.

"Oh no." She smiled creepily, "We still use traditional insemination methods for that sort of thing in our world. And of course, if you resist, your guardian will reap the consequences."

"I'd rather die." I bared my teeth at her, desperately trying to hide my horror as my stomach rolled so violently it's empty growl echoed through the cell.

"Don't worry," Sevran leered at me triumphantly, "we will harvest your body and mind until you want to anyway."

My powers rushed out of my body, wrapping around Sevran with a will of their own. Prying the device from her hand I threw it against the wall, smashing it to pieces. As Sevran's shocked gaze followed its direction I yanked her off her feet, propelling her away from me as rage rushed through me like a wave of destruction. The thwack of her body hitting the ceiling cutting off her shocked scream before it could even leave her lungs.

"Leil va aenat!" Still crouched on the floor, Lanest stared up at me in horror, his face washed white with fear.

"Help me!" I screamed at him, as I pinned Sevran harder to the ceiling. My mind thrummed, my powers roaring louder as they cut through the pain that permeated my every thought. Lanest rose hesitantly to his feet, his head whipping up and down between us both as he dithered over what to do.

"Release me. Please!" Hot bursts of fire stabbed into my brain, cutting into my concentration while Sevran thrashed against my hold, trying to get down and strangle me judging by the look on her face. She let out a high-pitched scream as the pressure forced the blood from her nose, her eyes bulging as they threatened to pop out of their sockets.

"Ahhh Siekaste!" Lanest cried finally. Rushing to the bed he unbound my wrists and feet with shaking hands. His face filled with trepidation, his eyes rolled nervously toward the ceiling as though Sevran might fall down on him in at any moment. The instant the last cuff fell off I launched from the bed. My loss of my sight altering my perception, I cried out in agony as I stumbled, the wound at my waist tearing open again. Gritting my teeth, I focused harder, still holding Sevran fast against the ceiling while my bare feet hit the hard floor of the cell.

"You've made things so much worse for yourself," Sevran stopped struggling suddenly. Looking up, I caught her maddening gaze as she hurled down her words with venom. "And you can kiss the life of your Guardian goodbye. You just sentenced her to death."

"Sevran." I squinted up at her hateful face. "What if you did have a child, and she was in my situation, in my world?" My voice shook with emotion, unable to comprehend her inhumanity. "What if we treated her like you have treated me? Is that the kind of universe you would have wanted her to exist in?"

The sneer slid from her face, a flash of uncertainty passing over her hard features, before she shook her head. "But it's too late. It's too late for all of us."

"But it's not! It's not too late for another way, another future!" I urged her, "It's you who has the power now to decide. Your people are terrified of your leaders. I can see it! Your generation could overthrow them! You could change things!"

Her mask dropping, anguish washed over Sevran's face as her eyes filled with the same hopelessness I'd seen in the eyes of the civilians. I watched her in silence, some of my anger subsiding as pity crept into my heart. I knew how to fight against resistance, but I had no idea how I could fight against utter despair, or hopelessness. Our training didn't cover emotional battles. As Sevran pulled her features back into the mask of disdain they'd taught her to wear, I felt for her. But I did not let her down. I knew these people better now, and their training was stronger than their hearts.

"It's too late for you now," Sevran warned. "The moment you leave this compound that chip in your brain is designed to explode. You'll be paralysed or brain dead in an instant. Or both."

"You're lying!"

Sevran fell, the connection severed as my hands flew to my head. The air whooshed from her lungs as she hit the bed, and I quickly threw my powers back out again, snaking the bindings around her own wrists and ankles before she had a chance to struggle.

"Abwarzians never lie," she hissed as she struggled against the straps.

Wheeling on Lanest, I searched his face for the truth, my hands pressing against my skull as though I could squeeze the microchip out if I pressed hard enough.

"I am s..sorry..." Lanest hung his head, unable to meet my eye.

"No!" I gasped.

"Itetch Avad," Sevran hissed at him reproachfully, "Abwarzians are never sorry."

"We have to go. Now!" Shaking off the fear rolling over my flesh, I grabbed Lanest's arm, as much to urge him and to try and steady myself. The room swum in and out of focus as the flames of pain seared through the cells of my brain toward my face. Panic bloomed in my chest as bloody ribbons flashed over my left eye. No. No. NO. I'd never get out of here if I went totally blind. I had to find Shay before that happened.

"I ca..nnot go," Lanest said simply as he gently pried my hand from his arm. "I must face my fate."

"They'll kill you." I stated the obvious in dismay as he backed slowly away from me, toward Sevran.

"I hope your pe..people d..d..defeat ours, for the s..sake of our yo..ung." Lanest smiled wistfully as his grey head shook, "But I... had e..nough of th...this world. I tired, and I jaded. M..m..my old b...bones are re..ready for rest, that I have ne..never known on this p..p...lanet."

My life on Como had been largely dictated, and I had resented it and fought it. But I had never felt the desire to give up on life, because I'd had hope. I'd been controlled but not crushed. But where there was no hope, there was no life. The soul itself would perish.

"They tell us that dy...dying for a good c...cause is n..no...noble. I think they are right...and I have finally found a worthy cause." Lanest nodded his head toward Sevran, his meaning clear.

"Please, Lanest," I pleaded, even though I knew it was already futile. "You don't have to die this way."

"But this be my will, I finally have co...control, and this is what I ch..oose. So you go. Quickly."

"Thank you, I understand." Tears burned my eyes as I backed toward the door.

"Go left," Lanest added as I turned and ran for the exit.

"Please stop her hollering at least until I can find Shay," I called over my shoulder.

"Wait!" Sevran shouted. I turned back, taking in her confused expression as precious time beat at my heart.

"Why didn't you kill me? You had the chance."

"I told you we want peace." I met her gaze with what little sight I had left, then turning on my heels, I ran left, for my life.

Chapter Five

Endless passages of yawning black windows greeted me at every turn as I crept from one corridor to another, through dark silent halls. The gloom merged with the darkness seeping steadily into my vision, and fear of losing my sight before I found Shay spurred me on as I raced against time. Weirdly, I hadn't come across a single soul, and panic and pain simmered in my brain like a deadly concoction as I peeked through every window. My heart hammered against my ribs in fear of what I might see.

At first all the rooms I passed were empty, and it seemed I'd been contained to an isolated area of the compound, where no one could hear my screams. But as I rounded a few more corners I came across my first inhabited room.

"Holy moga!" I shouted.

Ducking automatically, it took me a moment to gather my courage as I raised my head back up and peered through glass. Pale, bleak faces stared toward me, fear shining on grey gaunt faces as I gazed back. My heart twisted as I took in their deformed bodies. Some stared blankly past me, their gazes as vacant as the empty rooms. Others huddled in tight balls of bony limbs on their beds, huge dull eyes peeking out from over knobby knees, or behind shrivelled hands so malnourished I could see the blue veins running under their papery white skin. Hopelessness etched over faces too withered and weary for children so young.

A shudder rocked through me as I stared, trying to comprehend why they were locked up like this, like they were the enemy…like they were as hated as me. It wasn't right, on any planet, to treat your young like that, caging them like animals. It wasn't their fault they hadn't been born normal. It was their stupid leaders who were to blame; the very ones who now condemned them for their imperfections. Anger washed over me, my hands rising up to press against the glass dividing us as I contemplated freeing them. But where would I take them? How could I help them when I knew I couldn't even help myself? I had no plan, no formation of escape. I only yearned to see Shay, to say my goodbyes, to tell her I was so sorry I couldn't help her, that I could never take her home.

One of the smaller children climbed off his cot and took a tentative step toward me. His tiny face was pitiful with misery as he raised one arm and stretched it out toward me in a begging motion. My heart squeezed in sympathy as my powers began to thrum. Maybe I could let them out and help them to escape and find their families…

"Iiet! Iiet va Zadak!" Starting toward me at a run, the soldier reached for the weapon at his hip.

My powers rolled out in retaliation, connecting with a jolt as I threw him back into the wall.

"Oof!" The air left his lungs as my powers coiled around his weapon, yanking it from the holster. He yelped in horror as it whizzed through the air into my hands. The child drew back in terror, fleeing to the safety of the other children as the soldier slid down the wall to the floor.

"Zadak, querte sez!" The officer cowered against the wall and put his hands in the air, truly the universal sign for please don't hurt me, as I advanced on him.

Using the weapon, I pointed it first at him, then at the room full of rejected children.

"N…n..no… not with the da..damned." His eyes filled with horrified understanding.

"The dammed? You're euthanizing them?" I screeched incredulously. "What did they ever do to deserve death?" My heart raced so fast it felt like it would burst from my chest, and the soldier finally had the decency to look ashamed.

"They will never thrive here. It is not as cruel, as it is kind."

Maybe they were infectious, or maybe they just weren't good enough to live. Whatever the reason, my temper frayed as I pulled the trigger back. The sound produced the desired effect as the soldier scrambled across the floor toward the door. Pressing his hand on a panel on the door, it slid open and he practically threw himself in, as if he couldn't get away from me fast enough. The door slid shut, cutting off a final scene of his terrified face as the children surrounded him, reaching, and begging for life.

I broke into a run, trying to forget their faces as a distant shout informed me I'd been spotted again. The shouts grew louder, the sound of pounding feet behind me producing a desperate sob from my throat as I glanced over my shoulder.

Four more soldiers gained on me, step after pounding step; my weakened physical state no match against their pace as I stumbled stubbornly on, determined to die trying rather than surrender. I knew surrender wouldn't save me from death or torture on this damned planet, so there was nothing to lose. I pushed on a few more steps desperately looking into one last window before they caught up with me.

My heart leapt at the still form of Shay, lying in a bed identical to my own. Her eyes were closed, her face so ashen the flickering light on the hydration machine was the only thing assuring me she was still alive.

"Iiet!" a soldier shouted as I pressed my hand against the door opening. Nothing happened, my DNA or hand print unrecognizable as I beat my fists uselessly against the door.

"Prisoner, stop!" Ignoring their Comian, I stood back from the entrance, focusing my powers on the door. Reaching out, I felt through its volume, solid and dense. It would take a good amount of my dwindling energy, but I'd worked through a door as thick when escaping my own people back on Como. No time to hesitate, I threw the weight of my powers around the circumference of the door, and pulled with shaking limbs and mind.

"Iiet! Stop!" The door shifted off its hinges with a sharp crack of protest.

"Vadak!" I spun the door sideways as I levitated it out of its frame and toward me as I ran back a few steps.

"Iiet, Aiet un Avarkiez!"

My body strained under the weight of the connection, holding on with a thread as I lifted it over my head and got ready. As the soldiers rounded the corner I launched the door at them. Two were collected in one swoop, the door making a resounding smack against their bones as they were forced off their feet. Their bodies propelled backwards, into the next two soldiers with a satisfying crunch. At the same time, I severed the connection and let the door fall onto their tangled limbs.

Ignoring their screams, I hurtled into Shay's room, her name bursting from my lips in an anguished cry as I flew to her bed.

"Shay...Shay! Wake up!" The weapon fell from my hand, clattering to the floor as I grabbed her shoulders and shook her urgently, no time to be gentle. She weighed nothing in my hands. Her flesh clung thinly to her bones, her veins standing out like blue rivers on a white desert of deathly pale skin. As her eyes fluttered open and her dull blue eyes met mine, her emaciated face drained of what little blood there was left.

"Twell...no...oh no..."

"You have to get up, we have to get out of here right now." My brain automatically snapped the bonds like twigs, pulling the needle from her arm while I focused on lifting her up.

"Twell...no...please...stop." Her voice was so dry it cracked on each syllable, dismay filling my heart as she pushed weakly against me.

"Twell...it's too late, for me," she croaked, "please leave me...It's okay..."

"No!" My own voice broke as I gathered her stubbornly into my arms. "I won't leave you! I won't!"

"Twell, I'm dying...please..." Barely able to lift her head, Shay looked imploringly into my tear-filled eyes. "I raised you the best I knew how...but the Governing Body...they trained you even better than I ever could. Don't waste your training. You can still survive. Please. Please don't waste your life on something futile...try to save yourself."

"Shay, don't go! Just hold on!" Tears gushed down my cheeks, dismay and terror welling up in my heart. I didn't have the physical strength to carry her but my mind thrummed frantically, reigniting with a burst of power as I hoisted her into the air. Pushing her ahead of me, I made for the door, and stopped in my tracks as a dark presence filled the exit.

"I have to admit, your perseverance is somewhat admirable, for a lesser species."

My heart sank at the sound of her voice, then plummeted deeper still as I accepted how she must have escaped.

"You killed him."

"He was a traitor." Sevran spat in disgust. "He chose his fate." There wasn't an ounce of remorse in her tone as her dark eyes gleamed with violence. "And now I suggest you drop her and accept your own fate."

"I don't think so," I replied calmly although I was trembling all over. "I'm done doing what you want. My way now."

"Put her down." Sevran raised a weapon like the one lying at my feet. Pointing it at my head, the ominous click of a trigger sounded in the ensuing silence. My eyes darted from the weapon to Sevran, then back to the weapon again. I couldn't use my powers to grab it without dropping Shay. The ground was hard, and Shay's body a sack of fragile skin and bones, her head now flopped back in unconsciousness. Her bones would shatter, her skull sure to crack open when it hit the floor. Rather than the enemy, I would be the one who killed her off. The irony wasn't lost on me as I held her tighter.

"Vaero is no leader," I spat as Sevran advanced another step toward me. "He rules your people with force and fear. But my people obey out of loyalty. You'll never have what our world has learned, because you lead with your head and no heart."

"Very touching, and the reason your people are so easy to cull." Sevran sneered, as she took another step. "Such easy pickings when your kind are so distracted by this love business you value so much."

I was barely listening, my mind whirring with choices and consequences. If I let Shay go, she wouldn't make it. But if I didn't, and I failed to kill Sevran, she would kill us, and their army would never stop. It would never end, until we were conquered, our race extinct. I had to stop them to save my people. Shay's life, for the future of my world. My guardian sacrificed for the greater good. One death for thousands of lives. Way too much for a girl of less than 200 moons to have to decide.

"Love is what drives us. Yet your people don't even want to go on because they have no hope. I can see it in their eyes. In the end, you will lose, because hope is stronger than your weapons, and you can never destroy that."

"You can't win a war with words," Sevran sneered as she redirected the aim of her weapon at Shay's head. "Let me demonstrate how it's done."

"That's okay. I'm done talking anyways."

One heartbeat, I let go of my connection to Shay, letting her fall. Two beats, I slid under Shay's falling body. Five beats, I aimed the weapon at Sevran's. Her face grew more defiant and enraged as she leapt across the remaining space between us, her fingers finding the trigger as she moved. Six beats. I pulled the trigger on my own weapon and fired.

My body softened the impact as Shay's body slammed against mine, and Sevran's head exploded into a thousand pieces of flesh and brains, blood and bone. Her body continued to loiter in the doorway long enough to reveal the shocked faces of the soldiers behind her. Her knees folded as the rest of her body collapsed forward onto the floor. She twitched as her blood emptied out in a dark gushing river, flowing straight for me.

Meep Meep Meeeeeeeeeeeeep. Meep Meep Meeeeeeeeeeeeeep.

The shrill siren rose in a telltale wail throughout the compound, filling every atom of space with its ear-piercing shriek. Rolling Shay off me I crouched in front of her and got busy. I'd never seen nor heard of the weapon I held in my hands, but after that demonstration, I well and truly got the point. When the next soldier fired, I met the energy as it travelled toward me, blocking and reversing it in one swift pulse of power. Mushrooming back into the soldier, he jerked back, swaying for a moment before he looked down at the wide hole through his torso in amazement. I shared a moment's fascination with him as I gazed straight through his stomach at the bloodied wall behind him. As he fell, five more soldiers burst through the door and there was no more time to observe, only act. Sweeping my powers in a wide arc, I pushed through the burning in my brain as I collected their weapons in one swoop. As they stopped mid-air and turned on the soldiers they shouted in unified surprise, their mouths dropping open in shocked fascination as I swept my powers out again, this time knocking their legs out from under them.

Lurching to my feet I held my gun toward them with one hand while I continued to train their weapons on them. The effect was powerful. On their knees, their hands rose shaking into the air, just like mine had when they'd taken me.

I reached my free hand back without turning my head, feeling for the pulse in Shay's neck. It beat pitifully, but it still beat.

Meep, Meep, Meeeeeeeeeeeep. The siren wailed on, still insisting there was an emergency at hand.

"Do any of you speak Comian?" My voice was as course and dry as the desert sands as I forced it from my throat.

"Yes." The soldier climbed slowly to his feet. His sharp eyes pierced mine as my heart jumped in recognition.

"I don't wish to harm any of you." My voice shook treacherously as I addressed the soldier I'd once spared. "Do you understand? No matter what you've been told. I just want to leave with my guardian…on one of your spacecraft."

Silence followed. Did they understand me? Or were they planning their next move?

"Today," I rasped. "Take us now or I will have no choice but to force you."

The soldier's eyes did not leave me as he broke into a babble I had no hope of understanding. The other soldiers took it in, their faces reflecting different levels of reaction. Fear. Anger. Resistance. What did I do now? Did I need to make an example of one?

"You." I jerked my weapon at another soldier who was glaring resentfully away at me. "Come here.

My heart thudded so loudly it threatened to betray my bravado as he got slowly to his feet and edged toward me, muttering angrily. Keeping one hand splayed to hold the weapons over the remaining soldiers, I swivelled and pointed one at his head. He blanched, backing up a step as his features twisted with alarm.

"I will shoot this one, to show you I mean business if you do not direct the others to obey me." My voice shook, giving away my uncertainty.

"Doing that will change nothing," The soldier shook his head at me forcefully. "Don't you get it yet? Death in battle is honour in our world."

"You'd call several soldiers against one weakened prisoner honourable?" I barked a short bitter laugh, vaguely wondering how I'd come to a place where I was starting to sound as cold and harsh as they were, "Tell them I'll have no choice but to kill them if they try to stop me."

"So kill us," he replied tonelessly. "We have to follow orders or face the consequences."

"Where's Vaero?" I demanded, "I'll take out Mr. Creepy Control Freak for you. Who else do I need to blow up?"

At first the young man's face darkened as he contemplated my words. I watched wearily as confusion travelled over his features, then cleared as new possibilities seeped into his train of thought. "There are too many others who will reinforce our laws...loyalty or death."

"Listen," I replied impatiently. "Our people are going to fight your people, because you won't leave us alone. We've built our numbers and evolved our abilities more than you could ever know. There are many more like me, and even more with other powers you know nothing about. If you don't work with me, I will work against you, and so will my people when they get here."

The room fell quiet for a moment as his fellow soldiers gazed expectantly at him for interpretation.

"If you get back to your people, can you tell them there are enough of us who want to learn from you, rather than fight you, to stop this war.

"Yes."

"I can try and get you to a craft," he said quietly, "But after that you're on your own. You'll get shot out of the sky by our air patrol before you get far. "

"Let's go."

I stooped to pick Shay up, barely able to lift her as fatigue weighed down my limbs.

"I'll take her." The young man walked toward me, his arms

outstretched as the others gawked at him in disbelief.

"No," I snarled as I staggered back a step. "Don't touch her."

"You need your hands free to defend yourself, and it's obvious you can barely see!" the soldier argued. "I'm only helping you because of what you did for me."

"How do I know you won't try to kill me like Mr Blood and Guts predicted?"

"You don't."

I clutched Shay tighter to me, weighing up my complete lack of options as the soldier turned and relayed our conversation to the others. Their heads swivelled between the soldier and me in quick succession, then they jumped to their feet.

"Quick. Give her to me."

My heart dropped in dismay as the soldier darted forward, seizing Shay from my arms. I was so tired, I didn't resist as he stood beside me, grimly facing his own people with his jaw set tight. I was so incredibly tired. For a moment, I thought about surrendering, just so I could lay down again. But there was too much at stake, the life of my guardian, the future of my people.

Mustering the last reserves of my strength I prepared myself for my final battle. I was sure it would be death this time. I'd gone too far, and I was just too tired to keep fighting much longer. My headache was at full throttle, merging obnoxiously with the screech of the siren. My limbs were shaking in a way that warned me I was dangerously close to collapsing.

"Eiet atsilay acarn!" One of the soldiers shouted in a startled way as he lurched suddenly toward me.

The shaking grew worse, my legs starting to wobble as the floor began to buck.

"Acarn! Biest mazis!"

A deep rumbling reverberated through my bones as the soldiers pitched across the room. The soldier holding Shay dropped to his knees, his eyes wide with panic as he looked up at me.

"Prisoner, get down!"

"BOOM! CRACK!"

A symphony of deafening sounds filled my ears as I dropped onto all fours; the cloying smell of smoke assaulting my nostrils as I crawled awkwardly toward Shay. The room pitched again, throwing me off course as the other soldiers staggered to their feet. Without even hesitating, they turned and fled the room, in pursuit of the explosions cause.

The room shook as smoke streamed in from the hall and crept across the floor toward our abandoned party.

"We're being attacked." The soldier gaped at me incredulously. "I think your people have got through our defence force."

"Get me to a craft, quick," I urged him as I struggled to my feet.

"But they will think you're one of us, and shoot you down!"

"Moga, sh— I swore loudly, annoyed at my own stupidity. The chip in my brain appeared to be frying my brain cells, and I couldn't seem to think any faster as the smoke wound up our legs, climbing toward our lungs.

"But they brought yours back, I could try and get you to it..."

"Let's go!"

We moved, the smoke now so thick the air was choking with it. The soldier coughing violently as he tried to lead the way, struggling to carry Shay as he fought to breathe.

"Let me go first."

Overtaking him, I used my powers to push the smoke away. I'd managed the same trick once before; helping my friends escape the bomb that destroyed my school, and killed my best friend. The smoke obeyed the same way it had back then, billowing around us like a churning black tunnel as I cleared a path for us to move through. Up ahead, what looked like fire licked its way along the passages. The flames were a strange icy, blue hue, and they hissed rather than crackled. Ghostly figures of soldiers leapt away from it, rushing toward the exit, for safety, if there was such a thing on their forsaken planet. The siren screamed on, and I wondered if it had even been for me at all when another blast cracked sharply through the atmosphere, further away this time. The ground rocked beneath my feet as the soldier yanked hard at the back of my tattered tunic, forcing me to an abrupt halt.

"This way," he spluttered, holding his hand over his mouth as he pointed right. My gaze followed his gesture down a darkened narrow corridor, away from the direction the rest of his kind were running.

"Ummmm." I hesitated, years of being told not to trust his kind messing with my instincts.

"It's where we keep our war spoils. Trust me."

"You're kidding, right?" My conscience screamed unrepeatable obscenities at me as I dithered.

"Kidding? I'm not a kid, I'm the same age as you, I think."

I blinked, feeling foolish. "Oh..erm… that was a joke, you know? I meant how can I honestly trust you when our people hate each other?"

"Listen," he replied impatiently, "your aircraft is kept with everything else our leaders have plundered, so you need to hurry before it gets blown up as well." Ignoring my skeptical expression, he broke into run, leading the way as my heart galloped at the same pace inside my ribs.

"Wait! Stop!"

Wheeling around, his dark eyes burned into mine as I tried to read him.

"Why are you doing this for me?"

"Because I've seen enough!" Like lightening at night, his face lit with sudden fury. "Because I saw them torture and murder the other captives, and force you to fight. It made me sick to my stomach. It made me ashamed of my race. But mostly because you spared my life, when my own people would not."

Just like that, I finally understood that the rage burning in his eyes was not for me, but for his own people.

"So…can your generation actually see your leaders are screwing everything up?"

"Yes, many of us can see the vicious cycle. We are burdened with sadness, we hear the despair in our elders' voices as they tell us what it was like during the war."

"Well thank the heavenly realms, I thought you were all as brainwashed as your leaders."

"They try…but they can offer us nothing to hope for, and quite frankly, this world sucks. That doesn't leave us much incentive to keep on trusting them."

"I so don't want to shoot you anymore. What's your name?"

"That's a relief, and it's Ruvi-1067." He flashed his teeth at me in a sudden grin.

"Twell Anar, n…no number," I stammered, thrown by his genuine smile.

"Okay, Twell Anar, no number. We must hurry, we don't have much time."

Bemused I followed close on Ruvi's heels, as the sounds of warfare continued over our heads. Each rumble and groan of the Earth told me another missile had landed close by, and the siren wailed on.

As we turned down another corridor, I recoiled at the sight of a dozen pale and frightened faces peering out of the cells at us. Their palms banged in panicky rhythm against the glass. Their black eyes stared at us, huge and round, and full of fear.

"Wait!" I skidded to a stop. "We need to let them out, or they'll perish!"

Ruvi turned back. "There's no time and they're dead anyway," he replied, his features tight with urgency. "No one will help them, even if they do escape. They are all abandoned."

"Why?" The shrillness of my voice matched the wail of the siren.

"Because they're of no use to society, and therefore our leaders deem them of no value, apart from being used as decoys." Ruvi spat the words out bitterly, as his eyes darkened in anger. "They would never be allowed to procreate if they reached adult hood. But their life expectancy is only several moons longer anyway, if that."

"That could change…if…we…" My eyes stung as I trailed off. Ruvi looked at me apologetically, his shoulders shrugging. "If what? What do you think you can do? Rescue them all in one go? Break off the door and expect them to follow you? Expect my people to take them in?"

I knew that idea was as laughable as the concept of mercy in an Abwarzian, but still I couldn't seem to move. The fear and despair in their faces immobilized me as they pounded more insistently on the glass.

"Twell. We need to move. Now." Ruvi moved toward me, his hand reaching out to grab me as the fear grew in his own eyes.

"Wait!" I said again, as I halted him with the palm of my hand. Turning my palm toward the windows I focused on the glass. The children scrambled back instinctively, somehow aware something was about to happen. I let my powers roll out fast, slamming against the window with a crunch. The glass shattered into thousands of pieces, barely hitting the ground before the children dashed back to the frame, their instincts telling them they needed to flee.

"The soldiers will kill them!" Ruvi warned as the children clambered through the gaping frame. I was mesmerized by their dark shining eyes, the new hope in them holding me to the spot as I watched them drop to the corridor floor and advance toward us in jerky twisted moves of their deformed bodies. My throat tightened as they lurched toward me, their beseeching eyes demanding things I could not provide. Demanding life.

"Twell! Move!" Ruvi seized my arm and yanked hard, breaking me from the spell. I turned and fled with him, my heart sinking low in the pit of my stomach as their desperate faces haunted my mind.

Coming to a door at the end of the passage Ruvi slammed a palm against the security panel, jolting Shay in his arms as the door slid open. Rushing through without stopping I hurtled after him, my eyes scanning the room for any movement, my muscles coiled and ready to strike.

The room was unlit, but squinting into the gloom I could see it was beyond humongous. Hundreds of Comian lengths long and wide, every bit of space was filled with rows and rows of weaponry and flight crafts and other unidentifiable items from other unknown worlds. A chill snaked down my spine, the hairs rising on my arms as I moved past row after row of old world bayonets and knives, and new world guns and lasers. An eerie sensation seeped into my soul as I surveyed centuries and worlds of weaponry, tools of torture, and every way you could kill a person imaginable. I stopped in my tracks, frozen as my eyes fell in fascinated horror on a long, wide, glinting blade. I'd seen a blade just like that, in the hands of my own people, in grainy footage I was never meant to see. We'd used those blades to cut the heads off the Abwarzians.

"What are you doing? We need to hurry..." Ruvi appeared in front of me, his features tight with urgency as his eyes darted around us.

"We...we killed your people...with those," I pointed at the blade but I watched his face carefully, preparing for the anger I was certain would come.

"Yes. That was one of the first things they taught us," Ruvi shifted impatiently on his feet, as he adjusted Shay in his arms, "and then we conquered your people, destroyed your cities, and you surrendered the water."

"Um, not exactly," I replied cautiously, "We defeated your Army, because we had more numbers and haven't bartered since."

"Hmm, not quite the version we were taught." Ruvi stared at me grimly as a shadow of doubt passed over his sharp features.

"I think both versions hold truth and lies, according to our leaders' agendas." I looked away, down the rows of violence that seemed as endless as the fighting between our worlds would be.

"I think you are right," he replied solemnly as my gaze travelled back to his, "and that is why we are here. If we die, we die fighting for what we believe in; not what they have told us to believe."

I gasped as his words touched a place deep in my heart; speaking directly to my soul. How could the enemy be translating the words of my own heart, when my own people didn't seem to understand me, or refused to? Turning away, I began to jog, the urgency of the situation coming back into focus as I began to search for the aircraft I'd stolen.

'There! Over there!" I stopped, wheeling around to point out the craft as Ruvi caught up with me, Shay still flopping lifelessly in his arms. Pressing my fingers to the clammy skin on her neck I felt the faint bump of her pulse as she clung onto life. Maybe I had inherited something from her after all. Stubbornness.

KABOOM

Chapter Six

The deafening blast invaded my senses. Piercing my eardrums, the ground beneath me shook so violently I lost my footing and hit the ground hard.

Ruvi struggled to hold onto Shay, his grip on her lost in the confusion as the roof of the hall ripped open like fabric. Screaming in protest the metal shredded apart to reveal the bloody red sky. Fire roared over our heads, bursting into the hall like a hungry beast, gobbling everything in its path. Snakes of dark smoke twisted through the air and showered ashes like rain. I crawled toward Ruvi and Shay, and he raised his head, his gaze meeting mine for a split second before a horrific moan raised our eyes back to the skies.

"Look out!" I screamed. The Abwarzian craft crashed through the opening, exploding into a fiery ball of metal as it plummeted down on us. Springing to my feet I sprinted out of range then pivoted around, throwing both hands out in front of me. Gathering them both in my mind's grasp I dragged them unceremoniously across the ground toward me as the first piece of debris slammed into the place they'd fallen. Moments later the rest of the craft made impact; my connection to them breaking off as the explosion threw me into the side of something hard and unforgiving. My head smacked hard against the floor, and something or someone shrieked in fear as darkness pulled me down...

"Twell, get up! We need to get out of here. Now!" Ruvi's face appeared, hovering anxiously over me as I struggled to focus. Grabbing my hand, he yanked me to my feet, and then he was leading me back to Shay. Letting go of me, he stooped and lifted her back into his arms with a loyalty that made no worldly sense at all.

Ignoring the fatigue pulling at my limbs we broke into a jog, moving in motion together as the sounds of battle roared overhead. Reaching the craft, I raced up the stairs and opened the door manually, throwing myself into the pilot's seat by the time Ruvi caught up with me. Activating the ignition, the engine sprang to life. Punching in the co-ordinates for home with shaking hands, I jumped up again, rushing to kneel at Shay's side.

"Shay, please wake up!" I cried as Ravi crouched down beside me.

"Why?" Ruvi frowned. "I'm not sure she can, she's too far gone..."

"She has to." My voice cracked, my emotions beginning to leak out again. "The thing they put in my brain will kill me once we take flight. Once in flight the craft will follow the co-ordinates home. But she has to stay alive long enough to take off and land this thing."

Ruvi inhaled sharply before an awful silence stretched between us, no words sufficient to provide any comfort for my fate. I felt his eyes on me, studying my face as I continued trying to rouse Shay. He waited patiently until I was ready, even though there was no time to waste on my self-pity. Willing myself not to cry, I turned and looked into his eyes. My breath caught as I saw the spark of hope in his gaze.

"There is only death for me here now. Let me take her back to your people. Set the coordinates for me, and I'll deliver her home. If I can plead their mercy and tell them my people really do want the peace our leaders have refused us. If I can be an Ambassador for my generation, it's worth taking the chance."

"I don't know...I can't ask you to risk your life this way."

"There is more risk for me if I stay. And like you said, your people show mercy where ours do not. They won't harm me if I surrender to them, right?"

My eyes averted as I contemplated his words. My people painted themselves as people of mercy, but I had seen their hypocrisy and witnessed their merciless side.

"I know what they preach, but I can't promise what they will practice." My head hung in shame, unable to look at him as I smoothed away matted tendrils of hair from Shay's forehead.

From the corner of my eye I saw his hand reach out toward my face. I'd always expected Abwarzians to feel as cold as they appeared in the pictures, their temperature matching the ice in their eyes. But Ruvi ran hotter than me, and I inhaled sharply as his fingertips brushed my cheek; his narrow eyes widening in mirrored shock. His touch was the first kindness I'd known in a long time, and something I had missed more than I could have fathomed. My working eye began to burn in warning.

"I will take the risk, because it will give me peace in my heart, no matter the consequence."

"Thank you." My voice wobbled as tears threatened.

"Don't cry." Ruvi's mouth twisted up in a bittersweet smile, "It's a waste of fluid when you're already dehydrated. Trust me, I know."

I began to grin back when a sudden shout brought us to our feet. Rushing to the window of the craft, my heart lurched in dismay. Abwarzians swarmed the hall like black and grey insects, the pounding of their feet shaking the craft as they advanced toward our hiding place. Then I looked again more closely. Black and grey. Black was the colour of the Comian uniform. My uniform.

I gasped, my heart bursting with a mix of joy and adrenalin; fear and relief, as my fellow soldiers swarmed the room. They were really here, no longer just a dream. I pressed my hand to my chest, trying to contain my emotions as Ruvi reached my side. We watched as my own people positioned themselves throughout the hall and began to battle their opponents. The day had finally arrived. No more simulations. No more training. This was real warfare, and today we would all fight for our lives.

"Who…what?" Ruvi's tone was low with wonder as his gaze fell over the scene below.

"The Army of Powers," I gasped, my heart pounding in time to their boots hitting the stone floor of the hall.

As both armies spread out, they soon filled every corner of the great room as they picked their opponents.

Time seemed to slow down as the battles began in an elaborate dance of skill and power. Just outside the craft a Comian and Abwarzian soldier circled, sizing each other up as they prepared to fight. The Abwarzian aimed her weapon, the one I would now refer to as the human imploder. Before she could pull the trigger the Comian soldier threw out a bolt of power from his hand, blowing the weapon from her hand. Stunned but unharmed the woman lunged for the weapon but the Comian blasted it another bolt of energy. Exploding into shrapnel, they simultaneously dived for cover.

"He could have zapped her in the heart or head and disarmed her for good," Ruvi murmured. "You spoke the truth about your people."

I didn't reply as I crept back to Shay and checked her vitals once more. In my heart, I knew the truth wasn't as simple or easy as I wanted it to be. Some of us would let our consciences guide us in battle, or stay true to the morals they'd instilled in us through our educations. But deep down, feeling the stirrings of revenge in my own heart, I knew some of us would choose to seek our own justice. In the end, that would make us no different or better than our enemies. Picking up the weapon I turned back, handing it to Ruvi.

"You need this, but I think you should stay here with Shay. Will you use it to protect her?

"I will use it, against my own people, if it comes to that."

"I'm going to fight." I looked Ruvi steadily in the eye. "I have to defend my own…"

"You don't have to explain," Ruvi cut me off as a slight smile twisted his mouth, "As soldier to soldier, I understand. But you are weakened, so be intent and precise in your battles."

"Thanks for the tip." I almost laughed at the notion before reality sobered my expression. "I can never thank you enough, for everything…"

"Thank you's don't come often in my world. Consider it a pleasure."

I nodded. "I'll try to come back, but if we are defeated, hit this switch, and release that brake. The monitor will talk you through take off."

"Okay." Ruvi inhaled heavily as his eyes darted to the scene outside. "Go now. I'll try to watch your back from here."

Fighting my nerves, I crept to the entrance and surveyed the scene below. Powers pitched against weapons like a choreographed dance of war. Electrical current shot from the hands of my people, disarming the

Abwarzians, or sending them flying as the pulse hit their chests. Healers reversed their powers as they physically tackled their opponents, screams splitting the air as bones broke and tendons snapped. Hands and limbs were deliberately targeted to disable the soldiers, making it impossible for our enemies to even pick up their weapons. Looking up, the levitators were dive-bombing the Abwarzian soldiers, plucking their weapons from their hands before they even thought to look up. The soldiers with the power of speed attacked from the ground, moving so fast my eye could not keep up with them as more weapons were wrenched from the hands of our enemies, leaving them unarmed and confused. Cries of battle moaned in a spine-tingling echo throughout the hall, while fire jumped from one object to the next, or worse, from body to body as they screamed and writhed on the ground. Soldiers battled on beside them, too focused on saving themselves to help those who had fallen.

I watched as an Abwarzian shot a Comian with the dreaded toxic weapon they'd used to scar my own skin. Sure enough the Comian dropped to his knees, shrieking as the flesh melted from his bones. My muscles tensed as I moved into the doorway of the craft, my urge to help the soldier overcoming my fear of exposure. The next thing I witnessed was momentarily unexplainable. The Abwarzian's body jolted as his head snapped back in shock. No one seemed to have shot him, yet his eyes rolled back in his head as he crumpled to the ground unconscious. My heart began to race as the weapon in his hand rose up into the air, and a slight flicker of flying red hair flashed into view before disappearing again.

"Sazika!"

Launching myself down the ramp to the battle ground I raced in the direction of the bobbing weapon, then skidded to a halt as it spun and pointed at my head.

"Twell…"

Sazika materialized into full view, her arm dropping to her side in shock. She stared at me, her wide eyes huge with disbelief in her small pale face.

"You're supposed to be dead…"

"Not yet." I started to grin, but it faded away as I registered the

Abwarzian advancing toward us over Sazikas left shoulder.

"Disappear," I hissed, grabbing the Consciousness Deactivation Tagger from her hand.

Sakiza blinked at me once, then promptly vanished as I leapt toward the soldier and fired. Ducking, the woman sprang toward me, both of her hands aiming an obliterating gun at my head. I threw myself sideways as she fired, the heat of the energy's pulse palpable as it just missed my face. Hitting the ground at a roll I sprang back up to her left, my temper flaring. I'd had enough of these jerks trying to melt me or blow me up. Launching myself forward I crash tackled the soldier, ignoring her startled scream as I pulled her to the ground.

"Night night!" Pressing the CDT to her temple I pulled the trigger, her eyes popping wide in surprise before her body sagged under my weight.

"Sleep tight!" Sazika popped up beside me and handed me another weapon. It was a laser gun, good for slicing and dicing.

"Why've you only got a crappy CDT? I don't get it?" Jumping to my feet, I scanned the area for the next enemy.

"Because I insisted it was what I wanted." Sazika's tone was solemn as she scanned the opposite direction for movement. "They said no, but I pinched one from the training room anyway. It's my choice."

I was so proud of Sazika I wanted to hug her, but now just wasn't the time. She'd found a way to fight in a way she could live with, despite the Governing Body's rules.

"Stay out of sight," I warned her instead, "I don't want to see you sliced, Sazika."

Her grin was the last thing to disappear from view as I moved to the edge of the battle and selected my next target. He wasn't hard to pick, because he was trying to kill my genetic match.

My legs shook slightly as I prowled closer. Avin hadn't seen me, his body crouching low; ready to attack as his shimmering grey eyes fixed intently on his opponent. They swirled like molten steel as he tried to lure the soldier into his gaze. But the soldier was wearing some sort of protective eyewear that seemed to block the penetration of his gaze. Lifting the all too familiar weapon he aimed it at Avin's face.

"Avin! Watch out!"

Avin's head whipped in my direction, his gaze meeting mine for a split second before the Abwarzian shot a jet of acid at him.

"Get down!" Throwing my hands out I launched my powers at the cloud. It spread outwards, my mind meeting the sting of acid as I attempted to slow its movement. But the particles were so minute they mostly slipped through my grasp like air, continuing on until they touched Avin's skin.

His bellow of pain jolted through my heart as he dropped to his knees, covering his face with his hands. Fury rushed through my veins thicker and faster than blood, and I ran at the soldier with purpose, forgetting weapons as rage took over my senses.

"Oi!" My shrill warning served its purpose, distracting him from Avin as he wheeled to face me. Skidding to a stop in front of him, my powers kept going, barrelling on until they connected with his weapon.

"Vadak!" The soldier bellowed in surprise as I pulled it from his hands, his narrow eyes following its path into the air until it hovered directly over his head.

"Shower time for you," I snarled as my mind pointed the weapon at his head. "Let's see how you like it."

The man's features paled in understanding before he switched his gaze to look at me. Tears gushed suddenly from his eyes. Sinking to his knees he held his palms out to me, like he was begging. Because he was. I froze in horror as my heart hammered relentlessly inside my ribs. What was I about to do? He was disarmed, so why was I pursuing his death like this?

"Avar bable miet kar?" His tone was pleading, as his eyes pleaded with me for mercy.

Revenge raged inside me, battling with my conscience as the soldier cried openly on his knees before me.

"Don't do it." Avin's gasping warning registered vaguely as my mind pressed a little further on the trigger. "This isn't who you are."

Dismay filled my soul as I met his gaze. The flesh hung off his hands and face, the chemicals eating away to the bone. He must have been in agony, but it was his eyes that held the most pain. They burned into mine with emotions that ran much deeper than a flesh wound.

"Twell. Don't do this. Please."

In one look, I saw more than I could bear, not only anguish at who I was becoming, but even more scarring, his disappointment. I knew he could stop me with his powers if he chose. I was already so weak he could bend me to obey him in an instant. But he didn't. Once again, he'd chosen to give me my free will, and choose my path rather than control it. A cold dreadful sensation sank into my chest as the rage inside me ebbed away. Pivoting the weapon away from the soldier, I launched it as hard as I could, into a far corner of the flaming hall.

Getting to his feet Avin calmly approached the soldier from behind and tagged him unconscious. Stepping over his body, he moved slowly toward me, his shimmering grey eyes fixed on mine. I staggered back in panic, suddenly more fearful of facing him than the enemy.

"Don't run again, Twell. You've already broken my heart once that way." His tone was gentle but his words hit me hard, a small gasp escaping me as he stepped closer.

"You're emaciated." His voice cracked with sudden anguish, his raw hands starting to reach for me as his eyes roved over my bruised and bloodied body. "Your eye... damn them to hell, Twell, what did they do to you?"

"We don't have time to go over it now." I shook my head, swallowing the rising lump in my throat as I backed away again. "We have to finish this."

"Stay close to me then. You're weak," he replied tersely as his hands dropped to his sides. He must have been in shock because he didn't' seem to be in pain. The same adrenaline rushed through us both, blocking out any pain as we turned to rejoin the battle. There was no more time to think of anything but survival.

My training took over, and I was no longer a prisoner, nor a girl worrying about the people she loved. I was simply a soldier, fighting for my own life as the enemy closed in around me.

Nothing could have prepared me for the horrific sounds of battle assaulting my ears as I fought. Screams of terror invaded my senses as death chose its victims, wails and groans rising up in the last gasps of the fallen. As their blood pooled across the floor their bodies became a hazard, something to trip over or slip in whilst backing out of the enemies' range. I could not allow myself to look down as I leapt over them, too terrified a familiar face would distract me from my duty.

On autopilot, I tackled one Abwarzian after the next, wrenching weapon upon weapon from unprepared hands as they recoiled in shock. Some of them ran, not willing to tackle my powers bare handed. But others coiled and sprang, grim determination gleaming in their dull eyes as they too followed through with their training. Confronted with their willingness to fight to the death, there was no room for an ounce of hesitation as I used their weapons against them to render them harmless.

"Ahhhhhhhgh!" A soldier shrieked as I sliced off her outstretched hand with the laser beam. Blood spurting like a fountain, she continued to stagger toward me, her other hand raised to strike instead.

"Don't make me take your other hand!" I warned as I dodged out of her path.

"Achtiet!" Another abwarzian soldier's battle cry behind me was the briefest warning before he tackled me, the new blind spot of my right eye failing to detect him before it was too late. My back smacked against the floor, the air robbed from my lungs as he wrested my gun from me. As he pushed it into my cheek I clawed frantically at his hands, trying to pull it away as his eyes bore into mine, empty and as endless as a black hole in space. Panic overwhelmed my training as I struggled against him, imagining my face sliced neatly down the middle.

Then Avin was there, wrenching his head back as he stared straight into soldier's eyes with his own secret weapon.

"Get off her." Avin's eyes shone like silver pools of light, brilliant and inescapable as they pierced through the soldier's senses; capturing him in his deadly gaze. The soldier's body slackened in submission as his weight lifted off me, and like a vacant puppet on strings he jerked toward Avin, waiting for his next command.

"Leave here now. Do not attack again. Go and find your family." Avin's powers rolled out like a translucent wave, washing over the soldier with tangible force. His eyes glazed over as he dropped his gun. Pivoting away, he fled for his life.

Avin turned his gaze on me and I gasped at the effect, throwing an arm over my face to break the connection.

"Sorry," he muttered as he yanked me to my feet. Colliding into his arms, I felt his heart beat against my own chest for a fleeting moment before he released me and launched himself back into the battle.

Lurching after him with my hindered eyesight, I failed to see the body before it was too late, tripping straight over it. Hitting the ground at a practiced tumble, I rolled into a crouch as I scanned for signs of life or threat, and then recoiled in horror. Kaelin's dark eyes stared vacantly back at me, her mouth slightly parted in an incomplete scream as I sprang to my feet. Forcing myself to stay in soldier mode, I backed away. Now was not the time to let death sink in, or emotions distract me, or I would wind up in her place.

As the numbers dwindled and soldiers fell around me, the body count rose. On and on I fought, as the enemy came at me again and again; relentless and fierce, determined to the end. Wherever I could, I took a limb over a life, or disarmed them to discourage engaging with them in battle at all. But no matter how hard I tried to spare the enemies life, when the choice came down to their life or mine, I chose mine. Every time.

Like emerging from a dream, I finally stopped, exhaustion circling like another predator as I surveyed my surroundings. Everything was burning, intense heat roasting my skin as the flames licked along the floor, consuming the dead in an eerie blue glow.

As I picked up another soldier and flung him far down the hall, a familiar shriek caught my attention. Whirling toward the sound, my vision doubled before settling down to focus on one small dark shape, moving rapidly closer with each darting step.

"Mira!"

Mira spun toward me, her sharp eyes briefly taking me in. Her expression didn't falter as she turned away again, but her haughty tone was endearingly true to form as she tossed me a greeting.

"Glad you're not dead, but you'll probably wish you were once we get back to Como."

"I missed you too, Mira!" I grinned as I reached her side. She'd just electrocuted her opponent, and his hair was standing on end, a singed aroma rising from his uniform as he clutched his chest.

"Fight now, chat later," Mira muttered between gritted teeth as she selected another Abwarzian. The soldier yelped, catapulted into the air as she shocked him, yet I didn't wait to see where he landed, because I was too busy gawking at the huge machine rumbling through the battlefield. The screech of metal droned heavy in my eardrums as its sleepers crushed over everything in its path, chewing up bodies as it rolled toward us. As a huge hose like-nozzle emerged from its insides, my education of their weapons came back to haunt me.

"Meteor dust…they will pump it at you through a pressure hose that can shoot it about fifty Comian lengths…You would be fighting for air before you even had a chance to fight for your life."

And then the owner of those words was before me, my heart leaping as his gigantic form loomed over me. His eyes widened in disbelief as he took in my existence.

"Brazin!" I gulped, not sure if I should get ready to run or try and hug him as he lurched toward me. I cringed as his massive hands seized my shoulders but his eyes burned so fierce with a relief that it almost undid me.

"I don't know how you're still kicking kid, but right now we gotta stop that pump."

Turning, he ran at full speed, straight toward the machine as he shot at it with a laser gun. I ran after him, firing my own gun at the hose. But the beams barely scratched it, nor stopped its path as it halted, as its hose swung ominously toward a target. A target that turned my heart to ice.

Jonaz. Lost in the moment of disarming his opponent bare handed, he was entirely oblivious to my screams as I tried to warn him, my voice drowned out a thousand other cries, lost amongst the roar of flames, and whine of the machine. Adrenalin pushed my legs faster as I raced against time, trying to get close enough to flag his attention.

Surina and Talon leapt into my path, and I would have barreled straight through if Talon hadn't hurled his powers out to stop me.

"We have to stop it!" I gasped, ignoring their just seen a ghost expressions as I pointed in explanation. The hose shuddered, and catching on quick we all broke into a run, banding together as we prepared to merge our powers.

"Jonaz Maven! Move!" I screamed.

Jonaz's head jerked in my direction, his features wild with recognition of my voice. As his eyes met mine, the blood drained from his face. Staggering to his feet, he stood perfectly still, staring at me in shock as the hose expelled a jet of microscopically fine powered stone straight at him.

"Push it back!" I screeched to the others, my voice so dry I could barely force it out. Like a rope gathering strength with each strand, I felt Talon and Surina's powers weave with mine. Accelerating forward, we were pulled along by the force of our combined powers as they intercepted the spray. As our powers snaked around the nozzle of the weapon, I gave an extra hard pull, barely managing to shift the direction of the hose. Feeling it and understanding, the others pushed in the same direction, slowly but steadily pushing the nozzle up to the ceiling as a white jet of powder burst from the hose. Realisation registered over Jonaz's dark features as he staggered back, and as it settled over the room it swallowed up every figure still in its path, including Jonaz.

I ran straight into the billowing plumes of mineral, pressing my sleeve over my nose and mouth as I went.

"I can't see!"

"Aghh, it's burning my eyes!"

Screams fought their way into the air, only to be cut off in coughs and splutters as the fine particles seeped into our bodies. As I fought through the cloud, I saw some soldiers had pulled on breathers and eye protection, like we'd been shown in training. But I had no such protection. Covering my mouth and nose with my hand, I squinted through one streaming eye, pushing past other soldiers, Comian and alien, searching for the one face I yearned for. I opened my mouth to call for him, but his name choked in my throat as the fine dust clung to my lungs. They seized up instantly, my chest constricting like iron hands were squeezing my ribcage. Falling to my knees, I doubled over, gasping as my throat began to close up, and black spots danced across my eyes.

Black boots stomped toward me, halting abruptly as firm hands seized my shoulders. I tried to pull away as the soldier stooped down, but the hands shook my shoulder in a way that lifted my eyes to a masked face. Eyes as dark as night shone fiercely into my soul, making me breathless and shaky. Jonaz gazed at me like he never wanted to stop. His hands clenched so hard over my shoulders it hurt, but I didn't flinch, too lost in his expression. Relief was etched so deeply over his features, wild hope flooded my veins. I crouched there, unable to move or speak as Jonaz ripped off his mask and pressed it over my face. Taking my hand, he yanked me to my feet and pulling me along, leading me out of the deadly cloud as bodies writhed and gasped for air around us. Not so long ago, I'd resented Jonaz yanking me around the place like I needed his help. But now, half blind, and starved for air, I hung onto his hand like a lifeline. He gripped so tightly back I knew I never wanted him to let go.

I nearly tripped over Daelin. On his knees and handcuffed, the left side of his face was torn open, the muscles and tendons hanging out in a flap to reveal his exposed jaw bone. A dead Abwarzian lay before him clearly paying the price for disarming him.

His eyes met mine, frozen in shock and agony and I pulled to a halt, my powers fixing on his handcuffs. I had to help him, even if he'd betrayed me back on Como.

"Twell, No!" Jonaz yanked my arm so hard it almost ripped from its socket as he pulled me away.

"Stop!" I tried to pull free, but his strength far outmatched mine after so many days of torture and starvation.

Daelin pitched sideways, his head hitting the ground with a fatal crack as his eyes rolled vacantly up.

I tried to scream, to make him stop, but it never made it from my throat. Caught in the chemicals and wheezing in panic, Jonaz burst from the cloud, pulling me to safety as he aimed for a pocket of air that was breathable.

Yet the cloud was already dissipating, revealing tangles of bodies in its wake. An eerie silence had fallen, peppered by gasps and wheezes as survivors struggled for breath and life. Surina and Talon had caved in the hose, closing it off. Another figure stood on the front of the tank, fierce and determined. Using her powers Shanna yanked the driver straight through the glass window, throwing him so high and far across the hall I heard his bones shattering as his body met the bloody battleground.

Whimpers and groans filled my ears, piercing my heart as Jonaz stopped and released my hand. Then both of his hands seized my face, pulling my eyes to his as they scanned my appearance. His hands moved swiftly down, over my body, assessing quickly as he worked. Tears filled his eyes, sudden and fast as his hands came back up to my face and brushed gently around my left eye.

"Twell." His voice, the one voice I had been longing to hear, broke as he uttered my name, cracking under the pressure of fear, and grief, betrayal and loss.

"Jonaz I...I need to say I'm...I'm..." The words rushed out, strangled and small. The timing was wrong. All wrong. But I had to get it out. The guilt was like poison, killing me as slowly and cruelly as my enemies. But I was the only one to blame for my actions, my own worst enemy. Jonaz's eyes grew dark and murky, pain flashing across them like lightening. His mouth tightened into a grim line as his hands fell away. Looking away, he surveyed the scene around us and snapped back into soldier mode.

"We need to get out of here. This whole place is gunna come down." Leaving my plea unanswered he gripped my arm, spinning me around in time to see the roof peeling open like a tin can. The sky above was darkened with columns of black twisting smoke, and ashes fell like snow as a Comian craft hurtled past the roof toward land.

"We have to help them!" I broke into a jog, my fatigued muscles screaming in protest as my heart pounded with increasing urgency. As we ran, shrapnel rained from the exposed sky, falling all around. Jonaz grabbed my hand, propelling me faster.

"Look out!" I shrieked as a piece of the roof landed less than a Comian length in front of us. Jonaz swung me around the twisted metal without stopping as we headed in the direction of the fallen craft. All around us, soldiers abandoned their battles as the building collapsed around us. Flames licked up the walls, climbing for the sky as we ran through an open hanger door. The air was thick in my lungs, and my chest tightened as we made it outside, my eyes struggling to adjust to the eerie red light of the sky.

"Over there." Jonaz pointed toward the craft, which lay a hundred Comian lengths north of our location. I didn't reply, unwilling to waste oxygen as we ran swiftly toward the border of the Government compound. The other AOP followed Jonaz's lead, and in no time we made it to the metal fence. It stood at least five Comian lengths high, and was made of a thin greyish mesh.

"Is it electrified?" A soldier to Jonaz's left looked to me for answers.

"No idea." I shrugged. "But only one way to find out." Stooping to pick up a rock, I hurled it straight at the fence. There was no zap, no shattering of stone. But my insides tightened in warning. It could not be that easy.

"Let me test it." Mira's bossy tone gave her away before she appeared to my right. Marching up to the fence she placed her palms out toward the mesh and closed her eyes, as though feeling for a similar energy to the one she contained within her.

"It's not electrical," she confirmed. "But it sure is hot. Come closer."

We moved forward cautiously, palms out like one does when approaching an open flame. The heat was palpable from a human length away. There was no way anyone could touch it without burning.

"What now?" I looked at the other soldiers, who stared blankly back for a moment.

"I've got this." Mekai pushed through the crowd of soldiers, his grin larger than life as he winked at me. "Care for a lift, it will be just like the old days."

I grinned back in understanding as I hurried to his side. "We go over," I shouted. Anyone with levitation powers, step up now." Climbing onto Mekai's back to demonstrate, I shrieked once as Mekai shot off the ground, propelling us up, up, over the fence and safely to the other side. Mekai immediately sailed back over the fence, leaving me momentarily alone and exposed before one by one other soldiers were lifted and dropped over the compound fence. I exhaled the breath I'd involuntarily been holding as Jonaz dropped in front of me, his smile turning to a frown as he took in my expression.

"Jonaz, look, "I whispered, unnerved, "it's just like the hologram."

"At least they got some things right," Jonaz muttered as he led the way, his laser gun pointed out our path. The buildings sat as grey and gloomy as ones in the simulated training. There was little sign of life, no lights in the windows of the silent dwellings.

"Do you think they've fled?" I asked as we began to move up one of the abandoned streets.

"Hiding more like it, "Jonaz muttered as he swung his gun in front of him. "Or preparing to fight."

"Stay on this street, soldiers!" An Officer strode past us suddenly, his mouth set in a tight grim line as he trained his weapon on the windows as we passed. "Watch every dwelling. Do not hesitate to shoot if you perceive a threat."

"Do not hesitate?" I protested as the soldier crept up to the window of a home. "What about women and children?"

"What about them?" the soldier barked as he peered through the window. He was quiet for a moment as he scanned the interior, then jumping off the step he raised his weapon free hand to point at me. "Remember your training. You can't trust any of them."

"I remember," I retorted as Jonaz shot me a look of warning. "Doesn't mean it's the truth."

The soldier stopped in his tracks and stared hard at me. "You stand there looking at me, half dead at their hands, and you wonder if it's the truth? Maza was right. You're no hero, you're just a silly kid with a death wish."

"Hey!" Jonaz stepped toward the soldier just as the ear-piercing shriek of a new siren wailed over our heads. The sound echoed through the empty streets as we abandoned our argument and began to move faster. In the distance, more AOP soldiers were spilling from crashed aircraft, and they began to run toward us as our feet pounded the dusty red streets. The siren screamed on, mingling with smoke and fire, and muddying my senses. Fresh adrenalin flooded my veins, pushing me on until we reached the soldiers. But my relief was short lived, my heart freezing as a shadow moved past the window of the nearest dwelling.

"Someone's in there!" I shouted a fraction of a moment before the window shattered. A man's ashen face appeared for a moment, determination shining in his narrow eyes as he pushed the nose of his weapon through the window and fired.

"Get down!" I yelled as the jet of flame flared toward the officer. The soldier dropped on command, but the flame was faster, consuming his whole body so fast there was no time to beat it out. The soldier let out one panicked scream before rolling frantically on the dusty ground. Yet the flame wouldn't extinguish, and the stench of cooking flesh singed my nostrils as he writhed, his shocked silence more terrifying than the flames as the fire consumed him. Jonaz whirled back to me, his arms flying out to guard me as he simultaneously drew his weapon and fired at the window. The beam of his laser melted the skin from the Abwarzian's face on impact, his skeletal features staring back in shock before his body crumpled out of sight.

As more figures dove for cover behind him the Comian Army sprang into action, storming the dwellings in droves as the cry of battle reignited.

"Twell, come on." As Jonaz leapt toward the nearest dwelling, a dozen more Comian soldiers followed, pushing past me and storming into the building so fast I lost sight of him among the identical black uniforms.

"Still think the G.B are wrong about everything?" Mira shoved past me, stalking in the opposite direction. Her face was a mask of fury as she flew up the steps of a neighbouring dwelling.

"They think we're attacking!" Breaking away from Jonaz, I followed after her. "Wouldn't you do the same to protect your family?"

"Shoot now, ask questions later," Mira snapped before kicking the door open.

"Mira no!" my cry fell on deaf ears as she burst through the door. High-pitched frightened screams pierced my ears as I launched after her, and I raised my weapon, unsure whom I was planning to protect first.

I stopped in my tracks, my line of sight following the direction of Mira's laser into a murky corner of the room. Huddled in the corner, a woman and small child crouched, their faces lit by the dim light filtering through the window. The child peeked out from his mother's arms, so tiny and malnourished his large wide eyes appeared too large for his head as he surveyed us.

"Atchi ena mal ite!" The little boy strained to pull from his mother's arms. His mother's face screwed up with sudden anguish, as she clutched the boy tighter in her embrace.

"Stop!" Mira cocked her weapon at the child and pulled back on the trigger. "I will shoot."

"They're just civilians!" I edged to Mira's side, placing my hand over hers to lower her weapon. "They have no weapons."

"That you can see," Mira hissed, not taking her eyes from the mother. As she jerked her weapon upwards to shake me off, the Abwarzian woman let out a blood-curdling scream and sprang to her feet.

"Get back, or I'll shoot!" Mira warned, directing her weapon at the woman. But her hand was shaking, betraying her hesitation. My heart sinking, I swung my own weapon toward her, my heart beating fast as I reluctantly pulled the trigger back. The child began to whimper, as his eyes filled with shining tears.

"Azaste en et bastaz!" the woman shrieked, shoving the child toward us and holding up a small device in her hand.

"I knew it! She's rigged up the kid!" Mira screamed. But I already knew, my instinct to flee moving my legs involuntarily. The woman let out a long wail, a guttural mourning cry as tears poured down her face. As she squeezed her eyes shut and raised the device, Mira threw out her free hand and blasted the woman in the stomach. As the woman reeled back, Mira flew at her, wrestling her to the ground as she braced another hand against her chest and shocked her. The woman's body jerked like a puppet on a string, her bony hand locking over the device in a muscular spasm.

"Menae menae!" the boy howled. Trembling like a leaf, tears streamed down his face while a pool of urine seeped out around his feet. My heart swelled, choking in my throat as I lunged for him and gathered him up.

"What are you doing, you crazy moga!" Mira screeched at me as she shocked the woman again. The Abwarzian woman stopped struggling, her body still shuddering as the electrical currents attacked her nervous system. Mira wrenched the device from her stiffened fingers to inspect it.

"Trying to get it off!" I snapped as I assessed the bomb. It was wrapped snugly around the child's scrawny torso, hidden easily under his shirt. The little boy struggled and sobbed, trying to twist from my grasp as I attempted to unravel it from his waist.

"Hush hush. It's okay," My attempt at a soothing voice shook unconvincingly as the boy wailed louder.

"The device is on some sort of a timer, and I have no idea how to stop it." The first signs of panic finally leeched into Mira's tone.

"Can you blast it?" I gasped as I pinioned the child's flailing arms to his sides.

"Not without blowing us into the next realm." Mira looked me dead in the eye, her expression so unfamiliarly fearful my heart skipped a beat. "Twell, we have to leave the kid and run. Now."

I paused, gazing back into her brown eyes for what seemed like an eternity. I searched for regret. But all I saw was the same desire for self-preservation that was flooding my own veins.

Setting the boy back down, I bit back a sob as I backed away. The boy's eyes grew huge with abandonment as he staggered toward me, his arms outstretched toward me.

"Stop, get back," I warned him, my voice high and strangled as I backed rapidly away. The look on his face burned into my mind as we turned and ran for the door, a lonely and frightened wail rising from his chest like the howl of an animal as we abandoned him. Despair rose into my throat like vomit, and as I burst from the dwelling Mira was already screaming a warning.

"BO......"

The world exploded. One second I was on the stairs of the dwelling, the next, flying through the air into the street. The air whooshed out of my lungs as I hit the dirt, a high-pitched ringing pressing at my ears as I raised my head from the ground. Mira had landed nearby, and her left arm was twisted under in an unnatural angle. Through the persistent ringing, I lip read the curse word that formed on her lips as she struggled to get up. Her perfect hair was finally beaten, matted with the blood that ran from a gash in her forehead.

"Hey, Mira, your hair's a mess. Fancy that." I giggled hysterically as I climbed to my knees.

Mira glared at me like I'd lost my mind before surveying our surroundings. As the ringing slowly subsided I followed suit, surveying the burning buildings and the bodies, both Comian and Abwarzian that littered the street. My mind flashed back to the images of war I'd seen at the DUC. They were too similar, only this time all my senses were experiencing brutal reality. I could taste my blood in my mouth, salty and metallic, and reminding me I was still alive. Smoke billowed from the remains of the burning buildings, tightening my lungs, and hazing my view of the wounded. All around me they screamed in pain, their flesh hanging from their skin in flaps, their bones snapped like twigs. The smell of burning flesh was more intense than ever, and I leaned forward on my hands and knees, retching into the dirt. But nothing came up. There was nothing left inside of me at all.

A hand landed on my shoulder, and I looked up into Jonaz's face, the horror in his expression enough to bring me to my senses. Taking my arm, he pulled me to my feet, while the AOP reformed around us. As Jonaz brushed my cheek, his hand came away, sticky with my blood. But I felt no pain, my eyes travelling past him as my stomach turned to liquid dread.

Vaero marched through the street toward us, with three-dozen soldiers flanking him. His eyes were already fixed on mine as he walked, and I froze with fear before my muscles began to tremble. Not now. Not when I was spent. Following my gaze, Jonaz looked from Vaero, then back to me, taking in my expression.

"Who is he?" Jonaz whispered fast.

"The leader," I gasped just before Vaero and his soldiers came to a stop about ten Comian lengths away. His soldiers fanned out, forming a semi-circle around Vaero.

"Prisoners never leave Abwarz." Vaero's red eyes pierced mine through his barrier of soldiers, his teeth bared in a sharp gleaming grin. "But we will record your death, as well as those of your remaining troops, to show your citizens the consequences of fighting us, when we attack and defeat them tomorrow."

"Still delusional." I managed a shaky smirk as I stepped away from Jonaz, closer to Vaero. "You haven't exactly cleaned up around here.

Look around."

Vaero glanced at the bodies around him, noting the grey of the civilians clothing, that far outnumbered the black. I shivered as he gazed back at me, his eyes glowing like bloody embers. From the corner of my remaining eye, I saw our remaining soldiers creeping, pressing in all around me. My eyes widened fractionally as I noted my friends. Mekai was standing next to Sazika. He'd made it to the final showdown, his leg no longer holding him back from the war we'd all trained for together. Kina caught my eyes, her expression as serious as always, and finally appreciated. Beside her was Lavi, her hair as wild as her face was bloody. Innocence had been stripped from her features, war finally shattering her beliefs that something like this could never happen.

To my right, Mira crept in closer, her arm hanging uselessly at her side while she continued to aim her weapon with her right. Finally, my eyes fell on Shanna. Watching Vaero carefully, she inched slowly closer to me. I took my own step closer, emboldened by the presence of my friends. I sensed Avin was somewhere to the left behind me, but I did not look around. I could not afford to turn my back on Vaero. He would not be fair or merciful as he tried to kill me.

Forming a circle of their own around Vaero and his soldiers, the Army Of Powers pressed slowly closer, and Vaero noticed.

"Stop!" His voice rang out in Comian, slicing through the silence as dread gripped me like a vice. There was unexplainable victory in his tone, despite the odds. With dreadful clarity, I understood why. Raising an all too familiar device in his right hand, his fingers found the trigger at the same time he aimed his words at me.

"Let's see you fight after this,"

Click

The searing pain I now knew too well wove its familiar trail of fire, searing through my skull, slicing through every cell of my brain. It pushed at my skull as though it would shatter through bone to burst out of my body. I screamed once, a short sharp scream of agony as my right eye filled with blood, and I heard the pop of an artery as I went completely blind. My hands came up, scrabbling at my eyes as I sunk to my knees. The pain stopped just as suddenly, but my vision remained as black as Vaero's eyes and heart. My lungs rasped, my breathing fast and fearful as panic flooded my veins.

"Twell! What is it?" Jonaz started forward, his footstep thudding behind me before Vaero spoke again.

"Don't move," he commanded Jonaz, "or I'll press the button again to finish her off."

"I'm blind," I whispered hoarsely. "Just do what he says."

Jonaz's footsteps stopped abruptly as his breath drew in, sharper than any knife. Staggering to my feet I felt the ground swaying beneath me as I lurched forward uncertainly.

"Not so special now, are you, Comian," Vaero spat. "What a waste of that breeding programme your parents must have participated in."

"What are you talking about?" I spread my feet wider, trying to find my balance as the darkness threw my perception out of order.

"Come on now." Vaero's patronizing chuckle crossed the space between us, filling the tense silence with his scorn. "Did you really think your genes evolved in one generation without intervention?"

"We're anomalies." My voice wavered, shaky with shock. "A result of natural selection."

"Your parents would have been the first group experiment to produce gifted offspring." I could tell he was grinning from his tone. "Forced to create you to better the race. In the end, your lives are as controlled as ours. Only, we have never tried to deny it."

"You're lying," I retorted. "Nothing you say has any weight."

"As long as I lead my people, my words are law." Vaero laughed harshly. "A law you will now submit to, along with the rest of your world."

"Never," I hissed. "You survive, but you do not live."

"And under our control, you will barely survive. But that is better than death."

"Not in our world."

"Then you choose to die now?" I felt Vaero's smile, like a serpent slithering toward me in victory. I would be the example to control the rest.

I stood very still, listening to my heart hammer inside my chest as the silence pressed in at my ears. Everyone was waiting. For him to move, or to kill me. For the final fight that would result in our freedom or capture. It was now or never. I did not know if it would work, but I had nothing left to lose, apart from my life.

My powers stretched out, weak and shaking, and barely intact as they felt for the connection I knew I was looking for. My skin tingled as I met the solid force of Shanna's power, recognising and connecting silently.

Click

The sound of Vaero's trigger pulling back, masked the exact moment of another. Beads of sweat rolled down my face as my hands fluttered out in front of me, my fingers curling in anticipation.

"Today our people celebrate victory over Como and its inhabitants." Vaero's triumphant voice rang out over us all as his soldiers crouched and raised their weapons. "We will wipe out your Army of Powers before the sun has sunk tonight, and your civilians will be under our control by tomorrow."

My heart galloped relentlessly, determined to make a run for it as I secured my powers around her gun, lifting it noiselessly into the air at her side. I felt her stiffen, her hand reaching for the gun before releasing in understanding. I felt her power merge with mine like two threads, weaving to form a stronger rope. Ready to push the moment I was ready. Ready to be my eyes.

"Then kill me now. Right now."

"Twell, NO!" Jonaz shouted.

"Very well." Vaero laughed.

"Now!" Shanna screamed.

The whoosh of the gun met my ears at it travelled toward me, and I knew if I fumbled it was already too late. It hit my hand as Shanna screamed again.

"Fire now!"

It seemed like an eternity, raising the gun back into the air. Like pushing through water, the last of my minds strength pushed down on the trigger. I heard the laser beam ignite and shoot away in Vaero's direction, but I had no way of knowing if I'd hit my target, only the proximity of his voice and the sense of his dark presence to guess his exact location.

Twell and the Uprising

Every sound distinguished in an instant. Even the beat of my heart as I ceased to breathe. There was nothing. No gasps, no cries, no sound of pain, or victory, or death…until…

Thud.

Chapter Seven

"Nice work you moga, clean down the middle!" Shanna's deafening screech broke the spell as time moved forward again, and pandemonium broke loose. Shouts refilled the air as their remaining army turned on ours, and the battle reignited. They were not surrendering, even with the death of their leader. Something hit me hard from behind, dragging me to the ground as my gun clattered out of mid-air. Feeling for it, my hands closed over the handle as the body rolled over me and grabbed my face.

"It's me." Jonaz yelled in my ear as all pandemonium broke loose, "Don't move, until I come back for you!"

"Since when have I ever followed your orders?" I sighed to no one as he disappeared from my side. Pulling myself onto my knees I clutched the laser gun in both hands, casting out with my powers to detect any intruders around me. I sensed Jonaz, a few lengths away, and felt he was locked in battle. My heart jolted, the feeling of helplessness a new kind of pain as I tried to feel what I couldn't see. Every grunt of exertion, every clash of weapon seemed louder than normal to my ears, and I strained them further, desperately listening to their deadly fight for survival.

"How can I help?"

"Get down!" he snapped back.

"No!" I pushed to my feet. "Teamwork!"

"For the planets sake! Half dead, completely blind and... Stubborn. As. Ever..." the words were punctuated with three short shrieks of pain from his opponent. I heard another thud and then Jonaz was back, taking my hand and pulling me back into a run. I stumbled after him, towed along by the force of his grasp as we dodged and darted through the battlefield. Every few paces Jonaz jerked to a stop, and then a shriek of pain would indicate our opponent's fate as Jonaz used his free hand to strike them down. Jonaz let go for a moment, two hands required as he fought a stronger opponent. Desperate to contribute, I cast my powers out, feeling for intruders and pushing out to keep anyone from attacking us from behind. The sounds of battle were slowing, the noise fading from screams, to wails…to final whimpers as unseen lives were extinguished around me.

"How many left?" A Comian cried behind me.

"That's it! We have the remaining soldiers captured." I started as Brazin's voice in front of me began booming out directions. "Get them rounded up and taken to craft 502. We leave as soon as our dead and living are all on board."

"What will happen to the prisoners?" I shouted.

No answer. A slow creeping dread weighed down my spirit as I staggered forward toward the sound of his voice.

"Brazin?" I demanded. "What are we going to do with them?" The silence grew heavier, only broken by the occasional whimper or moan of the fallen.

"Jonaz?" panic began to build as I experienced the full isolation of my blindness. I staggered forward, my heart in my throat as I tried to feel for life, afraid of being left alone, but more afraid of being found by the wrong soldiers.

Sensing someone approaching, I took no chances, shoving them hard with my mind before they could come closer.

"Oof! Hello, not the enemy, you moga!?"

"Shanna?"

"Seriously? Forgotten the sound of my voice already?" I envisioned the roll of her eyes as her sneering tone hovered closer.

"How could one so easily forget such an irritating sound?" I retorted as she grabbed my arm.

"Well allow me to narrate the scene," Shanna went on unperturbed. "We have just kicked some Abwarzian butt. We have captured their remaining soldiers, and their leader is only half the man he used to be, thanks to you."

"Get her to the crafts," Jonaz ordered Shanna from a distance away. "I'll meet you there."

"Wait!" I cried as Shanna started dragging me away, "Shay's in the craft I stole. I need to get back to her, she's barely alive!"

"Where is it?" Shanna huffed as I pulled against her grip.

"The back of the building we were in before, at the eastern end."

"Come on then," Shanna said as she pulled me in the opposite direction, "we've rounded up the surviving enemy, but we need to get our wounded out of here ASAP."

I let her lead me, staggering slightly as I stumbled awkwardly beside her. All around me I could hear the pounding of feet as soldiers moved away from the battleground to our war crafts.

"I'll lead her." Avin's hand closed tightly over my free arm as Shanna let go.

"Shay's in her escapee craft," Shanna muttered hurriedly, "We'll take her there, then straight to 502. We're leaving immediately."

"Let's move." Avin's tone was dark and grim, his sense of urgency propelling me forward as our feet smacked in time against the ground. The heated fence had been blasted through with a tank, leaving a wide opening for us to run through as we retraced our steps. Avin led us back into the smouldering hall, his deep cough confirming the level of smoke as my own lungs struggled to receive air.

"This is too dangerous," Avin shouted through gasps. "This place is gunna come down any moment."

"Please, Avin, please," I begged as my chest tightened even more. "We have to try."

"Let's get on with it," Shanna snapped behind me. "We don't have time to argue about it."

Avin grunted in response, pulling me along with him once again as he searched through the hall for the pod.

"It's right here," Avin panted, pulling us to a sudden stop. I lurched ahead of him, my hands stretched ahead of me in search of the steps to the craft.

"Stop!" Avin yanked me back hard as he shoved in front of me. "You can't just go running blindly in there!

"No pun intended?" I replied drily, as I heard Shanna pushing past, her boots thudding heavily on the stairs.

"Oh. Sorry," Avin muttered distractedly as I heard the door to the craft groan open. There was a pause before Shanna shrieked, "Hey! Get away from her!"

Realization dawned too late, horror seizing up my throat as I forced out a warning.

"Shanna, no! Don't hurt him, he's…"

My words were drowned out by the short burst of a weapon, followed by a high horrifying wail of pain.

"Stop!' I screamed, "Shanna NO!" I staggered up the stairs and burst into the craft as a heavy thud sounded to my left.

"Ruvi!"

A faint moan rose up from the floor of the craft, and I threw myself at the sound, my hands landing on a warm damp torso.

"Ohforplanets sake, what's your issue now?" Shanna snapped impatiently. "We need to get out of here. NOW."

"Twell?" Avin's voice wavered uncertainly behind me. "I have Shay…it's okay…she's alive."

"No. No No…" My hands came away, sticky with his blood as it gushed from the hole in his chest. His agonized breathing wheezed faintly as his hand suddenly found mine.

"Ruvi…" A sob escaped me as I squeezed it with the last of my strength.

"Twell?" Avin's confusion laced with warning, "We need to go. Now."

I barely heard him as I bent over Ruvi's body. His lungs bubbled with blood, fighting for air as he tried to form words.

"A good thing… happened… today," Ruvi whispered through panting breath. "Our people… needed to be… defeated."

"I'm so sorry." I choked out, "I'll get Jonaz to come. He can heal you…"

"Twell…it was good… to know you. You showed me there could be ho…hope for my people…p..please. Don't stop fighting… when you return to Como. Your fight is not over…yet."

"I won't," I promised, "But you have to fight now. To live."

"It's too…late…" Ruvi's voice faded as his life seeped away, and the sound of the Comian war crafts hummed to life around me. "Help my people start… a new way…as I know you will help yours…"

"Ruvi, no…just hang on…" I begged. Avin's hands closed over my shoulders, but I shook him off, leaning close until my face was pressed against Ruvi's. As I felt the last of his breath leave his body, hands hooked firmly under my arms and hauled me to my feet.

"We have to go now.," Shanna barked unceremoniously. "We have your precious Guardian. He's dead. Leave him."

"You killed him, "I shrieked, lunging at the sound of her voice, "You stupid moga! He saved my life, and you killed him!"

"Are you brainwashed?" Shanna yelped as she dodged out of my way. Avin grabbed my arm, preventing me from lashing out again. "So what if he's dead?" Shanna snarled. "He's the enemy, and I thought he was going to kill your guardian."

"He taught me more truth about his people than our leaders ever did," I retorted as fury pumped through my veins. "And he could have taught us a lot more!"

"Oh, just when I begin to admire you, you go and spoil it with your idiotic notions." Shanna huffed and she stomped toward the exit of the craft. "You lead her back, Avin. I'm not apologising for dispatching the enemy." Her boots clomped angrily down the stairs as my head sunk into my hands.

"Twell." Crossing the space between us, Avin gripped my face gently as he pulled my hands away.

"I'm sorry. You know how she is, and I'm sorry she did it, but please, you have to come now. We have to get out of here, there's other lives to think of now. Including your guardian's." Without waiting for my reply, he let go, and I sensed he had crouched to gather Shay into his arms.

"How is she?"

"Alive. Barely. Now hold onto me." As he moved toward the exit, I reluctantly reached out to hold the back of his shirt as we disembarked and made our way out of the building and toward our main craft. The buzzing of agitated voices mingled with the drone of the engines as we neared, all shouting commands as they boarded the crafts. The smell of fuel turned my empty stomach as I followed Avin up another set of stairs into one of them. Jostled on all sides, streams of soldiers moving frantically past us as Avin moved at a slower pace. The incline felt like a mountain, my legs shaking with long overdue fatigue as the adrenalin seeped from my veins. I let go of Avin's shirt, reeling back on my heels, too exhausted to stop myself from falling.

Strong arms wrapped around me, lifting me off my feet and cradling me against a strong broad chest. His scent, though muddied with blood and grime, was so familiar I wanted to howl with relief, and grief all at once.

"It's okay," Jonaz whispered, his breath warm in my ear, "You can rest soon."

"I'm tired," I sighed. I felt tears rolling down my cheeks, despite my eyes no longer functioning in any other way. I wanted to go to sleep, but something niggled at the back of my mind, and each jolt of Jonaz's step kept me conscious.

"I know, Twell, shhh, you're going to be okay."

I felt us entering the massive hull on the aircraft, and after a while Jonaz lowered me flat onto a bench, not letting go until he'd strapped me in.

"Don't leave me." My voice rose in panic as I searched for his hand, my heart beginning to beat inexplicably faster. A stronger wave of fatigue hit me and my breath came in short tight gasps. Something was wrong, something I needed to remember.

"Hey," Jonaz seized my hand, his other coming up to cup my face. "I won't. I promise…"

"But I left you…I left you… I'm sorry…"

"Shhh, Twell hush. It's okay…we'll talk about it back on Como. Just rest." His hand smoothed my blood-stained hair, the warmth of his fingers burning a comforting trail down my cheek.

"I can't…I can't…there's something…" I struggled to sit up…the foreboding sensation so strong I felt sick to my stomach.

"Twell, stop." Jonaz pushed me firmly back down. "There's nothing we need to discuss right now. You're safe. That's all that matters…"

"No…there's something in my brain!" I gasped, realization hitting me the same moment the engines roared to life.

"What?"

"The microchip! It will explode once we're in the air," The air squeezed from my lungs, and I gulped frantically for more as terror chilled my limbs and heart.

"Avin!" Jonaz called sharply. "Come here NOW."

I felt Avin's presence before he dropped to my side.

"Hold her down." Jonaz yelled over the roar of the engine.

"Why?" Avin sounded slightly amused. "Worried she'll disappear on us again?" The engine hummed through my bones as it lifted off the ground…rising slowly up as it navigated a way out of the hall.

"More worried her brain will explode after take off if I don't remove the implant those monsters inserted into her," Jonaz snapped. "Now hold her!"

Avin inhaled sharply. A moment later his hands pinned my arms to my sides, and my insides flipped over as dread pounded my organs to mush. As the craft rose higher I began to squirm in understanding, sweat bathing my skin as my heart banged so hard against my ribs it threatened to burst straight through.

"Hold still, Twell. Don't move a muscle," Jonaz warned as he took my head in his hands.

"Wait!" Avin shouted against the whine of the engine. "What if you damage something…you could permanently harm her…or kill her…"

"If I don't she'll die anyway," Jonaz snarled. "Now hold her tighter."

As Jonaz clamped his hands like a vice around my skull, anticipation got the better of me, and I lost all composure. I began to struggle at the same moment a white-hot pain like a blade of fire pierced through the base of my skull. A howl of agony rose out of my chest like the ones I'd heard on the battlefield.

"What's going on here?" A booming voice rose over my shrieks as I thrashed in horror. The craft moved higher in a burst of speed as it cleared the hall, and Avin cursed uncharacteristically as we lifted higher.

"Help us hold her down. She's chipped!" Jonaz roared louder than everyone.

Brazin needed no more information. His huge hands held my head to the cot like metal clamps, and no matter how much I twisted and struggled my head remained still while Jonaz drilled further into my skull with his powers. The familiar smell of burning flesh assaulted my nostrils, the pain so unbearable a long scream ripped from my lungs, hushing every other soul on board.

"No, not again, no more, please! Let me go!" I could see them in a brutal flashback, the Abwarzins leering down at me as they tortured me…

"Twell, stop struggling and hold still!" Jonaz gasped, his voice tight and high with tension as I felt his fingers probing, searching, and then the scraping of bone as he located the chip. I felt the sticky warmth of blood trickling down my scalp. No one else spoke, only the sound of my screams mingling with the roar of the engine as we rose higher and higher. I'd felt enough at the hands of our enemies. And now, at the hands of those I loved the most, I wanted to die. It was too much.

"You're killing her!" Avin yelled, his voice hoarse with horror as another wail of agony echoed through the craft. I tried to buck Avin off me as the craft launched higher, the pressure joining forces with the pressing in my brain as I screamed again.

"Quit the melodrama," Brazin growled. "You're still a soldier…not a sook."

I sobbed uncontrollably, my body jerking in spasms as the pain consumed me.

"Please, Twell," The agony in Jonaz's voice was inescapable as he choked over the words. "I'm trying to save you. Just hold on…"

There was nothing but fire…fire travelling into my mind and burning up everything in its path. I stopped struggling, falling limp as I detached from my body, eager to get away from bones and flesh that could be torn and broken.

I felt Avin let go of my arms, feeling for the pulse in my neck. Then he gripped my shoulders, shaking them hard.

Too exhausted to resist, I felt myself rising up, climbing to the stars that twinkled around us, up and away to the promise of a place where I could no longer feel anything at all.

"Twell, no!" Avin shouted. "Jonaz, we're losing her! You have to stop!"

"I'm nearly there, I can feel it!"

"She's not breathing!"

"I have it, I'm trying!"

"Hurry, boy!" Brazin's voice rose up, strangely strangled and hoarse. "We're about to breach the civilian flight zone. That's her limit."

I drifted toward a brighter place, the tether to my mortal body stretching as I rose above them all. I felt warmer and lighter as I floated up. A sob ripped from someone's throat, but it was not mine.

"Twell! Hold on! Just hold on!"

But there was nothing to hold onto. The tether was about to snap, and I no longer had the energy to come back.

"Twell!"

A final blade of fire sliced through my skull, followed by a flash of light. It pierced through my blindness in one quick flash before the world around me exploded, obliterating the world, and plunging me into eternal darkness.

Chapter Eight

Soft hazy light pressed against my lids as the muffled murmuring of distant voices met my ears. The air drawing in through my nostrils was sweet, the temperature refreshingly cool as it caressed my skin. Gingerly flexing my limbs, a groan escaped my lips. I was very much alive. The afterlife couldn't possibly be this painful.

A dark shadow fell over the light, bringing a cold chill to my skin as a voice devoid of any warmth hissed in my ear.

"How are you not dead?"

Unwillingly, my eyes opened. The light hurt, burning my eyes like the sun as I blinked in protest. Far from perfectly returned, my right eye seeming to work better than the left, and tears spilled quickly, washing away the blur and grit as I glared up at a most unwelcome sight. Yet even the blurry version of Maza's disbelieving expression was still mildly satisfying as I struggled to raise myself to a sitting position.

"That seems to be the trending question at the moment." I shrugged. "I'm surprised as a leader you haven't obtained the answer yourself."

Maza's eyes narrowed, her countenance darkening like an impending storm. "Well, well, well. You mean to say they didn't cut that weapon of a tongue out of your smart mouth?''

"Obviously not," I sighed impatiently. "So can we just get to the part where you threaten my existence and happiness, and so on until you feel validated by the exertion of your somewhat questionable power?"

Maza moved over me so suddenly, I shrank back against the table. Her eyes were so black, so devoid of any humanity, it took me another moment to realise she was removing the tethers which anchored me to the cot.

"Get up," she commanded. "And don't even think about trying anything."

I moved slowly, experiencing a sharp pull at the back of my head when I raised my head from the bed. Recollection of what happened came flooding back as I gingerly probed the back of my skull with my fingertips. Discovering a small raised scar, I exhaled the breath I'd been involuntarily holding. He must have got it, because as far as I could tell, my brains were still inside my head.

"I said. Get. Up." Maza grabbed my arm impatiently, yanking me up so fast I cried out in pain. Anxiety clutched my chest as the room swam around me. I concentrated on deep breathing, letting the pure air fill my lungs until the floor slowly ceased rocking. As I glanced around the small sparce cell, I realised I was once again a prisoner of my own people. No better off than I'd been at the hands of my enemies. Despair rose up like bile in my throat, tears of frustration smarting my eyes before I forced myself to swallow my emotions back down and focus on the issues at hand.

"Give me a moment," I stalled, "I feel dizzy."

"Stop whining." Seizing my arm, she dragged me from the table onto wobbly legs, "I'm far from done with you yet. Walk."

"Where's Shay?" I demanded as she pushed me roughly ahead of her. I stumbled instantly, both from fatigue and from being unused to Como's gravity after so long away. "Is she alive?"

"That is of little consequence to you," Maza snarled. "Now move."

"Sure. When you answer me properly." I stopped and tried to anchor myself to the floor, my head spinning as Maza's blurry face formed into a viciously disturbing smile.

"How's those powers of yours, Twell? Let's find out? Shall we?"

Maza struck me so suddenly across the face I had no time to prepare. As I reeled back, she struck again, this time punching me hard in the stomach. The air sailed out of my lungs as I sunk to down on my knees.

"As I thought. "Maza's thin lips stretched over her sharp gleaming teeth. "They fried you good. Couldn't have done a better job myself!"

I gasped for air as a dreadful realization struck me. My powers had not ignited, and as I searched my mind for the familiar buzz, there was only anger and fear. Nothing more.

"Don't try to defy me again." Maza leered at me as I staggered to my feet, "or next time it might be someone you love that I hurt. Then it would be your fault, wouldn't it, Twell?" Giving me a hard shove toward the door, I went without further retaliation. But my blood boiled in my veins, mixed with a sickening fear that I'd possibly lost my powers for good. I couldn't help myself, let alone anyone I loved if she chose to go after them.

"I'm thirsty. I need water." I muttered as I shuffled along.

"That's too bad." Maza sneered, giving me another unnecessary push in the small of my back. My desire to hurt her welled up so hard and fast my teeth crunched together; my nails piercing the skin of my palms as I fought to stifle down my rage. Inhaling deeply, it took all my strength not to retaliate as Maza pushed me in front of her down a long white hallway.

I moved listlessly, dragging one foot after the other as Maza led me down endless identical hallways. They turned too many times for me to bother trying to map. I couldn't see the point. I had no energy to escape, and no idea where I would go if I tried. They would find me, no matter where I ran. I knew that now. It seemed there was no place free or safe, in my world, or any other.

Finally, we reached a doorway at the end of a hall. Maza opened it and pushed me roughly through it, grabbing my arm again as she practically dragged me across the room. It was a healing centre, or at least a room that had been converted into such, in order to treat all the wounded in battle. Rows and rows of white cots held soldier after soldier, and the room filled with the stench of burnt or rotting flesh, mingling with the soul piercing moans of the wounded.

"Like what you see, Twell?" Maza whispered coldly in my ear. "Because you're the cause of all this."

The misery of death hung over the place like stale air, sucking any spirit of hope from the room.

"What do you mean? It's not like you attacked Abwarz just because of me…" I trailed off as uncertainty overwhelmed me. I had no idea why they had finally attacked…it couldn't possibly be because of my actions..."

"We don't abandon prisoners of war." Maza hissed through gritted teeth. "No matter if they have abandoned us, their duties...their people."

No no no. I had never wanted this. I had never wanted to fight. And yet, my actions had caused Como to finally fight back. My heart pushed hard against my ribs, my senses reeling, as suffocating guilt and despair swelled in my chest.

"Did you really think there wouldn't be consequences because of your actions?" Maza grabbed my arm hard and yanked me around until I was forced to look at her. I flinched, barely able to handle the disgust that shone in her sharp rust coloured gaze.

"People died because of what you did. You will answer for it."

Something in her satisfied expression ignited my temper. I knew I shouldn't let her get to me. I would answer the GB for my actions. But I'd be darned if I would answer to her. She was as corrupt as they could come.

"They were going to attack us again anyway," I snapped pulling my arm from her grasp. "Better you fought them on their own planet than let them come here again and attack our civilians. So, really, you're welcome!" I lurched away from her then, ignoring her outraged gasp as I darted off down one of the aisles of stretchers. My insides churned with renewed dread as my eyes roved each cot for faces I knew

"Shanna!"

I barely recognized her war-torn features. Her short dark hair was matted and damp against her clammy skin, her eyes glazed with pain. Both of her legs were gone, amputated from the knees down, and a bandage around her waist was soaked crimson with her blood.

"Hey, is that you, alien lover?" Shanna's head lolled slightly toward me, a faint spark flickering in her eye as she searched for my face. Pulling out of Maza's grasp I moved quickly across the room, lurching toward her bed, reaching for her hand. I was still mad at her; I had not forgiven her killing Ruvi. But she was a familiar face, and I needed anything familiar right now.

I nearly dropped her hand in shock. It was as cold as ice, and her lips were a foreboding shade of blue.

"Shanna...I..." My brain swam, unable to form words that could match my thoughts.

"Well, I'd get up to greet you, but it seems I haven't got a leg to stand on." Shanna grinned weakly at the horror on my face. "Looks like you'll be making the next move on your own. Sorry."

"Oh Shanna...." I squeezed her hand so tight she flinched.

"No sooking, Twell." Shanna mustered the energy to pull a disapproving face. "We stood up for you when you ran off and abandoned us, so don't you dare let us down, or I'll come back and haunt you."

"I don't believe in ghosts," I retorted, "and stop talking like you're dying. The healers will help you."

"They already have," Shanna whispered tiredly. "They stanched most of the bleeding while we were flying home, but those filthy Abwarzians have some darn impressive bacteria."

"Do you have any family here?" I asked distractedly, one eye on Maza as she stormed toward me with a face like a thundercloud.

"Yeah, but she's not allowed in until we are all disinfected and no more foreign matter is detected. So no, I don't think my guardian will be coming to see me off."

"Don't say that!" I cried as Shanna grew paler before my eyes. "I need you to help me work out what to do!"

"Oh, don't be so needy; you already know you and I were never going to agree with how things went from here. You think we can be heard, and negotiate..." Shanna gave my hand a weak squeeze while her mouth pulled into a faint smirk. "But I know our leaders will never submit. You will have to crush them, and break their spirits like they broke ours. That's how power over another works. That's what power is."

"But I don't want power, I just want freedom."

"Power is freedom," Shanna's eyes burned with a mix of fever and fervour, her fingers tightening around mine. "But it's beyond your control now anyway. You'll see I'm right...in the end, it's already started, with or without you."

"What's has?" I whispered urgently as Maza closed the distance between us.

"The rebellion." Shanna fingers crushed mine painfully, her faint smirk stretching disturbingly across her pale face as Maza's hand clamped down on my shoulders like inescapable iron. "She can't stop you now, it's bigger than her, you, or me. It's everywhere."

Maza yanked me back so hard my hand was torn from Shanna's grasp. She didn't fight it, her arm flopping lifelessly to the bed as her hardened gaze met mine one more time.

"Don't forget, Twell." She sighed as her eyes began to close. "Make it count."

"Shanna!"

"Enough! More insubordination!" Maza hissed as her fingers dug into my skin. "You're not here to spread more poison."

"Then what for?" I snapped, my tolerance for her non-existent. She began pushing me to the far end of the room, past the gaping wounded, past the staring medical officers and healers. No one tried to stop her. No one said a word, the room falling quiet as they observed her in wary silence. She stopped in front of a medical chair, which sat in a small partition. I grimly noted the metal cuffs on the arms and legs, as well as the dark curtains making up the partition. As we entered the space she pulled them around us, closing out the curious observing faces, ready to conceal anything that transpired between us once they were drawn.

"We need to assess your physical capacity before we take you before the Governing Body," Maza said curtly. "Can't have you passing out, or gaining any sympathy during the hearing."

"Hearing?" I snorted as she shoved me into the medical chair. "Don't you mean judgement?"

"A just and fair consequence for your heinous crimes," Maza snarled, as she cuffed me to the chair. "And from now on," she leaned in so close her spit sprayed my face, "I'd recommend you watch that mouth of yours. With so many medical instruments around, I would love nothing better than to rip that poisonous tongue from your mouth."

I glared at her in bitter silence, hating her for hating me so much, despising the fear she still instilled in me after all I'd been through. I was so tired of feeling afraid, but the sensation followed me no matter where I went, haunting me like a restless spirit.

"Keep your mouth shut while the medic assesses you, or I'll make good on my threats." She hissed as a medical officer entered the partition. "Let me know when you're done," she barked to the medic. "She's not to be released from this chair."

With that she strode out of the space, leaving me with a nervous looking young medic whose hands were already shaking from the shock of all he'd seen.

Picking up a blood pressure cuff, he approached me warily, like I might try to use my powers on him. Closing my eyes, I tried to summon them, but no part of my mind responded, and only a dull aching pain filled my mind as I scowled in frustration.

"Leave here now. This medic is taking over, and you are needed elsewhere."

My eyes snapped open. The medic had already fallen under Avin's spell, his head nodding dazedly as he scurried from the room. Avin turned, towering over me as his molten silver eyes stared into mine. They swirled with his powers, capturing me easily in my weakened state. Realising the effect he was having on me, he abruptly switched it off, bending down to my eye level as I regathered my senses.

"How are you feeling?" He murmured, his hand resting lightly on my shoulder.

"Oh, Avin…" Tears sprung to my eyes as I took in the scars rippling over the left side of his face. Red angry lines ran down, streaking his cheek like he'd cried tears of acid. Maybe he had. His mouth formed a stoic sort of smile, trying and failing to hide the misery in his countenance as my heart filled with bleak dismay. His eyes clouded with the pain of loving someone who didn't love you back. Somehow, he had already decided my heart. Or read it in my own eyes as I held his saddened gaze.

"Don't worry about such things," he said tightly as he stood up again, moving away. "Jonaz will look after you now."

I inhaled sharply as Jonaz stepped through the curtain, dressed in the white medical gowns the healers and medics all seemed to wear. I didn't dare meet his eye as my pulse began to race. Shame bent my head, and my next words were muttered at the ground.

"Why hasn't anyone fixed your face, Avin? Surely a healer can do it?"

From my lowered gaze, I noticed Jonaz stiffen slightly.

"I did offer," Jonaz replied curtly, "but he declined."

I felt the tension in the room like a physical presence, and blood rushed to my face, making me squirm in my restraints.

"I don't want them to," Avin replied simply. "I don't want anything that has happened erased. I'll leave now."

"You don't have to go...." I trailed off, losing confidence as his expression shut me out.

"It's okay. Take care of her, Jonaz."

"Right. Because I take orders from you." Jonaz muttered under his breath as Avin walked from the cubicle. Avin's shoulders stiffened as he went, but he did not turn back to challenge him. And then I was alone with Jonaz. And as nervous as heck.

"How well can you see me, Twell?" Jonaz stood back, assessing me from a distance that felt as far as Como from Abwarz. His tone was so clinical, so unrevealing of any emotion, my heart sank to a low and lonely place, and I could not find the courage to look at him.

"I can see you," I murmured quietly to the floor. "A little blurry, and better from my right...but I see you."

I heard his steps across the floor before his touch jolted my skin like an electric shock. Tilting my chin firmly up, I was forced to meet his eyes. They pierced mine, dark and unrevealing, roving my face as his hand dropped to seize my wrist. My pulse beat fast against his fingers, and I swallowed hard as my cheeks began to burn. Nerves fluttered in my belly as he let go, his hand moving up to curve around to the back of my skull. Gently probing the tender exit wound of the micro-chip I gasped, jerking away as he flinched in response. Anger and pain flashed over his features like lightening, striking deep into my soul.

"Sorry," he muttered. "I need to monitor the wound."

"That's okay," I managed through clenched teeth.

"Here," Jonaz replied more gently. "Drink this."

I could smell it immediately as Jonaz pressed the vial into my shaky hands, the pureness of the Comian water igniting the incessant thirst like flames in my throat. Ignoring the dull throb at the base of my skull, I greedily gulped it down in one long pull, sighing with relief as it soothed the ache in my throat.

"Thank you." I gasped, as I felt my sluggish mind begin to clear. "Jonaz…where are we? Where's Shay? Is she…is she?"

"We're home, and she's stable, Twell, but she has some pretty serious damage. They're keeping her in an induced sleep for now, while we try to heal her."

"Thank the realms." I sank back into the chair with relief. "Back in Caran…you mean…we're home?"

"Not exactly. We're in Caran's healing centre. But you're under arrest for desertion, theft, oh…and inciting a rebellion."

"Oh good. Just a slap on the wrist then probably."

Jonaz's mouth twitched, beginning to form a grin that I yearned with all my heart to see. But just as quickly his smile ebbed away again, and the warmth in his eyes dimmed to a colder temperature as he stepped away from me again.

"You broke the rules. You knew what would happen." His tone was so patronizing, resentment stirred my spirit in retaliation. "They're going to charge you with everything they can. You have no idea what went down after you left."

"So tell me," I replied numbly.

"I warned you not to do anything. That wasn't the time. That it was too risky!" Jonaz ranted while he paced around the room. "And by ignoring me you started a rebellion that got so out of control we almost didn't have an army to come and find you let alone fight for our people!"

"What?" The air fled from my lungs like I'd been dealt a blow to the chest.

"Everyone went crazy, Twell. Crazier than us! Matches were breaking up faster than Maza could lock them up for insubordination. They rallied a protest and every single soldier involved was charged with treason against the Governing Body."

"And you, Jonaz?" I realised I was trembling as I searched his eyes. I looked deep, searching for the man I knew. Jonaz Maven. The boy who had once told me not to be afraid to love, no matter the cost.

"I was too busy thinking you were dead, to worry about anything else," Jonaz snapped. Holding my gaze, I gasped at the fury in his dark blazing eyes, feeling every ounce of his anger like a physical force.

"Jonaz...I'm so sorry you went through that...I never meant to hurt you this way...I...I." I hung my head, shame choking up my insufficient apology.

"Stop apologising, please. It's done, and I can't be long with you. But seriously, Twell. You're really in trouble this time. Maza's launched a smear campaign against you in order to control the rising resistance. There's no telling what lengths she could go to put you away, or shut you up for good."

"Well, it probably couldn't be worse than torture at the hands of my enemies," I muttered bitterly as the memories threatened to assault me. "But then again, after the way they've already treated me, maybe it could."

"You had to expect this would come of it," Jonaz replied tersely. "You knew how seriously they were reacting to the rebellion, even before you took off."

"So they treat me as badly as our enemy?' I leaned forward, pulling against the restraints in frustration. "Locking me up again? Taking away my rights for having a voice? An opinion? A heart?''

"And you think it hasn't killed me?" Jonaz's reply struck out at me, his eyes flashing with sudden rage as his frustration boiled over. "You think it hasn't almost destroyed me, not being able to save you from our own people...let alone our enemies?" Jonaz put his hands to his temples as his eyes squeezed shut. He grit his teeth, letting out a sharp cry as the veins in his temples bulged with blood.

"Jonaz, stop! You're hurting yourself!' STOP!" I gasped as a trickle of blood ran from his nose.

Jonaz opened his eyes, his expression as shocked as mine as he touched a hand to his nose, catching the blood in his hand.

"I'm sorry! I'm just so sorry..." my eyes burned with tears, my gaze tearing away in shame as emotions overwhelmed me. Jonaz closed the space between us in one long angry stride. Seizing my chin again, my eyes flew up to meet his, flinching at the torment swelling in his darkening gaze.

"You think my heart wasn't shattered, when you broke through that glass ceiling and ran away? Why run, without me? Why shut me out?" My stomach cramped at the pain in his voice. His dark irises burned into mine, bringing heat to my cheeks as I squirmed under his gaze.

"I know...Jonaz...I just wasn't thinking straight..." I gasped as his grip tightened, his mouth tightening into a frown as he shook his head vehemently.

"Yet you let him in?" Jonaz spat angrily. "Into your plans, and into your heart."

"No!" I stared at Jonaz in horror. "It wasn't like that! I didn't invite him into anything!"

"Well, he certainly seemed very invited last time I saw him with you," Jonaz replied, the anger draining just as suddenly from his voice as his hand dropped to his side. Betrayal and hurt haunted his features, and a throbbing ache swelled in my chest as I gazed desperately at the man I loved.

"I don't even know what to say. I don't know why...I...can you forgive me?" I trembled as I met his eyes, petrified of what I might see there.

"Do you love him?" Jonaz asked so quietly I barely heard him. His eyes fixed slightly off my face, his jaw so ridged the tendons in his neck stood out.

"No, Jonaz Maven. I love you."

Jonaz's eyes widened. His breath hitching as the words sunk in, and I realised I'd never uttered them before. But after all I'd gone through, telling Jonaz I loved him was no risk at all. I'd lost him, and my freedom. There was nothing left to lose now.

"Did he compel you?" Jonaz's response felt like a kick in the chest, the ultimate rejection as his rigid expression conveyed he already knew the answer. Shame struck me mute, and my heart seemed to pop in one painful burst. Our trust was broken, and some things could never be fixed.

"But you care for Avin." Jonaz exhaled.

"Yes. Because he's a good Comian. And he looked out for me...and maybe there is some sort of connection with him, because he's my genetic match...or maybe just because. But Jonaz, it's nothing like how I feel about you. I want you. I choose you. I'd fight for you...

I'd lose everything for you."

Jonaz heaved a sigh before he allowed his gaze to return to mine. "I know you think I abandoned you, Twell. I know you think I hate you for what happened between you and Avin. I saw it in your eyes just before you ran. And I see it even now."

"Yes, I did think that." My voice shook with regret. "And I couldn't bear to see it, to see in your eyes what I'd done. I wanted to protect you." I cried as I gazed into eyes full of anger and sadness. "I wanted to keep you out of the mess I was making. And so I ran from it, and you…and the hopelessness of everything."

"Our love wasn't hopeless." Jonaz shook his head furiously as he stood back to scrutinise my face. "Why did you get to decide our fate?"

"I…I hadn't decided anything." I trembled with dismay as my stomach churned dangerously. "I was upset and confused…I'd had my freedom taken from me, and you were part of that freedom."

"Were…" Jonaz replied stonily as he took another step back from me. "So you just gave up on us then." Looking away, he raised his wrist as he started stabbing my stats into his wristband." If you want to be with him. It's okay, "Jonaz forced the words from his mouth as though they tasted as bitter as they sounded. "I'll understand. He's meant to be perfect for you, after all."

"No!" I shouted, struggling against the restraints as frustration brimmed over, "I want you, Jonaz Maven. It's only ever been you who I've wanted."

Jonaz inhaled sharply, his eyes piercing right to my soul before he looked up in alarm, the hum of other patients and medics pausing as my voice travelled easily beyond the thin curtains of the cubicle.

"Shhhh! I'll have to leave now, I'll send the other medic back." He sighed, his expression a tangle of emotions as he moved toward the exit."

"No!" I began to yank hard against the restraints. "Jonaz! Please don't go!"

"Twell, please." Coming back, Jonaz crouched quickly in front of me as he met my stricken gaze. His own expression softened, the hardness fading away from the corners of his mouth as his hands covered mine. "Promise me you won't try to escape right now. Leave it to us this time. For the planet's sake, don't try and do things on your own, just one damn time."

"How could I?" I bit back the frustrated sob working its way into my throat, "I've lost my powers."

"For now." Jonaz squeezed my hands gently, at the same time rising to his feet as he glanced warily over his shoulder. "But you need more rest to allow yourself to fully heal. Don't give up hope they're still there."

"Thank you, Jonaz for saving me," I whispered as his hands fell away and he backed toward the opening.

"No need to thank me, Twell." Jonaz finally smiled. But it was a smile so bittersweet my heart twisted cruelly in my chest as punishment, reminding me it was still beating, if barely. "I'd do it again, even if I had to fight through another war to keep you safe."

With that he turned and left the cubicle, leaving me uncertain of his heart, and alone with the endless ache of my own.

Chapter Nine

"Twell. Open your eyes," a gruff voice whispered right in my ear.

I squeezed them more tightly shut in response, holding my breath the way I always did when I was afraid. But more than that, I knew it might hurt more to look in his eyes, and face all the disappointment and judgement I expected to see there.

"Twell Anar, wake up right now," Brazin boomed. A huge hand clamped over my shoulder and shook me until my eyes popped open.

"Okay, geez! OW!" My muscles coiled defensively for a moment before I realized he was releasing me from the cuffs. I bolted up like a stinging serpent had crawled in my pants, only to fall straight back down, swearing under my breath as I clutched my tender skull.

"Easy, Twell, take a moment when you sit up again. You're still recovering."

"My powers... do you think I'll get them back?" As I raised myself up again more carefully, my eyes dared to meet his. My heart beat quickly, not sure what I was more worried about. The loss of my powers, or his respect.

"We don't know yet, and I wouldn't recommend trying to find out until you are more fully healed...how well can you see me?" Brazin sounded more than a little irritable, the weight of my actions heavy in each word. I was getting really sick of being asked that question.

"Well enough to notice you need a good shave," I replied snarkily. It was true. Brazin was looking worse for the wear, his chin covered with thick black stubble while his bleary eyes scrutinised me closely.

"How do you feel?" Ignoring my comment, he tried not to sound as relieved as he looked.

"I have a splitting headache. Get it? Splitting?"

Brazin's mouth curved up momentarily, a ghost of a smile that faded too quickly away.

"Can you move?"

"I'd prefer not to. I'm feeling kinda beat."

"Twell, stop mucking around," Brazin barked, much more like his old self. "I'm here to take you to see your Guardian if you feel up to it."

I responded by sliding gingerly off the table, waiting until the room stopped spinning before I looked up at him.

"I don't need to tell you not to try anything, do I?" Brazin gave me a stern look as I began to roll my still blurry eyes.

"Curb the attitude." Taking my arm, he led me from the cell into the long white hallway. "I'm going against orders to let you see her."

"Why would you do that?" I asked his back as he pulled me along the passage. The harsh lights still felt too bright for my hazy vision, and I squinted as I tried to keep up with Brazin's long strides. He stopped for a moment, hesitating as I caught up to him.

"Tell me why?" I demanded again as my heart inexplicably beat faster.

"Because I'm not sure she's going to make it." Brazin looked at me, a flash of sympathy emphasizing the direness of the situation.

"Oh." I felt my throat closing up as my eyes began to burn.

"Pull yourself together, Twell." Brazin gripped my arm harder. "Say what you need to say to her, in case I'm right. But don't fall apart in front of her. You don't want that to be her last memory of you, after all she's suffered."

I stood frozen, trying desperately not to howl as my lower lip trembled in warning.

"Was it all for nothing then?" I whispered as I blinked back the threatening tears. "Was I too late?"

"She's been tortured for a long time, Twell." Brazin struggled to meet my eyes as they filled to the brim with more tears, but his hand released my arm for a moment as he brought it up to awkwardly pat my shoulder. "They had put her through too much, well before you came along. But she told them nothing. Brave and true to the end."

"Don't tell me it's the end!" I shouted. "It's not!"

"Keep your voice down!" Brazin snapped as he grabbed me again and began towing me to the end of the hall. Let's just get you in there to see her before they discover you're gone."

"Don't they have surveillance?" I muttered as I increased my pace to match his urgency.

"Yes. But it appears I still have some obedient soldiers who follow my orders...and you have some very loyal friends."

I really could have done with Sazika's presence right now. I knew she would be around somewhere, as always, trying to help me out of the huge pile of moga poop I was in. I needed a friend. I needed a hug. But then again, it would probably unravel me when I needed to stay strong.

"She's in here. Keep your voice down, you only have the shift change to see her, then I'm taking you straight back. Don't have a melt down and make me regret this decision."

"Yes, Sir." I sniffed as I looked up at his huge angular face. His eyes softened for a moment before he covered his emotions and gave me a small but firm push toward the door.

I entered on shaking legs, my stomach flipping over as apprehension overwhelmed me. Shay lay on a cot, not unlike the one upon which I'd woken. Her skin was waxy and as white as the sheets around her. Her face and body were so gaunt she was almost unrecognisable. Translucent lids closed over her eyes, and for a moment I stood frozen, unable to detect the beat of her heart inside her emaciated chest.

"Shay," I whispered. "Can you hear me?"

"Twell." Her voice crackled faintly through her cracked lips. "Thank the realms, you're alive..."

I reached out, pressing my palm to her cold clammy cheek. Her eyes fluttered open, a paler blue than I'd ever seen them. Faded and worn, the light that once lit them had dimmed, like her spirit was already seeping away.

"Shay!" I began to sob softly, "You can't die! I went there for you! I went there to save you!"

"And you did." Shay's smile was faint but sincere. "You saved me from dying in the enemy's hands, away from the world I love, and without you by my side."

"Let me get Jonaz," I pleaded as I took her face in both of my hands. "He can heal you! He's healed me before…he got my chip out! I'll go find him now, he must be here somewhere working on the wounded…"

"Twell," Shay whispered faintly as she held my terrified gaze. "He's already tried, as have others…but the Abwarzians poisoned me with something foreign. Our labs can't work out how to stop it, and the healers can't touch me without it seeping into them. But it's okay. I'm home, and you are safe. That is enough for me."

"It's not enough for me!" I nearly broke my promise to Brazin as a sob built up in my chest. "Please don't leave me!"

"You will be just fine, Twell. I know in my heart this is so. Please listen to me. You have always been right to follow your intuition. Keep following it, and everything will be okay."

"Please hold on, Shay," I begged. I stroked her face desperately, trying to rub my life into hers. "I love you." I wrapped my arms around her, lifting her into my embrace. Willing her to live.

"As I love you. Not as the child of my flesh, but the child of my heart."

I'd never heard Shay tell me she loved me. Not in my entire life under her care. She had shown me in many ways, but never verbalised it. Although she'd never been a hugely affectionate guardian, I remembered so well the look on her face when I did well at school. She would smile and congratulate me calmly, but her eyes would grow warm until they glowed with pride. That look over any words had meant so much to me. I'd loved the worry lines that had begun to crease her face as we grew older together, the grey in her hair unarguably my doing as I started to take more risks, and push her limits. But her biggest act of love had been remaining silent when she knew I'd broken Comian Law. More than that, she'd hidden evidence. Even though it went against her beliefs, she protected me, allowing me to pursue my own beliefs. I bit back a sob, choking it back as I drew ragged breaths to control my rising hysteria.

"Listen to me." Shays voice grew fainter as I held her tighter in my arms. "My soul is at peace because you are the last thing I will see and touch in this lifetime. You are reckless…but you are brave. Your heart is leading you in the right direction, and you will help change this world, even if you must suffer for it. I'm so proud of you, Twell, no matter what happens."

I held her tighter, trying to think of all the things I wanted to tell her. I wanted to tell her that I loved her as much as a child loves their mother. That she had been more than just a guardian to me, and had helped me to see the good in our world, while trying to protect me from the bad. But the words were stuck in my throat. Instead, my grief seeped through in a muffled wail as I buried my face in her neck.

"Twell, you need to take this off me and hide it, the moment I'm gone," Shay whispered with sudden urgency as she proffered her arm. A new wristband coiled around her skinny wrist, gleaming ominously as the light flashed over its silent face.

"I can't, they can track these things." I squeezed her hand reassuringly, but she gripped back tighter, her glassy eyes fixed on mine with growing urgency.

"Not once my pulse stops. It will deactivate and record me as deceased. Take it off the minute it shows you my status. You can activate it later, when you need it most."

"What? Need it how?" I leaned closer, trying to read the meaning in her words and decipher the expression on her face. But her eyes had taken on a clouded hue, the light slowly fading from them as her hand went limp in mine.

"Shay? Shay...!" I shook her slightly, willing her to look at me as her eyes lost focus and her body relaxed in my arms. "Shay! Please don't leave me!"

I felt her shudder once before her life slipped from her body. My entire being trembled with shock as I laid her back on the pillow, staring into vacant eyes that no longer looked back at me. Taking her wrist in my hand I stared numbly at the face of the wristband, my stomach rolling over as Citizen Deceased flashed impersonally on the screen. Shay was gone, to another realm, or maybe nowhere at all. And I had never felt more empty or alone in my life.

The door opened behind me, but I didn't bother to see who it was. I didn't care. A wrenching sound of grief ripped from my chest, releasing like the high-pitched cry of a wounded animal. Hands came from behind me, wrapping around my waist and pulling me off the bed. I tried to summon my powers, but they were either still broken, or my spirit was. My mind chugged numbly, producing nothing as I resorted to a feeble struggling that was easily overpowered by the strength of Jonaz's arms.

"No, not yet!!" I shrieked as I pulled the wristband quickly from her wrist and enclosed it in my fist. Then he was dragging me from her room into another one.

"You can't stay with her, I'm so sorry. They will be here to take her body for cremation at any moment." Dragging me down to the floor, he pulled me into his chest as the tears finally flowed freely.

"It was all for *nothing*." My words forced themselves between my fingers, strangled and hoarse. "I failed her. I failed you. I failed Shay! I failed, I failed, I failed!"

Jonaz pressed his own hand tightly over my mouth, stifling my cries as he pinned me tighter to him.

"You know it wasn't." His lips pressed against my scalp, his free hand firmly tilting my chin to look in his eyes. "You know she would want you to keep fighting. Don't give up, Twell. Keep fighting."

"What is there left to fight for?" I tried to wrench from his grasp. "I'm alone now. I have no one left!"

"You're in shock." Jonaz rose to his feet, his hands reaching for me, then pulling away as his uncertainty and concern grew. "Now's not the time to discuss this. You need to grieve."

"I need to go. Back to my cell. Now."

"Twell..." The pain in his voice nearly shredded what was left of my heart. But I spun away, lunging for the door and throwing myself back through the room where Shay's body lay.

"Twell, wait!"

I didn't look as I reached the door. I couldn't look. Barrelling straight into the wall that was Brazin's chest, one pitiful glance up into his stern features told him all he needed to know. Then he was marching me mercifully back to the safety of my imprisonment.

"Sorry, kid, you know I have to do this."

My tears dried up as Brazin reluctantly strapped me back onto the cot, my stony silence replacing my sobs as he locked me away in the cell.

"I'll be back, if I can..." Brazin muttered awkwardly as I turned my face from his toward the wall. My silence seemed to rattle him more than my tears, and he retreated from the cell, locking it quietly before I heard his footsteps receding down the hall. The remaining scraps of my heart deflated slowly in my chest as any remaining hope I'd had slithered off the table and disappeared into the murky shadows of the room. I felt more alone than I ever had as a prisoner on Abwarz. The two people I had loved most in the Cosmos were either dead, or unable to trust me. The searing pain of it made me breathless, even though I was lying down. Darkness swooped over my soul, suffocating any hope or will to go on that I'd been clinging to. Closing my eyes, the tears leaked silently down my cheeks as I willed myself to absorb into the emptiness of the room. I wished for a sleep that never ended. Where I would never have to feel anything again.

Chapter Ten

I awoke with a start, my heart pounding in the dark quiet of the room. No light had startled me awake, nor footsteps across the floor. Yet the slow cold sensation of dread creeping over my flesh told me I was not alone in the room.

"Visiting hours are over." I sounded much braver than I felt as my muscles coiled in preparation. "So if you don't mind, I'd like to get some shut eye."

"Oh, that troublesome tongue of yours," a contemptuous voice hissed in the darkness, growing closer as it approached my bed. "Maybe I'll rip it from your mouth right now, and silence you forever." Maza's fingers reached out like white bony claws in the gloom. Seizing my chin, she squeezed so hard her nails cut into my skin as she leaned down to threaten in my ear, "I could always say the Abwarzians did it."

"Like you did when you bombed our own cities?" As my eyes adjusted to the dark, I saw Maza draw back, her nostrils flaring as her eyes narrowed to furious slits.

"Careful, Twell." Maza bared her teeth in a sharp smile. "You're already charged with treason, but I don't mind adding lies against the Government to your list of offences."

"I have a right to explain my actions, and why I may have come to doubt the facts our leaders have been feeding us," I glared up at Maza as I quietly tested the strength of my shackles. "Regardless of whether you'll admit it or not."

"No one will be listening to you ever again you little traitor." Maza spat in my face as she drew closer. "I'll see to that if it's the last thing I do."

"You still aren't getting it," Raising myself up, I came so close to her sneering face, I could feel the heat of her hatred on my skin. "You

111

can lock me away, but you can't shut everyone up. My desires are not just mine alone. They belong to our generation, and we no longer want our lives dictated by our DNA alone. You need to allow us to love, so we have something worth fighting for, something to live for! Without the choice, we're merely robots, with no heart or spirit to fight.

"Duty and loyalty are all we require from you," Maza replied mechanically, but her rust hued eyes clouded with momentary uncertainty. "Why can't you simply submit like the generations before you?"

"We ruined earth with that mentality," I retorted as I strained uselessly against the restraints. My heart thrummed audibly in my chest, faster and faster as my powers refused to emerge. "Can't you see it? It's time to break the cycle."

"We need order!" Maza's shouted suddenly, jerking up. "Not love struck hormonal brats running after love and muddying our gene pool back to the disease ridden race we used to be!"

"We need a balance," I argued as Maza began to pace the tiny cell. "We can still be tested. But allow some leniency! Allow some normality. Allow us to just live!"

"Save your poetic dribble." Maza looked at me in disgust. "You can get it all out of your system now, because I'm the last person who will ever have to listen to your tiresome heresy."

"Ahhhh, there's the terrifying threats I was waiting for. But thanks for the small talk."

"I don't make threats, Twell. I make things happen. And I'm going to make you disappear."

"You can try, but you're not the Governing Body, are you?" I smirked. "At the end of the day they call the shots, and you answer to them, just like the rest of us."

Maza's features pinched up like she'd smelled something whiffy, and I enjoyed a moment's satisfaction before a new determined look washed over her brittle features. "You know, Twell, you're absolutely right. But I trust that I know how they think. After all, I've always looked to them for guidance and direction with the utmost loyalty."

"How touching." I replied, despite the sensation of serpents coiling through my insides. "I'm sure you're their shining example of a perfectly brainwashed citizen."

"Your rebellion is a poison." Maza leaned over me again, so close to my face her sour breath hit my nostrils as her spittle landed on my chin. I jerked my face away in disgust but she seized my chin hard and forced my head back to look at her. "I recognised it in you the moment I saw you. A toxin that will seep through society, and ruin the order and progression we've worked for three generations to create. Your nature is a genetic flaw that must be bred out. Or exterminated." As Maza finished her speech, she raised her right hand, brandishing a large syringe full of....

"Don't worry its only air." A slow smile slithered onto Maza's face, her eyes as beady and as unblinking as a Serpent's as they held my gaze. "At the very least, I will enjoy the satisfaction of seeing you brain dead before I leave this cell. But at best, you will die a more rapid death than you really deserve. Nothing that will show up in an autopsy though, of course." Maza's teeth bared wider, her eyes becoming shinier as she waved the syringe at me. "Did you know I have our ancestors to thank for the idea? Air embolisms were used on earth in POW camps to quietly dispatch the enemy in a way that was easier to hide from the public. Genius, really."

My heart stopped, refusing to beat as I tried to shrink away. My blood froze like ice in my veins as a deep dread shuddered over me. I knew without a doubt it would kill me, as clearly as I knew she'd intended to use it all along.

"And you call yourself progressive," I choked through the nausea rising into my throat. "It's still murder, no matter what you call it."

"A necessity, required to support the greater good."

'There will be no good in a world led by people like you."

"And no population, if led by the likes of you." Maza's eyes shone with excitement as she held the syringe up, flicking the stem with her fingers before suddenly clamping her hand over my arm.

"Aren't you forgetting something?" I blurted, trying to stall as I jerked my head toward the surveillance camera pointed right at us.

"You really think I wouldn't have thought to put a 'glitch' in that one before I came anywhere near you?" Maza snorted in amusement. I heard a click as my shackles opened, but Maza still held my arm in a vice tight grip as she leaned over me.

"You're weak, but you're still a highly-trained soldier, as well as an enemy of the G.B." A slow deadly smile stretched over Maza's thin mouth as her gaze darkened with intent. "So it's perfectly believable you viciously attacked me after I took you to the hygiene cubicle. I had no choice but to defend myself."

With that Maza stabbed me with the needle, the glass shaft puncturing the skin in my right arm in one easy thrust. "I had no choice but to do it, for the greater good..." Maza laughed, her laughter as crazed as it was shrill. A moment of shock slowed my reaction before I retaliated, bucking against her as panic flooded my brain. Maza laughed louder into my ear as she pressed down harder, bending over my arm as she pushed the needle further into my skin. 'I'm doing you a favour, really." Maza twisted my arm, looking for a vein. "All your reasons to live are gone. Your freedom...your silly little romance with the healer..." Maza's laughter stopped abruptly as a more frightening and maniacal grin stretched her thin lips. I thrashed and kicked, my size and weakness no match for her physical strength as she moved her thumb to the top of the syringe and pushed it a little further into my vein.

"And your guardian. Poor thing...really quite pathetic that you couldn't protect her, or save her in the end."

I stopped struggling as a roar like the ocean flooded my ears. Fury rose like a wave and crashed over me, flooding my veins before the poison in her needle could. Adrenalin surged through me with the force of a tsunami.

"*Get off me!*"

In one move I rolled off the table to my feet, the needle dropping from my vein and shattering on the floor.

"You little!" Maza rushed at me, her features twisted in rage as I blocked her instinctively. My mind buzzed with anger, drowning out any conscience as I seized her right arm with my left hand. Her mouth dropped open in surprise as I mashed my right hand into a fist and propelled it into her face.

Thwack!

Her nose made a satisfying crunch as she reared back in shock.

The blood spurted from her nostrils, a wild look of pure hatred stretching so tightly over her face, I crouched and spread my hands in front of me. I was ready. Ready to block, but even more ready to fight. My rage flowed hot and strong through my veins, as powerful as my powers had ever been. I no longer needed them, my need for justice coursing through me like burning fire as she lurched toward me again, revenge gleaming in her eyes. I swung my fist up again and socked her in the eye.

Smack!

"Come on then, Maza!" I cried gleefully as I danced around her toward the door. "Is that all you've got?" As Maza staggered toward me I leaned back on my left leg. Raising my right, I kicked her low in the abdomen, dropping her to her knees like a sack of spitting serpents.

"Owwwww, stop!" Maza clutched her pouring nose with one hand, and pressed the other over her stomach.

"Boof! Arghhhh!" The third kick struck her shoulder, landing her on her pompous rear.

"I think your own training's a little rusty," I snarled, circling her like prey. "Shall I remind you with a further demonstration?"

'Yowl pway fwor dis!' Maza tried to shake a fist, but quickly clapped it back over her streaming nose as she tried to get up. My anger drove me on, taking over like a parasite to its host, increasing my strength as supernaturally as my powers. Before I knew what I was doing I leapt on Maza, knocking her back to the ground where I straddled and pinned her to the floor.

"You went too far dishonouring the people I love." I shook with rage as I leaned over her, my heart pounding so hard it felt like it might explode. The possibilities of what I could do to her ran through my mind like a stampede of mogas, and as she opened her mouth to yell I knew I could easily silence her for good.

"Don't try it," I warned as she looked toward the exit. "I might be as dangerous as you say I am."

"Or what?" Maza struggled in my grasp, her rusty eyes matching the colour of her blood as they fixed on mine. "You know you won't get far. Your face is plastered all over the media. You can't hide. So don't bother running from us."

"It's only you I need to get away from." Reaching for a dangling restraint on the bench, I moved fast, clamping her hands together in one cuff over her head before she had time to fight. Then I stood up, some of the anger draining as I walked away from her. I'd wasted my breath for long enough. I knew now, that some people were so consumed with the desire for power and control they could never be changed, only stopped.

"You walk out that door, and your life is over anyway! Just like your Guardian's." Maza's screech scratched my senses like glass, her fury palpable as I stopped and looked back at her hate filled face.

"You know we could have saved her if we'd tried harder." Maza struggled to her knees, her diabolical grin revealing sharp teeth coated with blood. "But she was a traitor too, after all. She raised you to be who you are. You were both a blemish in our society."

I gasped, her words sharper than any weapon as they pierced my heart. Walking back, I crouched down, picking up a sharp shard of the syringe between my fingers. Maza struggled harder as I leaned over her, her expression flashing with horrified understanding as I forced her jaws open with my hands. I seized her tongue as a scream spilled from her throat, the scream muffling to a garbled wail as I stretched it from her mouth and positioned the glass. One clean slice, and she could no longer use her words as a weapon any longer; her own threats turned on her as I silenced her lies and hatred with ironic justice.

"So I have nothing to lose." Maza's eyes grew wide as she struggled to jerk free of my grasp.

Twell, this isn't who you are. Avin's words whispered in my ear like a ghost, and a shadow fell darkly over my soul.

"Stwaaaaaaaaaaaap!" Maza cried, trying desperately to pull away as I held her head tighter.

One clean slice, and I would be no different than the enemies I loathed, using torture and fear to get my way.

"Oooo arr ust lieeeeee nee awer awwwwl." Maza managed to cry as I bought the glass closer and her eyes filled with terror.

This isn't who you are.

Releasing her tongue, I dropped the glass from my shaking fingers.

"Too weak, I knew it." Maza raised her head shakily, the fear in her eyes instantly morphing back to hard balls of hatred. "If you're too weak to even stop me, you'll never convince the people to follow you."

My fingers closed into a fist. One more good old-fashioned punch later, and her eyes rolled back in her head, her body falling slack against the bench. Moving to the exit, I found it unlocked, another part of her evil alibi now my means for escape. Without looking back, I walked away from her toxic mind, toward my purpose and my fate.

Chapter Eleven

In the halls, the darkness loomed around me, playing tricks with my mind as I crept along the passages. Fatigue hit me as the shakes set in, and I wondered briefly if Maza had switched off the lights to further hide her intentions. A gloomy sensation lurked around my conscience as I realised I'd added harming an Officer to my lists of bad deeds. I doubted they'd believe it was self-defence, with my reckless reputation. Yet that was the least of my current worries as I rounded a corner and found myself nearing the medical quarters.

Pushing the door open at a glacial pace, I slunk through like a shadow, moving soundlessly as I crept past the wounded and the covered. The dead.

It was dark, save for the dim glow of the night-lights over the hospital beds. They lit the faces of the patients lying beneath them and the medics and healers who hovered quietly over them. Crouching out of the light beside the nearest cot I paused, listening to the laboured breathing of the patients and the soft whimpering of those who could not conceal their pain or trauma. Gentle murmuring soothed over their cries, and I realised some of the medics were using their hypnotic powers to comfort their patients. A voice travelled low and sweet toward me, and my heartbeat spiked as I recognised the compelling musical tone.

"Hush now. You are safe. You are well. Everything is under control."

Rising up, I peeked over the cot toward her voice. Several beds down, Stelli leaned over a female soldier, her perfect full mouth upturned in a dazzling smile, her fine golden hair pinned into shimmering plaits on her head. Her luminous amber eyes glowed directly into the girl's eyes, mesmerising and inescapable. The girl's expression cleared, the stress and pain draining away from her pale features as her whimpering ceased; her body sagging against the cot in relief. I made to stand up, wondering how to reveal myself without startling her, when the shock of Jonaz appearing by her side froze me in place. His arm curved around Stelli's shoulder, squeezing in comfort as she dropped her head briefly to his shoulder. They looked perfect together. The perfect genetically matched couple, everything our world needed to ensure the superiority of our future generations. If I left now, and never involved them, they could live out the perfect life I knew I would never have. They could be happy, and it would be easier that way. My head told me to leave, to run as fast and far as I could. But my heart lingered, weighing my feet to the floor as I remembered the promises Jonaz and I had made each other.

Nothing is easy when you're fighting for what you believe in... My own words came back to haunt me as my heart pounded in my chest, my body still refusing to move.

It's harder to give in. Jonaz's words, as he'd held me in the cave, before I'd even admitted that I loved him.

Had it meant anything? Our words? Our actions? Had he chosen the easier way, after all we'd promised, and all we'd been through?

"It hurts…my leg….owwwwww."

The patient I'd crouched next to lurched upwards so suddenly I fell back, my body smacking loudly against the floor. Cursing under my breath I scrambled clumsily to my feet, inhaling sharply as my eyes met directly with Jonaz's. Both of us stood perfectly still for a heartbeat, before I turned and ran.

"Twell!"

I weaved blindly through the hospital beds, trying to block him out, along with the moans of the dying.

"Twell, please!" Stelli's voice joined the chase, along with their footsteps as I searched desperately for another exit. I had no idea where I was, or where I would go. Anywhere but here was good enough.

"For the planets sake, will you stop her?"

"Gladly."

An electric force hit me squarely in the chest, lifting me off my feet and sending me sprawling backwards into an empty hospital bed.

Winded and dazed, I attempted to sit up, but an invisible force pushed me back down.

"You… Moga!" I gasped as Mira stepped smugly into my line of sight, followed by Talon, who had the decency to at least look apologetic for his involvement.

"Careful," Mira warned. "I'm in the mood to fry you again. And I do enjoy a good electrocution."

I was still recovering when Jonaz skidded to a halt in front of me, Stelli arriving just behind him. Stelli gaped at me in open-mouthed awe, like I was some sort of celebrity, or, more likely, a dangerous criminal. Jonaz's expression was unfathomable. His eyes tried to capture mine, but I tore them away, pressing a hand to the warm spot in my chest. I didn't know what hurt more, the electric shock, or the scene I'd just witnessed.

"Well at least she's saved us the trouble of stage one." Mira sighed as she smoothed her already perfectly tamed hair into place. "I'll still tell the others to meet us at the western exit as planned."

"What's going on?" I demanded as I scrambled awkwardly off the bed.

"We're taking you somewhere safe, Twell." Jonaz moved toward me, his gaze solemn. "Until the GB can guarantee you a fair trial."

"No!" I backed away from him, unwilling to decipher his expression. "You all need to get away from me. I deserve whatever happens to me, but none of you do!"

"Here she goes." Mira sneered. "Even after all this she still thinks Como revolves around her."

"Save it!" Jonaz snapped, suddenly losing patience. "We need to get her out of here. *Now.*"

"You're not listening to me!" I looked wildly around at them all, my chest tight with anxiety. "You can't do this!"

"Again, not about you!" Mira snarled. "Think bigger picture, if you can get over yourself for long enough. If you are silenced for life, then we lose. Then we all still suffer. Not just you! Get it?"

"Let's go!" Jonaz commanded. There was no more time to argue as everyone ran toward a door at the far end of the hospital wing. Jonaz seized my hand, the contact of his skin along with his sense of urgency flowing from his skin into mine like another shock.

"Let go of me." I tried to wrench my hand from his grasp, but he gripped tighter, pulling me along so fast I fought to keep up.

"No. And I'll throw you over my shoulder and carry you if I have to. Stop being difficult and trust me. If that's even possible."

"Trust you?" My feet stumbled, my lungs burning from unfamiliar exercise. "I thought it was me you don't trust..."

"Quick!" Talon shouted from up ahead. "Someone's coming!"

Skidding to a halt just before the exit, we pressed silently up against the wall on either side. As the sound of multiple feet thudded toward the door I closed my eyes, trying to gather my thoughts enough to try and summon my powers. But nothing happened, not even a feeble pulse.

"I still have no powers," I whispered breathlessly, "And I've exhausted myself, physically fighting Maza."

"It's okay," Jonaz replied. "Watch Twell's back everyone. She can't defend herself."

"I wouldn't say that," I retorted. "I'm just a little disadvantaged right no..." Jonaz pushed his hand over my mouth, hushing me just as three bodies pushed simultaneously through the door. In moments, we'd surrounded them, crouched and ready to fight.

"It's us! It's us!" Surina squeaked as the light fell on their faces. I froze, like I'd been caught in floodlights under Avin's gaze. They glittered like ice, and I shivered as he broke contact and swivelled toward Jonaz and Mira, the obvious leaders.

"The exit route is clear now. We have to move immediately, or the guards will be back any moment."

"I kinda forgot to mention I just knocked Maza out, and tied her up," I added.

"You what?" Mira screeched so loudly several patients nearby moaned in empathy. "Nice one, Twell, adding assault of an Officer to your ever increasing list of crimes. Because you weren't already perfecting the whole bad girl thing."

"She was trying to kill me!" I retorted. "You know, that whole silencing me for life thing. Turns out she was taking it literally."

"Ohmyrealms." Surina gasped as Jonaz's head whipped toward

me. His eyes fixed on mine, so dark with emotion a shiver rolled down my spine as I tore my gaze away.

"Busting Twell out is just as serious, Mira," Avin finally spoke. "It doesn't matter anymore, we're all in this together now. And Maza's evil, she deserved it. So please, let's just go!"

This time we all moved without protest, filing out the door in silence, moving like shadows along the dark dim halls, the lights flickering occasionally to illuminate the way. I decided I had a passionate hatred for hallways of any variety. Whether schools, government departments, enemy cells or civilian hospitals, they spelled no good, and I experienced an intense yearning for fresh air and wide-open spaces.

I found myself closely guarded by both Avin and Jonaz as we moved. It was hard to decide if the danger or the awkwardness of the situation was worse, the only place safe to look being straight ahead.

"Where are we going?" I muttered as we rounded another corner and moved swiftly toward another door.

"Running now. Questions later," Jonaz grunted from my left.

"Said the control freak."

"Maybe attitude later as well?" From the corner of my eye I saw his head shaking, as a slow smirk crept onto his lips, and I pursed my own in annoyance.

"What about camera surveillance?" I shot back as I looked over my shoulder in apprehension.

"It's taken care of," Jonaz replied shortly, as I pushed myself to keep up with the group.

"Trouble ahead." Avin's warning mingled with a shout as two guards walked right through the door we were headed for.

"Arghhhh!" the first guard went down as Mira stuck him in the chest, his hair standing up on end as electricity raced through his body.

"Hey, whatareyou…" The second guard's yell cut off as Talon picked him up from a distance away, pinning him against the wall as we all ran past them. Avin stopped, looking deep into the guard's startled eyes, capturing him in seconds.

"You want us to get away. You support us. Say nothing."

The guard nodded sluggishly, his eyes glazing over as he slumped to the floor.

We ran on, bursting into the night as the fresh air came to greet us. I gulped it in as greedily as water, the chilled air kissing my skin like a familiar old friend.

"This way!" Mira urged us as we ran into the darkness. Unaccustomed to the darkness I stumbled, my hands stretching out instinctively to steady myself. Jonaz's hand caught mine again, his grip unarguable as he towed me into the inky black.

"There it is!" Surina called softly as a dim shadow took the form of something tangible. The black aircraft camouflaged with the night, crouching in silence, waiting for us as we pelted toward it. My lungs heaved with effort as we reached the pod, not stopping as we all piled into it. The moment the door slid shut behind us the craft rose up so suddenly I was thrown down the aisle, straight into Avin's arms.

"Sorry," I looked up into his vast grey gaze, my heart beating hard as my body fought for balance.

"Here, sit down." Avin pushed me into a seat, his hands firm, but his eyes not unkind. Pulling down beside me, we buckled up as everyone followed suit. Once I was secure, my eyes traitorously sought out Jonaz. I squealed in surprise.

"Sazika? Mekai?!"

"You didn't really think we'd abandon you, did you Twell?" Mekai winked as his hand curled around Sazika's.

"She's speechless." Sazika smiled. "What did they do to her up there?"

"You guys…" I sniffed as my eyes started to burn in warning… "You all…"

"Yeah—Yeah." Mira groaned as she rolled her own eyes. "Save the warmandfuzzies for another time. Getting to safety is more imperative right now."

"Hey…." As I did a head count, the math didn't seem to add up. "Who's flying this thing?"

As the pilot turned in his seat to grimace at me, my mouth dropped open, words failing to come to the rescue.

"Looks like we're all in big trouble now, kid." Brazin grinned so defiantly it took my brain a moment to catch up as I gaped at him.

"What about all those timing speeches you drilled into me?" I gasped finally.

"Fat moga lot of good they did!" Brazin replied cheerily, "Carpe diem, as they used to say a very long time ago in the old world."

"Carpe what?" Stelli piped up? "Weren't they aquatic scaly creatures back on earth?"

"Never mind." Brazin snorted as he turned back to his navigation. "It's time to act now. No turning back."

"Now will you tell me where we're going?" I looked at Jonaz, a few seats down, finally allowing myself to look at him

"Remember the old underground water caverns?" His tone was hesitant, as if he knew the memories would come flooding back to try and drown me. I gasped, as if the stale air was already filling my lungs. I'd almost died there. It was not in my top ten picks of 'Places Twell would like to hide.'

A heavy silence descended the craft, everyone but Avin and Stelli lost in memories that haunted us all. I finally realized Brazin was flying without lights, and assumed he was using either his exceptional skills as a pilot to navigate the skies, or infrared GPS. Either way, as long as we were not discovered sneaking through the skies, I was happy. Jonaz got up, his gaze resting on me for a long moment. My heart kicked in reaction as I felt my cheeks warming. His eyes held so many things, concern, frustration…and other emotions I was unwilling to explore. I looked stubbornly away, gazing into the twinkling night sky as I heard him sigh. Moving into the cockpit to sit with Brazin I heard them conversing, their voices mingling so low they were drowned out by the hum of the engine. But it was clear by his tone that Jonaz trusted Brazin as they discussed whatever our next moves would be. I jolted as Avin's hand brushed over mine, and my eyes met his again.

"I know it happened there," he murmured quietly. "I know it won't be easy."

"Nothing has ever been easy, from the day they signed us up for this war." I sighed as sadness settled over my spirit. "I've been fighting for my life since this began, with enemies no matter where I turn. I'm tired, Avin. I feel like I'll never be able to stop fighting, unless someone stops me forever."

Avin squeezed my hand, the comforting swirl of his gaze soothing me as they lulled me with or without intention. "No one can fight forever. This is going to end on our terms, no matter the cost."

"You don't hate me?" I whispered. I didn't care who was listening, or watching, although the loud hum of the aircraft muted conversation. I didn't know when I'd have the chance again to seek his forgiveness. I needed to know he was okay.

"Twell, I could never hate you." Avin's smile pierced my soul like the sun through storm clouds. "You've only ever been honest and true to yourself."

"I'm so sorry, Avin," I stammered, struggling to meet his gaze. "That you got lumped with me, and that I just can't submit to the laws like everyone else.

"I just need to know, Twell." Avin's tone dropped low as he leaned in close. "When you kissed me, before you ran away... was it because you wanted me? Or was it because you knew I wanted you."

I held my breath as I gazed into his eyes. They searched mine deeply as his thumb stroked the back of my hand gently. My heart clenched as I exhaled slowly, struggling to form the right words, even though I knew there were none. "I felt something for you, but I was confused. I still am..." I stammered as I lowered my gaze. "Maybe it was because I just didn't want to keep disappointing you."

Avin exhaled heavily, and once again I felt his disappointment as he turned his face away to the window. He swallowed hard, and my heart squeezed in turmoil. "Avin, I'm so sorry. I never wanted to hurt you....I wish...I just..."

"Hey...it's okay." Avin turned back to look at me, his gaze dark with understanding, "I can see you love him, so it doesn't matter in the end. I would never stand in the way of your happiness. No matter how I feel for you, we would never be right unless you chose me too."

I turned my hand, grasping his back, squeezing my thankfulness into his palm because I could not speak. Tears burned threateningly. Avin was a good person, and I hated to see him in pain.

"Please. It's okay, Twell. I won't lie. Maybe I still hope that one day, when you are free...then you might change your mind. But for now, I am realistic enough to withdraw my advances and settle for your friendship."

"Your advances?" An embarrassed smile twisted my mouth as warmth painted my cheeks. "Did you learn that from your grandfather as well?"

"Well, of course." Avin smiled a small smile that did not quite reach his luminous grey eyes. They dimmed like mist over the ocean, heavy with sadness. As he withdrew his hand, the warmth of his touch, and the comfort of his gaze seeped away, the darkness pressing back in around me as we sailed through the night to a darker place, and more danger than we'd ever been prepared for.

Chapter Twelve

The descent into the caverns was every bit as bad as I thought it would be. The chill seeped through my bones as we plunged underground, and I couldn't control the deep shiver that followed. The air seemed to grow thinner before we were even half way down, and as stale as the cells on Abwarz. I took exaggerated breaths, trying to quell the irrational panic growing inside of me. As a hand cupped the small of my back, my fear spilled out, disguised as retaliation.

"I'm fine!" I moved away from Jonaz, backing myself into a safe corner.

"You're not. Just breathe." His eyes were traps that I was unwilling to fall into. I looked stubbornly away, over toward Sazika who shrugged back uncomfortably.

"I am." I sighed finally. "I don't need your concern, thank you." The lift stopped moving before Jonaz could reply, and the doors slid open, a blast of damp cold air slapping us in the face as we stepped out into the gloomy opening to the cavern.

"This is creepy." Stelli shuddered, her liquid eyes shimmering with anxiety. "I don't know how you can all come back here…"

"It's okay, Stelli." Jonaz turned to her reassuringly. "It's safer here without any signal. We're off the map unless they work out where we are."

"I know," she whispered, smiling back at him in a way that annoyed me to the core. "I want to be here, with all of you. This is right."

"We're not here to bond and braid each other's hair you know, Stelli." Mira sneered. "Our actions have serious consequences. Like, life imprisonment if this all backfires."

"You don't need to keep spelling it out," Jonaz turned on her

127

angrily. "She gets it."

"So protective," I muttered. Jonaz wheeled back to me, his eyes burning into mine so intensely that I instantly regretted my words.

"Keep it together soldiers," Brazin grunted. "I've prepared a place to camp out, that's not even charted. So let's just get there."

We followed him quietly, our steps and breath echoing slightly around us as we made our way through the small winding tunnels. It was weird seeing Brazin in civilian clothes, though he was still a giant. His muscles rippled under his dark clothes as he strode at twice the pace as the rest of us. I felt my chest growing tight and knew it was fear not lack of air as the rocky tunnel narrowed and the ceiling lowered. A small gasp of anxiety escaped my lungs as I pushed my legs harder to keep up. Fatigue nipped at my heels as I stumbled over a rock.

"Are you okay, Twell?" Sazika appeared at my side, her face full of concern as she read the weariness on mine.

"Nothing a year's worth of sleep wouldn't fix." I smiled wearily back.

"You can rest as soon as we get there." Brazin called over his shoulder, "Just keep moving."

I focused on putting one foot in front of the other until Brazin finally rounded a corner and called back once more. "Wait here a moment." A muted orange glow seeped out into the passage just as a wave of dizziness hit, and my legs buckled.

"Mekai," Sazika shouted as she grabbed my arm. "Can you help?"

The next minute I felt hands hooking under my arms, then my feet leaving the ground as Mekai lifted me into the air. He sailed past the others and around the corner into a small but adequately lit cavern. Fire lit the walls, burning out of metal cylinders every few feet. I'd never seen fire used in such a way, apart from in earth history lessons. The fire emitted a pleasant warmth, stealing the chill from the air, while the light touched every nook and cranny, and scared away the dark.

"You're a lot lighter than the last time I lifted you, "Mekai commented as he lowered me onto one of several thin mattresses lined up against the northern wall of the cave. Crates were stacked neatly on the eastern side of the cave, hopefully full off whatever we needed to survive underground for an unknown period of time.

My hands were shaking, I realised, and I clasped them together to stop the tremors as I tried to slow my breathing. The air was thin, and I was trying hard to stay calm as the cave walls seemed to press in around us. I'd hated this place the first time I'd come here. It wasn't getting any more appealing.

"What can I say, the starvation diet did wonders for me."

Mekai tried to smile but it ended up more of a lopsided grimace.

"Ahem…So what now?" I asked as the others selected mattresses. Sazika flopped down on the ground to my left, Mekai flanking her other side. Avin moved to the last mattress at the end of the cave, with Talon and Surina alongside him. I went very still as Jonaz took the spot to my right, his dark eyes meeting mine with fire of their own as I opened my mouth to protest.

"Don't argue," Jonaz said simply. "I'm not letting you out of my sight again."

"You'll be busy then." I nodded over toward Stelli who had hunkered down next to Mira and Surina. "What with looking after her as well. Who's going to watch your back?"

"It's not what you think." Jonaz leaned in close, his eyes burning a hot trail over my face. "You always did make too many assumptions."

"And you never could see how she feels about you." I rolled my eyes childishly and turned over, away from his look of frustration.

"Stubborn as ever…never listens…" I heard him muttering as he stood up and stalked off to where Brazin and Talon were rifling through the crates.

Despite myself, a little smile crept onto my mouth before I looked up and caught Sazika shaking her head at me.

"You do have it wrong, Twell. You know that, right?" Sazika whispered as she lay down beside me. Her red hair shone like burnished metal in the glow of the flames. Her wide eyes met mine patiently as I ignored my niggling conscience.

"I know what I saw." I sulked. "Why mess with their destiny, when I already know mine."

"Because none of us have chosen our destiny, Twell," Sazika replied seriously, "That's the whole point. We all gave that up when we chose to fight for our rights."

"But you didn't see them?" I argued weakly as my face grew hot with shame.

"I did, actually." Sazika replied solemnly, her eyes suddenly bright with tears. "When you were gone, and we thought you were dead, it was like he died too, for a while. Like a ghost walked in his place. You didn't see him Twell…he was inconsolable."

"Oh…" I trailed off as my gaze flicked over to Jonaz. He was bent over a box, pulling out weapons I was too tired to want to know about it at the moment. His chiselled features took on even more shadows and angles in the eerie light of the cave, his mouth curved down into a troubled frown. My heart thumped hard in my chest, swelling with feelings I fought to smother." I'm sorry you had to…"

"It doesn't matter, Twell. It's done. But I'm telling you now he never looked once at Stelli that way. She was just the only one who was able to reach out to him and draw him back out of his grief. She was the one who told him not to give up hope you were alive."

"She did?" My mouth dropped open in surprise. "Why on Como...?"

"Because you've always been Stelli's hero, Twell." Sazika grinned as she rolled her own eyes. "She's always believed in you. Even when she never believed in herself."

"Ohdearcosmos." I groaned as the truth sunk in. "Why am I such a moga?"

"You're not a moga." Sazika chuckled as she gave me a small affectionate push. "Jonaz was right though. You do make a lot of assumptions…but I know they're based on fear of getting hurt."

"Well, seeing as my fears keep turning into reality, can you blame me?" My eyes burned with threatening tears as an image of Shay flashed through my mind. I pushed it away, but the emotions lingered.

"I don't. But you can't let fear destroy you." Sazika reached out, her palm connecting with my cheek as her small voice grew suddenly fiercer. She met my gaze with that old defiance which still never ceased to surprise me. "That's what they want. We can't let them win."

"I know," I whispered. "We can't."

"We won't," Sazika replied firmly.

"Rest now." Brazin's bark echoed too loudly, bouncing around the cave and vibrating through our eardrums. Sazika's hand fell away and she lay down on her back, and I rolled onto mine as sudden exhaustion pulled at my conscience. It smelled musty, and the padding was thin and too soft to stop me feeling the uneven floor beneath it, but still it was better than the cold hard benches my flesh and bones had been accustomed to for the last few moons. A million thoughts and emotions vied for first position in my brain, but none of them won as sleep claimed me fast. It was the first time I really slept in moons.

Chapter Thirteen

There wasn't enough air. The cave was like a tomb, slowly suffocating me as I gasped for breath, staggering blindly through the dark tangle of tunnels. My heart pounded as I ran, sweat trickling down my back as I searched for a familiar path. I was lost. Each twist and turn led me further into the endless system of caverns, yet I had no GPS. No way to navigate, or tell one path from another.

"Hello?" I called out, panic pitching my voice much higher than normal "Where are you all?"

I forced myself to stop and listen. My rapid breaths sounded loud in the low tunnel, but no answer came.

"Where are you all?" Rising hysteria crept into my call as I broke into a run, stumbling over the uneven ground in the gloom. "Jonaz! Where are you?"

"Here. I am here," a voice hissed through the cavern, low and faint.

"Jonaz." I increased my pace, my heart leaping with relief as I ran toward the sound.

"Here. I'm right here," the voice whispered again, closer this time. I broke into a run, rounding the corner so fast I failed to stop before slamming into the stony wall.

"Ow! What the…?" It was a dead end. Confusion and frustration tangled my thoughts as I whirled around. I was sure he had called out from this direction…

"I'm right here, Twell Anar."

A ghostly form slid around the corner from where I had just come. The smell of rotting flesh growing stronger as the figure moved toward me. I pressed back against the wall in fright, horror rising in my throat to form a scream as the thing loomed over me and I saw its face.

"No..no…you're dead." Disbelief choked the words to a strangled whisper as my body froze in terror. The rotting corpse of Raze glared down at me with milky white eyes, the flesh hanging decayed from his bones, the muscles and tendons exposed. The stench of death assaulted my senses as I cowered, my heart fluttering frantically as it tried to keep me from fainting from shock.

"You never should have come back here." His bloody mouth bared into a grin that revealed his smashed and jagged teeth. "But I won't rest until I have had my revenge. I will bury you alive now, as you did to me." Raze's fleshless hand grabbed me suddenly, the bones of his fingers digging into the skin of my throat like knives. My breath was severed as my windpipe was crushed. The scream I'd been forming was cut off as I stared wildly up into the sightless but deadly gaze of my former trainer. My hands closed over his, the gooey wetness of them barely registering as I fought to pry them off.

Raze growled like something inhuman, lifting me off the ground by the neck without effort. A strangled wheeze expelled from my chest as the darkness of the cave pressed in. I kicked feebly as the lack of oxygen exhausted my struggles, gasping for air that would not come.

"Twell!'

My clawing hands scrabbled at my throat in a last desperate bid to live, my body jerking in spasms as darkness swooped over me.

"Twell, wake up, you're dreaming." A hand much warmer than Raze's gripped my shoulder, shaking me out of a place much darker than the cave as a strangled cry broke off in my mouth. Bathed in a cold sweat, my eyes opened to gaze directly up into Jonaz's. His expression was filled with pain as his hand rose up to smooth my damp hair away from my face.

"It's okay, Twell, you're safe."

"For how long?" I whispered imploringly. My heart still hammered in my chest,

"For as long as I'm still breathing." His mouth formed a bittersweet smile as his warm fingers traced a line down my cheek.

"Jonaz...I.."

"Everyone, up." Brazin ruined the moment with his unnecessary volume, and I cringed as I raised my shoulders off the thin mattress. Jonaz pulled away, jumping to his feet in one swift move.

Talon approached, pressing a vial of water into my hands and I croaked my thanks before gulping the liquid in one long pull. It tastes like the best thing on Como.

"Fresh from the river." Talon grinned.

"Cold, that river." Jonaz winked over his shoulder before striding off to talk with Mekai and Surina. They were mixing up a protein meal, and my mouth began to water, despite knowing they lacked much taste.

"So what's our plan of attack?" I asked Brazin as our group merged and sat around the crates to eat.

"There will be no attack," Brazin replied calmly as he shovelled in his protein mush.

"Then what are we doing here?" I stared around at them all.

"What do we all share in common, that other civilians do not?" Brazin asked as he scraped out his bowl.

"Um....our abilities?"

"No. Something even more powerful than that." Clanking his bowl on the ground Brazin stood up. Covering the ground between us in one long stride he towered over me, tapping the side of my temple with one giant finger.

"Think," he ordered me.

I flinched, glaring up at him in annoyance. He smirked back, staring me down while I wracked my brains. Mira sighed, twitching impatiently as if my stupidity was physically hurting her.

"Oh." I picked up what he was putting down. "We have knowledge."

"Finally," Mira sniped. "We're all aging here."

"Why are you even here?" I wheeled on Mira, suddenly fed up with her renewed crappy attitude toward me. "Let's face it, you're the biggest champion of the Governing Body in this cave. You love the law. Maybe even more than you loved Chaz!"

The collective gasp included mine as I realized what I'd said. Mira staggered back like I'd physically struck her, her face draining of blood as remorse flooded my own veins.

"I'm sorry, I didn't mean that." My hands flew up, pressing over my mouth in horror as Mira's face tightened into a look of fury.

"Here we go," Brazin groaned as he stalked back to a box and sat down. "Righto. Get it over with girls, and make it quick. And fight properly if you must. Don't disappoint me like you did last time."

"Do you see my partner here, Twell?" Mira hissed, taking a shaking step toward me.

"Erm. No." I gulped. Taking a quick step back I pondered how I could deflect her powers without my own functioning. But only her words hurtled toward me, sharp and piercing to the core.

"Do you not see that I always have your back, even when I don't like what you do, or how you go about it?" Mira stood in front of me, her face flushed with emotion as her eyes narrowed to angry slits.

"But you said we should submit to the partnering. And to everything else they want." My argument weakened as guilt wrapped its tentacles around my heart and squeezed hard.

"And yet here I am. With you. I've helped a criminal, and now that makes me one too."

"So why did you do it? You didn't have to get involved."

"Ohletmesee…Because obeying the law didn't save Chaz. Because obeying the law made me miserable. How about because following their laws means denying my heart for the rest of my life…Oh and finally, because I can't obey leaders who have done the things I know about, including what they did to you!"

"Then why are you angry at me." I stepped closer to her. I wanted to reach out and touch her, to show I was sorry, to somehow erase the tortured look in her eyes. She'd hidden that pain for so long, but somehow it had overcome her now, her heart no longer resembling stone.

"It's not you I'm angry at." The frustration in her eyes grew wilder as she raked her fingers through her perfect hair and ruffled it for the first time possibly ever. "It's the system. I hate them for what they allowed to happen to Chaz. They failed us then, and they have failed us now. And you keep reminding me how bad they really are. You're tangible, and much easier to take it out on. Plus, I think running away to our enemies and risking your life like that was just the stupidest most self-indulgent thing you've ever done."

"Fair enough." I nodded. "And I think I was duly punished for it."

"I know." Mira looked at me seriously. "And when you're ready to talk about it, I want to know about it."

"I don't. Ever." I avoided the weight of everyone's gaze as I shuddered, my arms crossing protectively over my chest as I kept my gaze on the floor of the cavern. "I mean…I just can't…"

"Well…I'm sorry you went through that…even though you kinda asked for it."

I laughed so loudly it burst off every wall and came back to ring through my ears as the others cringed and covered their ears.

"Please don't change." I snorted as I lightly punched Mira's shoulder.

"Not planning on it." As her red lips parted to reveal her perfectly white grin, everyone else sighed in unison, visibly relaxing. Brazin got up at a leisurely pace, yawning rather theatrically as he stretched his arms over his head.

"Well, that was underwhelming. Now. Let's move on to more important issues if anyone's interested."

Suitably embarrassed, I moved toward him, hunkering down as the others gathered around.

"The only currency we currently have is our knowledge of all the GB's secrets." Brazin's low tone filled the small cavern, the low flames casting eerie angles over his hardened features. "They know how much I know. They suspect how much you all know, and are fearful, "Brazin jerked a thumb at me, "thanks to your excursion to enemy land."

"But is it a currency?" I challenged, "Or a death warrant?"

Surina's sharp intake of breath spoke volumes. They had to know the danger we were now in. They had to know the price they could pay if they stuck with me.

"Do you really think they won't try to silence us?" My gaze travelled slowly over my friends, assessing the fear flickering over their pale faces. "Look at what Maza did just to silence me. She tried to bury me alive just for wanting a boyfriend! How far do you think our leaders will go to shut down a rebellion that could change everything?"

"I think it's realistic some of them will want us killed." Avin's fluid tone delivered the words like a cold chill, and I shivered against my efforts. "There's good and bad leaders in our world, and the only way we can tip the scales is if we expose the truth to everyone, and let every citizen in Como decide where their heart lies.

"He's right," Sazika agreed softly. "It's not our secret to keep, or our decision alone to make. The truth affects everyone. Our families, our friends…" Sazika flashed a shy glance at Mekai. "Maybe our future children."

My eyes met Jonaz's, like two magnets unable to pull apart. Heat blazed over my cheeks as I stopped breathing, trapped in the endless dark depths of his gaze. Part of me wanted to run away, all embarrassed and clumsy. But another part of me wanted to sink to my knees and cry. I'd never wanted children. Not in such an ordered world that strove for perfection over happiness. But what if our world changed, because of us? What new things could I feel safe to desire? And what of the desires I'd buried deeper than Maza tried to bury me?

"We need to infiltrate the GB's communications," Talon ventured, "and share what we know with all of Como."

"But how?" Surina trembled, her large, green eyes round with anxiety. "How can we even get close enough to do that? We don't even have our wrist-coms anymore. Or the chips."

I hadn't even realised. But now I saw their wrists were as naked as mine, severing them from the society we'd run from. More than that, when I looked closely, I saw the wounds on their arms, freshly raw.

"The microchips." I gasped. "How did you…"

"We did it in the hospital, with a numbing gel," Jonaz assured me. "Then we planted the chips inside the collars of several medics who are living there while they tend to the worst wounded. If the GB's looking already, they'll be running around in the hospital for a while before they figure it out."

"That's brilliant." I tried to smile, but there were ramifications to our loss of connection. We were isolated in every sense of the word, and I was pretty sure smoke signals had died out in the old world, more generations ago than I cared to count.

"I uninstalled the Com-screen in my pod so they couldn't track us," Brazin replied. "But I can reinstall it to send messages. Right now, the pod's hidden out of sight under an overhang of rock, and untraceable. But the moment I reactivate, we're back on the map.

"But you can only contact known contacts in your data drive, right?" I asked as I stood up to stretch my legs. "Not much reach surely?"

"On the contrary, "Brazin said as he grinned. "It's an ex-army pod a couple of models old I got through my position. It's still good to contact all local councils in case of emergency as well as broadcast to all citizens in the event of an attack.

"Well. Where were you when the Abwarzians bombed Caran?" I couldn't help blurting. "Could have used a warning then."

"As could have I." Brazin lurched to his feet, and began pacing, his features twisting in such sudden rage I was scarily reminded of his former persona. "But you weren't the only one who was let down by our leaders. I never called the shots. I just followed them."

"And do you believe it was Abwarz who attacked us that day, Brazin? Or do you know if it was our own people, the same people who instructed you to kill the ones we found in these caves?"

"What?" Sazika gasped.

"What are you saying?" Mekai demanded as he reached for Sazika's hand.

The air seemed to suck from the room as Brazin wheeled around. Drawing himself up to his full height, he towered over me, his bulk and sudden aggravation forcing me to take a step backwards.

"Do not confuse what I know, with what I have done." Brazin barked down at me as I struggled to hold my ground. "I'm here because like you, I've seen enough, and done enough, but worst of all, kept silent for too long because I put my faith in a huge lie. I've carried that weight around long enough, and now I intend on doing what I believe is right."

"I'm picking up what you're putting down." I raised my chin defiantly, trying not to envision how easily he could throttle me.

Avin slid between us as fluidly as water, his back to me as he challenged Brazin's angry gaze.

"Don't try it, kid." Brazin growled. "You never went through my training."

"We're all here for the same reason. Let's remember who the real enemy is here." Avin's calm tone rolled over us all, defusing the tension while Jonaz appeared beside me, ready to defend me, like always. Guilt washed over me as I stepped away, retreating to a safer distance from them all.

"I didn't mean to make accusations. I just wanted to know the truth."

"Twell, you know more than I," Brazin growled as he ran a giant hand through his closely shaved head. "I think it's time we pooled our knowledge, and everything you gleaned from the Abwarzians if we're to have any impact on our people. And we need to act fast, before they find us. It's only a matter of time before they think of this place."

"Where else can we go?" Talon voiced the question on everyone's mind. "We can't go to our homes, or endanger our families. Maybe we already have…"

"Of course, they'll be searching for us there," Mira added, "so the civilian flight zones are out."

"You're right." Surina pressed her hands to her temples as her face drained of blood. "We're fugitives now. Who knows what they're telling society about us."

"I think I know." The answer shot through me like Mira's electricity, the hair on my arms standing to attention as everyone looked at me expectantly.

"We need to break back into the DUC," I replied calmly despite the quickening of my pulse, "If we can get to the Mainframe of intelligence, we can hijack the system and share the truth to the whole of Como." My words hung in the air like static, zapping us all as we eyed each other cautiously.

"Back in?" Avin's eyebrows shot up before he swung around to gauge Brazin's reaction. Talon and Surina gawked at me like I'd just notched up another level of crazy.

"Yes, they were that reckless." Brazin flicked his gaze at me as his face filled with unexpected pride. I knew it. He'd known all along. Just as Shay had known. She'd kept quiet out of love for me. But Brazin had kept quiet because his ideals matched our own. "Although the DUC wasn't ready for them that time," Bazin continued, "now it will be harder, especially since they've increased their security."

"And I don't have Shay's wristband anymore," I murmured in dismay as the realization hit me. I'd didn't know when I'd lost it.

Possibly when I'd fought Maza off me.

"You mean this wristband?" Brazin's held it out in front of him like it might bite.

"Oh, boy," Sazika exclaimed, shooting me a wary glance.

"Couldn't leave it just lying around," Brazin grunted, looking uncomfortable. "You dropped it when I returned you to the cell, after...well. After saying goodbye to her."

No one spoke for a moment as they acknowledged my loss. I shifted my weight uncomfortably, not sure where to look as everyone waited for my reaction.

"Could we really use this again?" I walked toward Brazin, palm out. He placed it into my hand and I inspected it closely. The dark blank face stared back at me empty of life and revealing no trace of its former wearer. I pushed away the heart wrenching grief that lurked like fog in the shadows of my heart.

"Yes. I can activate it again. We'll need it to connect to the mainframe because they've removed the passwords and inserted them into the wristbands. Not even the workers know the codes. But just like any Comian technology, it will instantly reconnect to the mainframe and alert the GB where we are. So we can't use it until a moment before we break in. Even then, we'll only have a short window of time to complete our mission before they come for us."

"Is everyone ready for this?" I let my gaze travel over each somber face as knots of fear coiled like serpents in my belly. "This isn't just breaking the rules anymore. We're stomping all over them, publicly."

"We know," Sazika replied softly. "We know we're choosing to fight our own leaders."

"This isn't just about our freedom." Mekai added. "We're fighting for everyone now."

"But what if they're happy with the way things are?" Surina replied. "What if they don't back us at all?"

"They will," Talon answered with such certainty that I looked at him with hope. "You saw what happened at camp after Twell took off."

"We're fighting for the right to choose our futures anyway," Avin said as he came to stand beside me. "We're not making their decision for them, we're just giving them the freedom to make a decision at all."

"Yes, yes, well articulated everyone." Brazin interrupted, looking like he couldn't stand another moment of our emotional convictions. "Now let's get planning while we all still have a pulse."

Buried underground, in the faint light of the flickering flames, we crouched in the dirt like our earthly ancestors, and plotted against the people we'd once trusted with our lives. Only now, they threatened our existence and we would fight back to protect ourselves, and those we loved. I looked at my friends, their faces older and harder than when I'd met them, wiser to the ways of our world, and the ways of war.

My heart was heavy with the knowledge that we hadn't evolved much further than the generations who'd destroyed each other on earth. No matter our good intentions, no matter our advances in technology or sustainability or knowledge, we could not seem to advance our minds or our hearts. We were neither immune nor shielded from hatred. War would never end if we could never change. But there was no choice now but to fight or die. When it came down to it, we were all designed with the primal instinct to fight for our lives. So I would again, and I would until I died. Because I knew in my heart I'd always fight for freedom, and that could only be right for us all.

Chapter Fourteen

Time crawled in the caverns, one day feeling like a month too long. My hatred for the underground clung around me like a heavy cloak as I dragged the thin stale air into my lungs, trying to stay calm. We'd made a plan and it was crazy and dangerous. We were leaving as soon as the sun went down. We knew we had to act before they expected us to, and it was fine with me. I wanted to get it over with, to face my enemies before they hunted us down. Waiting was far worse than knowing my fate.

In one of Brazin's crates, were enough weapons for each of us. CDA's, as well as laser guns.

"Laser guns? On our own people?" Sazika said the words we were all thinking as I stared at the guns, aghast.

"I can't use these on another Comian," I stated flatly to Brazin as he went to pass me a laser gun. "I don't want to harm anyone to that extent. I know we may have to fight them, but I want to disarm and defend, the way you first taught us."

"That's very noble and all, "Brazin smirked grimly, "But if they try to slice your leg off so you can't run, will you still feel the same way? Take one as back up at least."

"No. I won't." I held my palms up, refusing to take the proffered weapon. "I want them to see that I mean no harm, and that my intentions are not violent. I can't make that point with one of those dangling from my belt."

"Your funeral." Brazin shrugged as he holstered his own in one swift move.

"Nice." Avin shot a dark look at Brazin as he took a CDA from the crate instead. "She's right, though. We need to do this as peacefully as possible, unless it comes down to them or us, or we are only offering our people more trouble and pain. Our message will be lost."

"Thanks, Avin." I flashed him a tentative smile. "My point exactly."

"Well. We have to stick together like glue, and watch each other's back. No heroics okay, Twell?" Jonaz strode toward me, his expression so serious I didn't know whether I wanted to laugh or back up fast.

"I've learned my lesson, okay?" I retorted. "We're all equal in this. I'm not interested in leading. I never have been."

"But you are, Twell, whether you like it or not." Jonaz held my gaze as he held his ground. I squirmed in discomfort as my cheeks began to burn.

"No, it was Shanna who was really running things, "Avin butted in without candor. "She had a mouth to represent a rebellion perfectly."

"But you were always the ambassador." Ignoring Avin, Jonaz gripped my arm and I froze at the intensity in his expression. "Now more so than ever. You're the girl that survives. Not only did you escape death at Raze's hands, you defied death at the hands of our enemy in their own world, and came back alive! You defied the impossible, and now they want you to do it again, by leading the fight for our liberty.''

"And really, right now I'd be happy to fight for a good hot shower.'' I laughed shakily as I shook his hand off, my heart skipping a few too many beats.

"You should. You smell like a herd of Mogas." Mira sneered. "Least the GB was right about one thing. They really don't have water on Abwarz."

"Thanks for that." I pulled a face at Mira, relieved to break the tension. "I'm going to go for a swim in the river." I made to head off, but Jonaz blocked my path, his face full of alarm.

"No way. Remember how easily the current took me away?"

I stared at him for a long moment as the memory came flooding back. I'd thrown Jonaz in the river to save his life. The current was impossibly strong, but his love for me had been stronger. We'd saved each other that day. But I'd also killed Raze to save him, myself, and protect the others. I shuddered as the image of him screaming under the rubble shrieked through my mind.

"Of course I do," I replied quietly, suddenly afraid to meet his eyes. "I'll just wash at the edge."

"I'll come with you," Stelli offered as I moved past Jonaz, my eyes safely trained at the ground.

The sudden stillness in the room highlighted the awkwardness of the situation. Stelli and I had barely been friends before I'd learned of her match to Jonaz. I had no issue with her, apart from the fact she was clearly into Jonaz and I was insanely jealous of her physical appearance. Well, Okay. Maybe I had a few issues.

"Oh. Um. That's okay, Stelli, I'll be fine." I raised my brows at Sazika as I kept walking, and she hid a grin behind her hand, shrugging unhelpfully.

"Well, I'm coming anyways, I need to wash too."

I looked at her sharply, taking in the nervous expression on her flawless face. Yet her amber eyes glowed with determination rather than hypnotic powers, and I knew I was about to have a conversation I really didn't want to have.

"Suit yourself." I stalked past Mira mid smirk, resisting the urge to shove her as I went by. Stelli followed close on my heels as I took a few turns down a couple of narrow dark passages, following the sound of rushing water through the cavern walls. I was careful to memorise the path as I went. I hated to admit it, but I was glad I wasn't going alone, even if it was Miss Perfect Match. I didn't know what was more off-putting, the rapidly darkening tunnel, or Stelli quietly following me like an irritating shadow I couldn't shake. The roaring of the water grew louder as I turned left down another tunnel; the sound amplifying to a deafening volume as we came to the mouth of another small cavern. The river ran through it, dark and deep, churning fast and furious. Swimming? What was I even thinking?

Ignoring Stelli, I moved cautiously to the river's edge, crouching down to steady myself before I dipped a hand into the icy stream. The current dragged my hand and I pulled it out as I quickly stripped off my shirt and pants, down to my underwear. Self-conscious of my half-starved frame in comparison to Stelli's generous curves, I ignored her harder as I squatted down and splashed the freezing water over my face. She was already clearing her throat by the time I'd used the sleeve of my shirt to wash my upper body. By the time I'd got to my legs she'd knelt down beside me and was staring at me so obviously I had no choice but to acknowledge her.

"Jonaz still loves you, Twell. There's nothing going on between us."

"But you wish there was, Stelli," I replied bluntly. "It's okay, you can admit it. I've always known it."

"I know you have." Stelli smiled patiently, no trace of hostility in her golden stare. "But you also must know he's never had eyes for me, only you. Ever."

My damp skin wasn't the only reason I shivered as her words prodded at my heart. I wanted to run from the pain it caused. But I lingered, unable to stop wanting it to be the truth.

"Why side with us when you have every right to fight for him, Stelli? He's your match. It's your legal right."

Stelli snorted, rolling her eyes so uncharacteristically I widened my eyes in surprise.

"Come on, Twell, genetics means nothing over love. Even if I was chained to Jonaz by the wrist, I'd get dragged all over Como while he followed you. What kind of a life is that? I do have some dignity, please give me some credit."

"Oh." I blushed, probably glowing in the dark like a firebug. I was decently ashamed that I'd yet again underestimated her intelligence.

"You need to sort it out with him, before we go and do this. You need to fight in this cave for what we're about to go and fight for, out there. Don't miss the point, Twell. This is why we're doing this; because love like yours and Jonaz's has given the rest of us hope. It shows us why we need more freedom over our lives. You might not get the chance after we leave this place. You don't want any more regrets."

"You're right." Guilt flooded me as her words stung my heart. The truth often hurt. But if I went to fight for everyone else, without fighting for myself, then I was a hypocrite.

"I know!" Stelli beamed, her face shining in the dim light like some beautiful other-worldly spirit. "I am smarter than I look. Sometimes."

"I just don't get it, Stelli." My eyes began to burn unexpectedly as a lump formed in my throat. All I have left is a trail of destruction." A strangled moan escaped from my mouth, surprising us both as I pressed a hand to my heart. "I've killed so many people, Stelli. Did you know that? I killed Raze, right here in this cave. Do you know how much blood I have on my hands? And it won't wash off in this river...it won't ever wash off..." I plunged my hands into the icy rush of water to emphasise my point as I grew more upset. "Why would anyone support or follow my lead?" Drawing my hands out of the water I pressed them over my mouth, trying to stifle the howl of agony as it burst from my chest. But it forced its way through, filling the cavern in a haunting echo of grief. I felt Stelli's hand on my back, patting it as a mother comforts a child. The floodgates opened, the tears rushing faster than the river. I covered my face with my hands and cried like I had been needing to for more moons than I could keep count.

"I watched them killing her," I sobbed as Stelli's patting increased in tempo. "Ohmyrealms, Stelli, they killed her slowly and there was nothing I could do!" I could barely see for the salt in my eyes, my chest heaving as I braced my palm in the dirt and let the cries wrack through my body. I'd wanted to grieve alone, when I had a safe and quiet place to do so. But my body clearly had other ideas, or maybe it just knew that there would never be that time, and so it had to be now. "So I killed as many of them as I could to save myself."

"You had no choice. You know that. We all know that." Stelli's voice was soft and soothing, lulling me slowly into calm as my sobs began to run dry. "I'm so sorry about Shay. We all are. But I know in my heart that if I was in your position, I would have done the same."

"You would have charmed them all into submission before you needed to shed any blood." I hiccupped as I picked up my shirt and wiped my face with it. My eyes felt swollen. I knew I was not a pretty crier, so I was finally glad about the darkness to hide my puffy face.

"I would have done whatever I had time to do," Stelli said so seriously I looked finally into her glowing amber eyes. "Survival is an instinct before it's a choice. That's why humanity will never lose the urge to fight for life. It keeps us from going extinct."

"Planning on a teaching career?" I couldn't help but smile at the sincerity in her gaze. "Because that's the voice of a humanities teacher right there."

"Maybe one day." Stelli grinned. "But I think my powers might still be required for a while yet."

I exhaled slowly, feeling exhausted yet somehow lighter. "Sorry about that. I guess it was coming sooner or later."

"Please don't be. Take all the time you need." Stelli patted my back one more time reassuringly as she got to her feet. The sense of calm that surrounded her withdrew as the sound of her steps retreated behind me.

"Where are you going?" I jumped to my feet, no longer pretending I wanted to be in this eerie airless tomb alone. I swung away from the water, toward the sound of her rapidly retreating steps, and collided straight into Jonaz's arms.

"Oh" I squeaked as I looked up into eyes as deep and dark as the cave. Painfully aware I was shivering in only my underwear, I tried to squirm from his arms.

"Sorry. I didn't mean to scare you," Jonaz muttered, not sounding very apologetic at all as his arms stayed around me.

"I'm not scared," I retorted weakly, as I pulled away. "I'm confused." My heart pounded so hard against my chest I was sure he could hear it as I darted for my clothes.

"Twell. Talk to me. Please."

I flushed, as I dressed self-consciously before him, the cold no match for the burning intensity of his gaze.

"I just don't understand why you want to fight now. You told me it wasn't the time for us to fight for us. That it wasn't safe." I stepped away from him, closer to the edge of the swirling black water. "Now it's more dangerous than ever."

"Well. I figured if you can't beat 'em, then join 'em." Absorbed by the growing twinkle in his eye I barely registered him closing the space between us, step by careful step.

"I've lost so much already..." Tears burned my eyes again, blurring my vision as my hands rose to my face in distress. "Oh, the realms, Jonaz... First Chaz, then Shay. I can't handle you too. That's more than I can bear, that you might lose your freedom, or your life, because of me." I started to tremble, unable to remain aloof. "Is this

147

really what you want?"

"You're what I want." In one swift move, he seized my arms and swung me safely away from the water. The look in his eyes took the air from my lungs, the rush of relief so overwhelming I covered my eyes with my hands once more, the tears rushing, hot and fast in an apparent endless supply. My skin tingled in warning before his hands closed over my own, pulling them away from my face.

"You were right, Twell. There was never going to be a good time. Or no time at all if we died in battle. I'm so sorry I didn't support you..."

"Because you wanted to protect me. I get it," I whispered in echo of my earlier reasoning.

"Yeah...at least we both meant well." Jonaz smiled ruefully. Lifting a hand, he traced a finger down my profile. A burning wake of longing radiated through my whole being, and I tore my eyes away as emotions threatened to overwhelm me. But when Jonaz framed my face with his hands again, the look in his eyes sent a jolt of electricity through my body that struck straight to my heart.

"I love you, Twell Anar. And I'm already charged with disloyalty to our leaders. I see no reason to obey them any further, or stop fighting for us. Losing you is a price I'm still unwilling to pay."

Another sob broke from my lips before it was stifled by the crush of Jonaz's mouth against mine. His hands wove tightly through my hair as he kissed me hard enough to erase the sorrow in my heart. Crushed against his chest, Jonaz held me so tight I gasped for air. But I didn't pull away. I never wanted to leave his arms again. Raising my head to look into his eyes, a thin pale reflection stared back at me from Jonaz's dark irises. The longing in my expression was softly illuminated by the firebugs dotting the roof of the cave.

"This could be our last time alone together," I whispered. "Our last night of stolen freedom."

"We should make the most of it then," Jonaz murmured huskily as he traced my profile with his hand. His gaze deepened, stirring forgotten places within me. My skin tingled as his fingers trailed softly down the curve of my back, my knees shaking as his mouth pressed to the nape of my neck. Sparks igniting within me, melting the chill from my skin.

"I am yours," Jonaz said fiercely as he drew back to look at me once more. "No matter what they say!" I gasped as Jonaz reached for me again, his mouth quickly muffling my cry as his arms caught me in an inescapable embrace.

Lost momentarily in time that was fast running out, it no longer made sense to deny each other anymore. We both knew some needs were bigger than our own desires, and the freedom of Como was worth more than our own lives and hearts. The greater good mattered more than our individual yearnings.

Yet the fire roared within me, exploding in irrepressible desire as Jonaz pulled me to the floor of the cave. I was burning, all my senses consumed as we tangled as one in the deep depths of the cave. The churning waters muffled our cries, the dark depths of the cavern hiding our final crimes against the Governing body as our bodies rebelled, ready to surrender completely to each other.

But there was still something not right in my heart, a small voice screaming at me to stop as my urges overwhelmed me. Lost in the sensation of his touch, I knew I was on the brink of no return, every cell in my body screaming at me to surrender. Yet the whispering warning in the back of my mind grew louder as I struggled to pull away from Jonaz, breathless and shaky. "When the time is right, and we can take our time…" I panted, my voice trembling as I recited his words back at training camp.

"I don't want any regrets, Twell," Jonaz gasped, his gaze burning with intensity as he reached for me again. "I want you to know how much I love you. I want to show you how much."

"Then show me by waiting." I pushed him gently away, "Wait until we don't have to hide our love. Or hide at all. I don't want this moment to be a shameful secret, something we have to conceal like we've done something wrong. Never again. No more! Not after everything I've been through."

"I'm not ashamed of wanting you," Jonaz replied fiercely as he captured my face in his hands. His touch reignited the flames in my belly, his gaze so heavy with desire my heartbeat took off again. "I want you. Now. While we can. I don't know if I can protect you out there, I don't know if I'll ever have this chance with you again."

"That is our whole hope, the reason we're going to go out there and fight!" I cried as his gaze burned a trail of longing deep into my soul. "I can't relax until we make it happen. I can't rest until we make it right." Captured in his gaze, my words pleaded for mercy while my body still yearned for surrender.

Jonaz drew in a ragged gasp, his hands still holding my face as his expression softened. The fire in his eyes died down, smouldering like embers as he stroked the tangled hair back from my face. "Then just let me hold you awhile." He scooped me up, crushing me to his chest until we were heart to heart. "Let me remember the way you feel in my arms."

Burying his face into my neck, I felt him shudder, his mouth pressed against my skin as he fought for control. I clung to him until our breathing slowed, stroking his hair while his arms held me like a vice. Gradually, he relaxed, and our limbs softened together, melting into each other as our hearts beats returned to a normal pace. A sense of peacefulness washed over us as I inhaled deeply, memorizing his scent. His hands roved slowly over my skin, gently memorizing every inch of my body.

"What are we going to do now?" I said quite a while later. I shifted until I was lying in his lap, staring up at the twinkling firebugs as though they were stars.

"We're going to fight, Twell. Side by side."

"Till they tear us apart?" I grinned up at him.

"Something like that." Jonaz grimaced, ignoring my amused expression. "Maza won't be happy you're still alive. She would have preferred the Abwarzians killed you."

"They nearly did," I whispered.

Jonaz's eyes filled with instant anguish. Swallowing hard, his fingers curled into fists at his side, the muscles in his jaw tightening as he took a deep breath to calm himself. "No matter the cost, I won't let you down again. And I can assure you we won't be alone. Things have changed, and none of us can go back to the compliant and ignorant lives we knew. We've come too far for that."

"They want a different life on Abwarz too, Jonaz. The youngest, like our generation. I saw it. I felt it. They feared their leaders, like us. They want peace and negotiation. Just like we do."

"Let's work on our own freedom first, girl." Jonaz smirked, "That's going to be one heck of a fight on its own."

"Walk in the wetlands." I winked.

"After everything…you still haven't lost that spirit…" Jonaz stroked my cheek, his gaze full of such tenderness my heart squeezed in response.

"And neither have you…thank the realms."

"How did you defy the impossible, Twell? How can you be lying here, in my arms, right now? I feel your heart beating." Jonaz placed his hand on my chest. "I felt your breath on my face before I kissed you." Jonaz traced every curve of my mouth with his thumb, his eyes burning into mine with a depth of emotions far too heavy to bear. "And I feel these scars on your flesh just now…" He shuddered as he gently stroked the puckered angry flesh that scarred my arms. "Twell…how in the realms are you alive?"

"Because I was capable of more than I believed," I replied thoughtfully as I rose up to kneel in front of him "But also, because they are not everything we were raised to believe. Their leaders are the issue, as I said. Just like ours.''

"So it's time for change in both our worlds," Jonaz murmured as his hand moved from over my heart to lift me from his lap. "We better go. The rebellion can't really get started without us." Getting to his feet, I followed his lead as I fought the sudden urge to laugh.

"The rebellion. Like, that's the name? Seriously?"

"Admit it. You live for it." Jonaz winked over his shoulder, catching my hand as he led the way back from the cave. My amusement evaporated as reality pressed back in, as dark and smothering as a nightmare. Only I knew I was awake, and reality was far more threatening than any dream.

"I just want to live," I whispered, as I followed him back to the others.

Chapter Fifteen

The gloom of the caves hid my mortified blush quite nicely as knowing grins greeted our return to the others.

"Feel better now?" Mira smirked.

"Did you get lost, Twell? You were ages!" Mekai snickered.

"Shoosh now." Sazika shot a warning look at Mekai but she was trying not to laugh.

Avin's face tightened as he turned away, suddenly busy with a box of supplies. Stelli moved over to him, her smile for him empathetic. As he turned to her his profile softened, and his hand came up to rest on her shoulder.

"Okay, listen up soldiers," Brazin barked, filling the cave with his presence. "We need to go, so arm yourselves now, and fuel up. You'll need your full strength to utilise your powers when it comes to that."

We all knew it would. There was no other way. We ate and drank quickly as we grabbed up the weapons, securing them to our belts before we headed back to the main entrance, single file and silent. Jonaz's hand rested on the small of my back as he brought up the rear, the heat of his touch warding off the chill circling my heart. But as we all stopped at the lift, darkness fell over my spirit like a cloak of doubt and I shivered with dread.

"Could there be another way?" I squeaked, my concern growing as I took in Surina's wide eyed stare.

"I can't think of one," Talon replied grimly. "Not this soon, and we can't wait to act. That's the reality of the situation."

"We need technology to help us." Mira sighed as she met my gaze. "I think smoke signals might be lost on our generation."

"So if they catch us before we can do anything?" I let the idea hang in the air before the screech of the lift sliced through the silence.

"Then we all go down together, or keep on fighting whatever way

152

we can" Jonaz replied firmly as his hand moved around my waist, pulling me close.

"And fight for each other," Sazika chimed in softly. We all nodded in unison, sure of one thing at least.

"Okay, enough of the feel goods, let's get a move on." Brazin grunted as the lift door slid open and we all trooped in.

The flight back to Caran was as tense as the flight away from it. Only this time any fleeting sense of fleeing had evaporated as the lights of the city twinkled into view over the plains. A sudden pang twisted low in my stomach. I didn't know if I could still call it my home. I doubted I'd ever live there again, apart from within the confines of solid impenetrable walls.

The pod dipped with a sudden jerk, the descent so steep we were flung against our harnesses.

"It starts this far out?" Surina gasped as the air whooshed from her lungs.

"Of course," Brazin replied, "No point in escape tunnels unless they truly help you leave the city."

"How many people know about these tunnels?" Avin asked as Brazin swooped down for a quick landing.

"I don't know," Brazin muttered. "I'm not meant to, but my father was high up in the first Army of Como, and he told me before he went into battle."

"I didn't even know we had an Army back then," Sazika replied softly, her eyes wide with realisation. "I thought we were unprotected when they attacked us…"

"None of us knew. That's the whole point, isn't it?" I retorted as new anger stirred in my veins. "And why did we need escape tunnels in the first place unless we knew we might have a reason to hide and run?"

"I don't know any more than that," Brazin replied tersely as he focused on where he wanted to land. "I guess my father only told me because he wanted to make sure our family could leave if we had to. Even if he stayed to fight."

"And did he?" I asked as the ground drew nearer. "Did you use the tunnels while he stayed?"

"Yes." Brazin grunted. We fell silent while the belly of the pod bumped into the soft marshes of the Caran plains. I waited until we'd come to a stop before I resumed my interrogation.

"Did he come and find you?" Brazin turned around and met my curious stare, his expression so unfamiliar it was momentarily confusing until he spoke.

"No." Brazin's voice dropped wearily as his eyes filled with memories. "He died trying to protect our citizens, as he was trained to do." No one said anything more, unsure how to deal with the emotions of a man who'd exhibited more resemblance to a robot throughout our training. We un-clicked our harnesses and moved quietly off the craft into the chill night air. I shivered from nerves over the cold as I blinked against the dark. It was pitch black, the faint glow of the city doing little to light the ground under our feet.

"We need to push the craft into the bog over there," Brazin ordered. "If they spot it, or try to track it, they'll work out where we are straight away."

Talon and Surina focused their powers on the pod, wrapping them around the pod in a binding pull that dragged it quickly into the dark lake. The night was silent, apart from the squelching and sucking sounds as the pod slowly disappeared from sight. After a while, only the faint ripples on the surface gave away any indication of what lay beneath.

"There's really no going back, is there?" I turned to find Stelli's shaking silhouette behind me.

"You know we can't." Avin moved to her side, his arm visible across her shoulders as my eyes adjusted enough to take in her frightened expression. "We can't hide forever, and we can't help anyone if we hide."

"I know, I know." She sighed finally. "But I'm not brave like the rest of you. If I freeze up, don't wait for me. Just keep going."

"No. I won't." Avin gripped Stelli's shoulders, turning her around to face him. "You are as capable as all of us. You know how we can use our powers, and you will. I know you will."

"Stelli, you're brave in your own way, and we still need you." I backed him up as the others nodded their support.

"Follow me, and don't talk until we're underground," Brazin said as the whites of his eyes flashed warily upwards to the twinkling night sky. An ominous feeling settled over our group as we hurried across the soft wet marshes, our feet gathering mud that added weight to every step. I found my own eyes rolling frequently up as mist blew cold and stinging from my breath. If they spotted us now, we were completely vulnerable to attack. The marker was obvious, if you were looking for it; a pile of tall pale boulders, looming up like ghosts in the night.

"Woah. Remember this place?" Jonaz pulled to an abrupt halt in front of me, I stopped beside him as the huge grey boulders emerged in front of us, pale and ghostly, and eerily familiar.

"Unfortunately," Mekai replied, his expression as wary as my own.

"Oh no. I don't like this." I felt my stomach contract tightly, reminding me of the hide and seek type game we'd played when we'd first begun training. But Raze had hunted me, pursuing me into a cave where Jonaz had helped me to fight him off. We'd already realised it wasn't a game for Raze before he tried to hurt me.

"He's not here." Jonaz looked back at me quickly as he assessed my expression. "He's dead."

"And I killed him underground," I muttered as I walked reluctantly toward the rocks. So he'll probably be waiting down there to haunt me."

"Ghosts are as non-existent. Our ancestors dreamed them up." Avin rolled his eyes as he moved past me, Stelli sticking closely to his other side. "Even my grandfather told me they were mythological."

"And anyway," Mira said as she strode past, her tone annoyingly condescending. "If he was going to haunt you it would have been back in the aqua ducts where you actually killed him."

"Ohmyrealms!" I squeaked in alarm. "She's right!"

"Cut it out!" Brazin growled as he wheeled around, glaring threateningly, "Redirect your focus and ready your powers." Turning back around, he strode toward two thin, tall boulders. They leaned together like old lovers, creating a gap at their base just wide enough to slip through, or in Brazin's case, to squeeze between with much grunting and an impressive amount of cursing.

"Umph...Tighter... than I... remembered." Brazin grunted as he disappeared from view. Jonaz moved in front of me, taking my hand as he pulled me through the alarmingly tight crevice, gripping so tightly I had no choice but to push through before my mind and lungs could panic. Emerging through the rock, we found ourselves in a small circle of dirt. In the middle, Brazin was already brushing dirt off a hatched metal door in the ground, with Mekai and Talon's help. Jonaz and Avin moved to help them pull the heavy looking door open, pushing it back on its hinges to produce a small yawning black hole.

"Mmmmm, that looks inviting" Mira commented, a flash of nerves finally striking her features.

"You first then." I grinned as she flashed me a dirty look.

"I'll go first," Brazin cut in, as he moved to the side of the hole. "There's steps here, but they're steep."

As he dropped down the hole, we all moved to the edge, shining the lights on our weapons down on him as if he were our target. The steps were carved from stone, rough and rushed. They were also barely wide enough for one person at a time, and cut so high even Brazin hesitated as he placed his feet carefully before dropping to the next step.

"Who built this ancient death trap?" I snapped. "The same people who build the pyramids on earth?"

"Steep," he said. "Steps, he called them." Jonaz failed to hide his sarcasm as we all assessed the height we could essentially plunge should we slip.

"That's broken bones height, at the very least." Mira smirked as she pushed past Stelli and plunged down the hole. A few long moments later her voice wafted faintly up through the hole. "Yep, definite brain damage potential here folks."

"Let me go next," Mekai offered. "If anyone slips I can fly up and catch you." Turning to Sazika, he grinned widely. "All aboard!"

Sazika giggled as she climbed onto his back and a moment later they jumped through the hole, her gasp of fear followed by muffled laughter as they landed at the bottom.

"Why can't we do that?" Surina whined as Talon helped her over the edge.

"No thanks!" Avin and Talon replied in unison as they followed her into the yawning hole.

"Lucky last, you go ahead and I'll spot you," Jonaz suggested. His hand reached up, smoothing back a tendril of my hair as he gave me a reassuring smile. Gritting my teeth, I clambered carefully down onto the first step. Grabbing Jonaz's hand, I moved sideways from step to step, leading with my right leg and trying not to look down as the lights of the other's weapons shone up to help light the stone path. I sighed with relief as the ground appeared beneath me, and letting go of Jonaz's hand I jumped the last few steps onto the ground.

Jonaz landed beside me as Brazin pulled out a map from one pocket, and a strange looking object from another. Holding it in his palm, he tuned and faced what I thought was east.

"What is it?" Avin peered at the item.

"A compass." Brazin flashed a sudden smile, "They used them on Earth to navigate, and they are completely untraceable."

"Wow." Avin's face lit up with interest. "Can I have a go?"

"Sure." Brazin passed it to him. "We're heading east, down this passageway. There should be a crossroad of sorts about three hundred Comian lengths from here. At that point we need to turn north, then keep choosing all north tunnel splits to get to the base of the DUC."

Avin studied the map for a moment, then held the compass out until the dial swung eastwards. "Okay, got it." He took off, leading the way as we jogged after him. My heart pounded with the effort, my body still no way near as strong as I needed it to be. A small whiny voice in my head nagged in time to my steps. What if you're too weak to fight? What are you going to do without your powers? How will you protect the others? I blocked it out as I pushed on, only matching Sazika's pace as her short legs struggled to keep up with the others. Stelli also dropped back, simply not as fit as the others due to her lack of training. We walked for a long time, only stopping long enough to sip our flasks of water before resuming our urgent pace. My legs ached, the muscles protesting with fatigue as I pushed on, while Jonaz looked over his shoulder so many times to check on my progress it was a wonder he didn't trip over his own feet.

When the tunnel opened into three separate paths, Avin stopped, his head dropping to peer at the compass. Then turning left, he darted around the corner, and we were forced to speed up again to keep sight of the others. Beginning to jog, we moved from one tunnel to the next based on Avin's careful study of the map, and the direction the arrow on the compass seemed to be pointing. Our breaths almost synchronised as our feet pounded in time on the rocky ground. Just when my muscles were beginning to scream in protest, Avin slowed down, coming to a stop as the tunnel opening into another small round cave. Another set of stone steps led up to an identical round hatch in the roof of the cavern.

"This leads us straight into the main communications room," Brazin warned. "Once we're in, we'll have to disarm whoever's in there. They never leave it unmanned anymore after your little visit."

"Darn." Mira huffed. "I told you all it was a stupid idea at the time. But no. Noooooone listened, did they."

"And thank the realms we didn't." Stelli smiled patiently at Mira. "Or we'd have no knowledge at all with which to fight."

I stifled my grin as Mira's face screwed up in surprise, and Jonaz smirked openly at her.

"Get it together, ca-brats, we're movin'," Brazin hissed. Moving up the steps so fast we had no choice but to pursue him. At the top, he pushed his plate-sized hand against the trap door, and looked at Talon and me.

"I'm sorry…I still have nothing." I hung my head, unable to look him in the eye and see his disappointment again."

"It's fine, Twell," Brazin grunted. "Just give Talon some space so he can give it a bit more juice."

Talon patted my arm sympathetically before he moved in front of us, his eyes bright with the power that shone through them. Facing the hatch, he struck at the door in one sharp burst. Everyone cringed as the metal shrieked and twisted off its hinges and launched upwards, into the room above us. Before it landed, we'd spilled out of the hole, launching into the dimly lit room so swiftly, the workers had barely the time to spin around in their seats. I trained my weapon on the closest worker, watching him consider his limited options as he gazed fiercely back.

"Nobody move!" Brazin roared to the startled workers. They gazed blankly at us until recognition set in.

"It's them! The wanted!" one woman hissed as she slid numbly off her chair to the floor.

"What do you want here?" The man I was aiming at stood up slowly, his palms out as he stepped toward me. "You must surrender."

"Thanks, but no thanks." I drew back the trigger as he moved slowly toward me. "Don't come any closer. Get down on the ground, we don't want to harm you."

"You won't get back out of here," the man suddenly snarled as he looked at me with hatred. "The place is set to go into lockdown the moment you're detected, and I hope they lock you up for life. Your guardian would be rolling in her grave if she knew what a traitor you are." He lurched toward me so suddenly I froze, screams erupting in the room as Brazin shot him in the temple. As he fell, Surina threwher powers out, only just stopping him from striking the ground face first. The other workers gasped as I rushed forward and took his weight, lowering him carefully to the floor.

"He's not dead, he's just unconscious. It's for your protection, so you can't be held accountable," I said as we approached the others. Some whimpered in fear before we shot them, others glared with eyes full of reproach and judgment, but they all passed out the moment the voltage of the CDA's touched their temples. After we lined them all up against the wall and out of the way, we moved straight to the mainframe. Pulling Shay's wrist-band from my pocket I snapped it onto my left wrist.

"Here," I thrust my arm at Brazin. "Let's do this quick."

Seizing my hand, his fingers worked amazingly fast over the tiny screen, despite their size. I felt the heat of its activation a moment before it lit up, then it buzzed against my skin as it hummed to life.

Whirling around, I looked for the new activation point. At the base of the screen was a slot for my hand and wrist to go, and I shoved my hand in without hesitating, feeling it pull my hand upwards, with a strong magnetic force as it clicked into some sort of vice to retrieve the data. The screen lit up, straight on the home screen, with no further requirements. Using my right hand, I tapped into the screen, already knowing where to go. I pulled data out at a furious pace as everyone leaned in around me, the tension so thick I began to sweat as I collected a montage of images and reports.

The first things I found we could use were communications from the Abwarzians imploring we supply them with water, and detailing how their civilians were mutating and dying without our continued support. Next, I complied the files where we had denied any further help, based on the Governing Body's decision to barter with another world that could supply us with protein grown from crops we had not yet managed to cultivate on Como. Then I found the report we'd read before, about the defects and abnormalities their children were developing as a result of mineral deficiency. I grabbed several images of weapons our people knew nothing about. Weapons that were in no way peacekeeping and could only result in violence, injury or death if used. Lastly, I grabbed several reports on the prisoners we'd captured, highlighting the parts where they mentioned the POW camps.

"Don't forget the pictures of those camps," Sazika whispered as a hush fell over the room. She didn't have to remind me. I'd never been able to shake those images from my mind, and the ones I knew would have the most impact, because they portrayed the war crimes of my own parents. A tight sharp pain pulled at my heart as I found the one picture that changed everything I'd ever known about my origins. There they were, in their Army uniforms. They gazed out at me as the familiar chill worked its way down my spine. She still wore the same solemn expression as they stood over the dismantled bodies of the Abwarian prisoners. He still stared at the camera without an ounce of guilt in his proud expression. I hesitated as my hand hovered over the faces of my parents.

"You don't have to use that one, Twell." Jonaz's hand rested on my shoulder. "Everything else is enough."

"No, it's not." I turned to him regretfully, "They need to see this picture, to know the truth has been hard for us too. They need to see I'm ready to expose the truth even if there's a cost for me. I'm willing to pay for their sakes."

He nodded in response as he squeezed my shoulder, and I clicked on the image, dragging it into the file with the other POW photos. They clearly displayed the proof of our crimes, the blood curdling atrocities we'd committed against the prisoners. I felt my eyes begin to water, still affected by the despair and fear on the faces of the Abwarzians as they prepared to die. We had not shown them mercy, and all of Como deserved to know what we had done. A gasp of horror sounded behind me, to my right.

"I never really wanted to believe you guys, you know," Mira whispered behind me, her tone heavy with dismay. "But seeing it for myself, I just can't believe it..."

"Confronting, isn't it?" I flashed her a sympathetic glance over my shoulder. Her face was paler than usual, the look of betrayal in her expression pulling at my heart.

"Horrifying." Mira's eyes gleamed with tears. "Those children...They were..." Mira's voice was strangled with a sob she was desperately trying to quell. She looked at me a face full of remorse. "I was wrong, Twell. Now I get it. It makes it easier to understand now why you have chosen this path."

"What about the images of what they did to us?" Surina asked suddenly. My head jerked from Mira's to Surina's as she stepped back from us all. "Surely, they have those too, worse than what they ever showed us at school."

"You're right," Mira replied as she eyed Surina warily, "But if we use those, we weaken our message."

"But then we also sway it to our own agenda, and our whole aim is to show there are two sides," Avin argued. "Without both sides, they might think it's just propaganda."

"Make a decision, soldiers," Brazin barked as he spun around toward the middle of the room. "Some of you need to help me watch the exits. They will be here any moment. There's no more time."

"Show the post bomb photos, but align them with our prison camp photos, and show the dates," Mekai suggested before he moved to guard the main exit door with Brazin. "That way it shows their crimes in chronological order, as well as our own. It will speak the truth more clearly than anything we try to say ourselves."

"Okay," I replied shakily. I matched up the timeline of events and hit download. As it processed, I found the main universal communication portal, and dragged all of the data into the screen. No

161

one moved a muscle as I hit send, unable to believe we'd just messaged the whole of Como in one fell swoop. The collective sigh of relief was so loud I giggled a little hysterically as I went to remove my wrist from the slot.

"Hey," I tried to yank it free, "I can't get my hand out."

Jonaz seized my arm, pulling so hard I squealed in pain as my hand held fast inside the device.

"It's a trap!" I cried out as realization hit. "They must have known we took her wristband!"

"They would have known we are here the moment you inserted it," Mira gasped. "They're already here." Everyone froze, staring at the exits in anticipation. There was no alarm to warn us. Or the sound of pounding feet to prepare us. Yet the silence smothered us like a net, ensnaring us in a spell of shock.

"Let me try." Jonaz moved aside as Brazin strode over. Winding his hand around my wrist he pulled hard as he tried to release me.

"Owww!" I gasped. "Stop! It's hurting!"

Brazin slammed his huge fist down over the slot several times, my body jolting with the impact as I pulled with all my might. Still it did not budge, and I looked around at my friends as panic flooded my veins.

"You guys have to run." I gasped, "You still have time. Get out of here while you can."

"No!" Jonaz yelled. "If you have to leave that hand behind, you're still coming with us. They'll take more than your hand."

"No way!" I shrieked, losing all remaining composure at the idea." Don't you dare!'"

"Stop! Stop it!" Sazika screamed as Jonaz closed his hand over my wrist and I tried to fight him off. Avin leapt to my defense, trying to pry Jonaz's desperate grip on my arm. Stelli jumped in, pulling at Jonaz's waist, trying to drag him back.

"Please!" I sobbed as everyone began to yell, and push and pull. I stared desperately into Jonaz's frantic wide eyes, willing him to listen. "It's me they want anyway. Please, please go!"

"I'm not leaving you!" Jonaz shouted so furiously I flinched. "Don't you get it? I'm never leaving you again. Ever. No matter what."

162

"For the planet's sakes! Get out of the way, Jonaz Maven, you big stupid hero!" Mira shocked him so abruptly, he let go as he flew backwards and landed on his backside in the middle of the room.

"What are you doing you crazy bi…

"Twell, get down, now," Mira cut me off, her tone demanding and unarguable. Her face screwed up in a look I knew all too well. Dropping to the floor I looked up just as Mira placed her hands over the slot. A resounding 'CRACK!' was followed by a bone rattling jolt as the power travelled through my arm. My body slammed against the machine as electricity shot through every nerve in my body. Black choking smoke filled the air as sparks flew up and the screen blinked and stuttered. The putrid stench of burning plastic surrounded me soon coating my lungs. I gasped for air as I covered my face with my free hand as the glass on the screen shattered. Everyone dove for cover while I huddled into a ball as best I could. Stunned, I hung limply for a long moment before my hand slipped from the device, and I slumped to the floor.

Jonaz scrambled over to me, lifting me onto his lap as the all too familiar smell of burnt flesh permeated the air. The wristband had melted onto my wrist, and Jonaz pried it from my skin before I could even think to scream. Covering the bloody wound, he quickly began to heal it before the sound of pounding feet diverted my attention. My heart began to gallop as I stared at the others. They were coming.

"This is it, soldiers. Flee, fight, or surrender?" Brazin stood in the centre of the room, commanding our attention as he raised his weapon at the door. "How does this end?"

"We have to surrender," I gasped as Jonaz pulled me to my feet. "We have to face them in peace. Violence does not resolve violence." Around me, the others nodded, fear etched starkly over their faces. Our weapons clattered to the floor in unison as we moved toward Brazin, meeting him in the middle, and facing the door. My heart pounded to the rhythm of their steps as they burst through the door, weapons raised, faces grim with purpose.

"Get down! On the floor!"

I felt Jonaz's fingers interlacing with mine as we sunk to our knees. They circled us in moments, at least twenty law enforcers. My mouth went dry as I recognised their weapons were laser guns, and not CDA's, like they'd always used against those who broke the law. Surina let out a small sob of fear, and Talon put his arm around her shoulder, his face grim as he caught my eye.

"Shoot them now?" one of them asked, looking toward their leader. My blood ran cold as my eyes followed his direction and landed on Maza's victorious face. She was already staring at me, her hatred palpable as she moved forward from the ring of soldiers and stepped toward me.

"What!" Mekai shouted. "We've surrendered! Are you going to murder us in cold blood?"

As I turned to look at Mekai, the first thing I noticed was the absence of Sakiza beside him. I twisted around, scanning for presence, but she was gone. Or invisible for now. It wasn't part of the plan. But now, as I watched them closing in on us, I willed her to run for her life. If she could escape, she might be able to tell everyone how we were murdered in cold blood. It was up to her to tell our story and try to convince our people our Government was as corrupt as the Abwarzains.

"CDA's only." Maza's tone dripped with disappointment, her beady red eyes never leaving my face as she switched her laser for the CDA in her holster. "They must appear before the G.B, as per our orders. They must be seen to be trialled."

"Seen to be, but not actually," I spat as I glared up into her cold hard face.

"Appearances are everything after all, on Como." A creeping smile twisted her lips into a sneer that made my skin crawl. Jonaz gripped my hand so tightly it was almost crushing. "I've prepared a nice cold cell with your name on it." Maza's eyes gleamed sadistically. "I hope you're not claustaphobic…Oh wait…but you are."

The soldiers shot my friends all around me before I could even react. They slumped to the floor soundlessly, and my eyes sought Jonaz's, his beautiful brown eyes meeting mine just before the charge of power hit him. His body went slack, his hand releasing mine as he pitched sideways and slumped to the floor. The only one left, I knew she'd planned it that way as she closed the space between us, forcing me to tilt my head back as she loomed over me.

Twell and the Uprising

"Order is everything." I flinched as Maza pressed the cold metal of her CDT hard against my temple, her grin glinting as sharp as a blade. "And you and your friends will never jeopardise that again."

A sharp sting bit my temple, the force knocking me hard to the floor. The light fled my senses, and once again my old foe, darkness, came to greet me.

Chapter Sixteen

The cold chill from the tiles crept into my skin, awakening me abruptly as a shiver rattled my bones. I rolled onto my knees and stayed there for a moment, waiting for my head to stop spinning before I looked around my new confinement. Not quite as cosy as the pit Maza had once thrown me into, it came a close second, with barely enough room to walk two steps in any direction. There was a small bench along one side, opposite a heavy iron door that looked thick and impenetrable. But I was willing to give it a try. Standing up, I waited for the sensation of nausea to ebb away before I stared at the door, wondering if I should try my powers again…

"I wouldn't do that." An unrecognisable voice piped over my head. I looked up, straight into an audio camera. "There's a collar around your neck. Feel it."

My hands flew up, grasping the thick metal cuff encircling my skin. It was so tight I couldn't believe I hadn't noticed it.

"If you attempt to use your powers, or escape, the collar will sense it and insert a toxic agent into your jugular vein. It's a new development, and you are our first to trial it, so we aren't entirely sure of the long-term effects. But we do know it's at least toxic enough to paralyse you for a moon or more."

My heart began to race in response, the beat of the pulse in my neck pushing against the collar as I ran my fingers all around the smooth metal, trying to find the join.

"Same goes if you try to remove it," the voice warned without emotion. "So I suggest you sit tight until the trial. You won't have long to wait."

"Wow," I answered back, "it's amazing how quickly you people can move when you really think there's a threat."

The voice either chose not to reply, or had gone off somewhere else, because all I got in response was the cold silent stare of the camera and the horrible sensation that the collar was already choking me.

"Is anyone there?" I called out, trying not to sound panicked. "Jonaz? Mira?"

"Twell, I'm here! Can you hear me?" a voice called faintly through the wall to my left, and I scrambled over to put my ear against the cold stone.

"Avin? I can hear you. Do you know where we are?"

"At Caran's Courts Holding, for offenders against Como," Avin's voice travelled back to me, the sombreness of his tone not filtered down through the thick walls. "I heard some guards talking. They aren't even going to give us a trial. They don't want anyone to know we're even here."

"Oh Avin…" My heart sank like a stone, my knees buckling as I slid to the floor of the cell. "This is it then. They've won."

"Haven't you read our world history?" Avin chuckled suddenly, the sound hauntingly beautiful as it echoed into the room. "Evil never wins in the end. There's something inside us all that will always keep fighting against injustice. Some of us just realise we are oppressed sooner than others. Some of us need to lead the way, showing there's a battle that needs to be fought. Some of us need someone like you, Twell."

"Oh stop." Blood heated my cheeks so fast I was glad he couldn't see me. "You should have been a historian, not a soldier."

"And when we are through all of this, I will be," Avin replied so firmly I leaned back against the wall, hoping his certainty might seep into my own spirit.

The door screeched loudly as it dragged open. I leapt to my feet as a law enforcer appeared, his laser gun thrust in my face as he gestured for me to move. I left the cell without argument, swallowing the rising lump in my throat as the others emerged from their cells. There was an enforcer for each of us, solemn and grim as they marched us down a long grey corridor. No one spoke, nerves drying our already parched throats. Jonaz turned to look back at me, but the enforcer pushed him hard in the shoulder, forcing him to watch where he was going as we quickly arrived at the end of the passage. Another huge door slid open before us, the enforcers rushing us through so fast we barely had time to register we were already in the courtroom.

We were pushed to the podium like a herd of mogas, the soldiers only retreating to the edges of the room after we climbed into the accused box that faced the judges. To the left, standing on a separate podium, stood Brazin. His head turned slowly, encumbered by the collar as his gaze caught mine. The defiance I saw in his eyes emboldened me, and I moved first to the end of the podium as the others filed alongside me.

Twelve judges stared back at us, split into two rows, with the second raised behind the first. All my life I'd tried to imagine what they looked like. They never revealed themselves, preferring to remain anonymous and safe from personal attack as they dictated our lives.

"Just like the Great and Powerful Oz…" Avin murmured more to himself than to the rest of us.

"I can't believe it but I actually know what you are referencing for once in my life," I muttered back. We'd covered famous literature from Earth, and I knew what he meant.

As they surveyed us, I realised they looked nothing like the big powerful images of them I'd imagined as a child. Instead, apart from their black official uniforms, they were as regular and plain as any civilian. They did not look powerful or in control. And yet, up until now, they have made the entire population of Como believe in their promises. It just went to show how well we bought anything we watched or heard in all the media messages. We'd never questioned anything they'd taught us in school. Maybe our complacency was much more dangerous than they had ever been. Maybe their power lay in knowing how easily people would follow a leader when they were too lazy to search for the truth.

As I contemplated their success, I became aware of one person amongst the judges that I couldn't believe I'd missed. Sitting at the end, in an attached witness box, Maza's lips pulled into a smirk so prematurely triumphant, I considered how long the poison would take to paralyse me if I were to leap from my box to hers and wipe the smile off her face permanently. Someone's leg trembling against mine brought me back to the present, and I turned to look into Surina's fear struck eyes.

"I can't do this," she whispered. "I'm so afraid."

"Shhh, it will be okay," I lied as I took her hand and squeezed it firmly. Then the judges were standing and I turned to the front to face them.

"Twell Anar," began an elderly man with thick silver hair and a stern tone. "You are hereby charged with escaping solitary confinement, desertion of The Army of Powers, theft of Army property, the act of illegally absconding from Como in the stolen craft, trespassing in neighbouring planets solar systems, and inciting acts of rebellion against our Government."

"Oooh, didn't know about the trespass one, but that's cool." I grinned despite the knots twisting in my belly. "I'm sure you could also throw in damage to the Army storage facility, breach of the partnering law, oh and assault of an Officer. How's your nose, Maza? Looks a little wonky from where I'm standing."

"Careful, Twell," Brazin growled at the same time Maza lurched to her feet. Her eyes blazed with such hatred I would have incinerated on the spot if the fiery daggers she was shooting at me were real.

"You may not speak, traitor," Maza hissed like a serpent ready to strike. "You will be silenced and your rebellious following stamped out."

"Sit DOWN, Officer Maza," an elderly member of the G.B shouted. "You're a witness here today, and still only a training member of Government. It is not your place to read their verdict. It is ours."

Maza's face reddened and her face screwed up like she'd just dropped some gas. She sunk slowly back down, as though it physically pained her to do so.

"So this isn't a trial, is it." I looked at the members of the Governing Body in disgust. All my life they had seemed like an invisible power, never in the media themselves as they spoke to us through our wristbands and billboards, and intercepted our pod radios to tell us how to live our lives. I'd imagined powerful impressive looking people, with wisdom and strength to guide us all. But now I saw them clearly. They were nothing but a bunch of old bullies from prominent families who'd been allowed to get away with it for too long because of their bloodlines.

The old man stood up in turn, clearing his throat before he looked at me and spoke again. "Trials are for deciding if there has been a breach of the law. That is not in question."

"But why don't you question why I did it?" I looked at them in dismay as my heart sank into my boots. "Why not ask yourself why I felt I had to break the law."

"It doesn't matter what you felt," the man replied impassively. "We are looking at your disregard for the law and order we have put in place to regulate a safe and prosperous civilization. If we allow you all to go running about chasing after your emotions, we will wipe ourselves out purely through muddying our gene pool."

"How can you expect loyalty from us when you clearly don't care about us at all," I shouted, ignoring Jonaz warning hand on my back. "Loyalty is earned and built on respect. And you've lost that with our generation."

"She's right!" Talon spoke up as I trembled with anger. "You can stop us, but you can't stop everyone. We want change. We want the right to choose who we match with. Love gives people a purpose to live and protect this world, not perfect genes and empty hearts."

"What nonsense." Maza snorted contemptuously from her witness box. "They are all clearly brain washed, most likely at the hands of that so-called officer over there, "Maza stabbed an accusing finger in Brazin's direction. "The whole lot of them need to be exterminated if you ask me. Their thinking is more dangerous than the weapons we put in their hands."

"That's enough!" the man turned and glared at Maza in way that convinced me he wasn't in her fan club either. "Genocide is a dangerous suggestion to be using in our presence. We are not still the barbarians our ancestors were and your thinking is sounding dangerous itself."

"Here, here!" I clapped my hands and cocked my head at Maza just to provoke her a little more. If they were starting to see how many stars short of a galaxy she was, then there might be some hope for us yet.

"Order!" another Govenor interceded sharply. Lifting his hand, I saw the device he was holding and instinctively clutched at my neck. You will not speak unless we permit you. This is not acceptable!"

"And threatening us with poison is?" Jonaz growled from my right side.

"Be silent," the Govenor snapped. But he raised the device and looked at our necks as though really considering them for the first time. "It's merely an aid to ensure our safety. We know what you are capable of doing to us."

"Well of course you are," I sneered. "You designed our abilities, after all. Regretting it now?"

"Just press the damn thing and be done with it." Maza couldn't help herself as she glared at the collar around my own neck with longing. "It's the only way to shut that one up, and I would know."

"Yes, do we get to talk about that?" I retorted as my gaze swung back to the GB. Do I get a chance to tell you about how she imprisoned me and tried to kill me at the Army camp? Any interest? I have witnesses. Oh look! They're all right here in this box!"

"What's she talking about?" a lady Govenor standing beside the older man looked at him quizzically. "I wasn't aware of these facts...perhaps we need to hear what happ.."

"Lies!" Maza screeched. "After everything she has done, would you really listen to a word that comes from her lying lips?"

"Officer Maza, I order you to stop interrupting," the old man said fiercely as he glared at her. "Those details aside, we are still looking at the immediate and proven crimes conducted by these accused." Swinging his stern gaze back to me, he continued. "Because you have coerced your fellow soldiers to aid your escape, they will be sentenced alongside you, to a life of solitary confinement and the disabling of your powers. You will wear the collars permanently."

"No." Surina gasped, hands clutching at her throat. "Please...can't you listen?"

"Silence!" the Governor commanded. "Any attempt to use your powers, any attempt to escape, will result in instant paralysis." The man frowned, his tone still as formidable as he glared at Surina. A sharp wide grin stretched across Maza's mouth as she looked directly at me. I was momentarily too dismayed to respond, victory shining in her eyes as the others reacted around me.

"Hold on..." Another man in the Governing box muttered. "It's not decided yet...we are meant to make judgement today..."

"There is no better solution! What is there to discuss?" Maza hissed, spinning toward him in her seat with an ominous frown.

"So we get no chance to defend ourselves?" Jonaz spat across the open space between them and us. "You will not even listen to our side of the story, or why we were compelled to act as we did?"

Some of the G.B looked at each other, hesitating for just long enough for us to witness their discomfort. It was obvious they were not united in their beliefs, their lack of unity evident in the chaotic way they were trying to rush through our sentencing. But the uncertainty in some of their expressions was beginning to unravel my idea that they would not or could not change.

"How can you ever justify betraying our laws?" another judge who had not yet spoken replied uncertainly as Maza tried to intimidate her with a arctic stare. "How can we let it go unpunished, without losing control of the people? If we show you mercy, we show our citizens that it's acceptable to defy us. Then our leadership is threatened."

"But don't you get it?" I blurted, not caring that Maza looked ready to leap over the barrier and come at me, "it's already threatened because it's in our nature to desire free will. It's always been within us, just as our history on earth shows us. People will always find the strength to fight for what they believe is right in the end."

"Well. We will just have to stop them before they even try." Maza slammed her hand on the barrier so hard the woman behind her flinched.

"I won't warn you again, Officer Maza!" the elder Governor snapped. "Be silent until you are asked to contribute," the old man continued. "You, Officer Brazin, are charged with aiding these young subordinates', and will be stripped of your rank and imprisoned until further trial."

"A just sentence!" Maza saluted the air, her face smug with satisfaction. "How can you even call yourself an Officer of Como?

You're as big a traitor as these infidels."

"Fair enough." Brazin barked as he stared the Governor down. "But I will not be interrogated by the likes of you, woman. Your power tripping is an embarrassment to the Army. I'd rather be a traitor than a dictator."

"Well said!" I chimed in until Brazin flashed me another warning glare.

"Nonsense and slander!" Maza hissed back before she turned her head in our direction, "and as for you, we will be broadcasting your fate throughout Comian media as an example to show them what happens to those who threaten the order of things."

"I said SILENCE!' The Governor finally lost his temper as he shook his fist at Maza. "You are being INSUBORDINATE!"

"No!" Surina shrieked so suddenly I jerked away from the sound. "You can't do this! You can't! It's not fair! I can't live in isolation...I won't!" She began tugging frantically at the collar, yanking harder as her hysteria grew. "Get it off me! Get it off me! I've done nothing wrong! Please take it off!" None of us saw it coming. In one swift move, Surina vaulted over the barrier and hit the ground running.

"Surina! Stop!" Talon's face contorted in horror as she sprinted toward the exit. The rest of the G.B jumped to their feet in alarm as she sprinted toward a guard.

Chapter Seventeen

"Surina! No!" I leaned so far over the barrier Jonaz seized my arm to keep me from falling. But Surina was beyond listening, her fear the only thing driving her. Raising her hand toward the closest guard, the soldier flew back against the wall in a short burst of Surina's power before she pulled to a sudden halt. Her piercing scream filling the room as she clutched at her neck. Her eyes bugged wide, dawning comprehension flashing over her face as the poison entered the main artery in her neck. Her body stiffened, her limbs rigid as she jerked and twitched. Her fingers curled like claws over the collar as pain and fear filled her eyes, and her mouth gaped open, her scream now as frozen as her body.

The soldier darted forward as she fell, catching her just before she hit the ground. Flipping her over, he laid her face up, unblinking at the ceiling. The blood drained from her face so fast the soldier stepped quickly away, like he'd touched a corpse. He nervously looked toward the G.B for further direction.

"Ohmyrealms..." Stelli sobbed quietly beside me, burying her face in Avin's shoulder as Mira pressed her hands tightly over her mouth, trying to stifle her growing terror.

"You told us, it would just be a little shock and sedation!" a woman in the panel stood up, her voice shaking as she stared at Maza in horror. "What have you done?"

"You are accountable for this!" Brazin boomed in sudden fury, shaking his curled fist at Maza before he turned his rage on the Governing Body. "This Officer's leadership leads to war, not ours. Her way is death, and there will be no future for you or anyone who listen to her."

"This hearing has gotten way out of hand!" The elderly man rose to his feet as well, glaring furiously at Maza. "You have taken unapproved liberties and withheld the full force of those collars. This was NOT approved. This is unacceptable!"

"Is she still alive?" Talon asked very quietly, his body trembling with too many emotions to list. The room fell silent, as Surina lay abandoned and untouchable on the floor. "Somebody help her...please..." But they seemed just as shocked, staring at her body with horrified expressions.

"She chose the wrong reaction and reaped the consequences," Maza replied, her tone dripping with self-righteous justification. "There is no sympathy or retribution for those who resist our laws."

Jonaz's hands seized my arms from behind, knowing me too well. But my fury reared up like a wild animal, snarling and vengeful, eager to attack. Rage filled my soul like a blinding flash of lightning. It washed over my senses as the fury ran through my veins. My powers thudded to life, my fingers tingling with power as I glared at Maza's sneering face. I could lift her out of the box and dash her brains all over the ground. It would only take a moment, before the collar got me, but I could be quick enough to finish her for good before the poison took over.

"Twell, "Jonaz voice was tight with warning, "not her way."

"What good will any other way do?" I hissed, swinging around to look in his dark pleading eyes. "What good has surrendering done us? They won't listen to reason; they will never show mercy over their stupid laws. Don't you see?

They'll do this to all of us. No one will ever know and all of this would have been for nothing. At least let me take her down before it's too late."

"Please, Twell." Jonaz's tone was too low for the G.B to hear, but it was firm as his hand touched mine, urging me to stop. I held my breath, feeling my heartbeat pounding away inside my ribs as his eyes burned into mine. "Trust me on this. Wait."

"For what?" I whispered. The pounding seemed to expand from my chest until the room seemed to rumble. I gazed into eyes so bright, they warmed my soul like a fire. "What is there left to lose?"

"Do you hear that?" Mira said suddenly, her shrewd dark eyes

175

darting toward the exit. As she spoke, a rumbling sound caught my attention, followed by the sight of the panel's water vials shaking in their holders.

"What is it?" Avin muttered as he turned toward the sound. The floor began to shake as a pounding vibration rocked the podium so violently we gripped the edges in alarm.

"What's going on?" Maza demanded as the G.B struggled to keep their footing. "Somebody go see what that…" The sudden blasting of the door several Comian lengths into the room reduced the need for questions as it sailed past the G.B's faces, their expressions unanimously stunned as it crashed into the wall on the other side of the room. I stared, dumbfounded, as our people forced their way into the room. Their faces full of fury, their voices raised in a shout of protest as they filled the space between the two podiums, pressing in closer as more and more Comians tried to push their way in.

Talon leapt over the edge of the box, disappearing into the crowd as he fought his way through the crowd to where Surina lay. As he dropped to his knees, he disappeared from view.

"Civilians retreat immediately!" the soldiers tried to yell above the noise of the crowd. "We will shoot! I repeat, civilians retreat immediately!"

But the people ignored them, emboldened by each other as they forced the soldiers right back against the walls. A shout went up as weapons were wrenched with invisible forces from the soldier's hands, shooting up into the air and bundling together in a way that made my heart leap as my eyes sought the source of their removal.

"Look!" I cried. The army of powers framed the sides of the room, their black uniforms creating a striking border against the clothing of the regular civilians.

Jonaz winked at me as my jaw dropped.

"You knew? How did you know they were coming? And the civilians?" I gaped at Jonaz who seemed to be enjoying the moment immensely.

"Because I knew they'd want answers once we leaked the information and come looking for it. And because I knew Sazika would make sure they knew where to find us when they did." As he finished his smile grew wide as he stared past my left shoulder. "There she is."

In the centre of one of the lines, and shouting orders, was Sazika.

"She's here, Mekai, she's okay!" I pointed across the room, Mekai eagerly following my arm until his eyes came to rest on his match. The relief on his face almost bought tears to my eyes as a grin broke over his face like sunshine after a storm.

"They're on our side!" Mira gasped. We gazed in awe as the Army of Powers dashed the soldier's guns against the walls, breaking them into useless pieces that rained down over the crowd. The soldiers, forced to retreat, found themselves forced to their knees with various techniques of power, and then the room was full.

Citizens of Como pressed into every inch of space, their anger crackling through the room like electricity. Even the corridor filled up, people crammed so closely together I was sure they would be crushed if there was a stampede. The noise was deafening, everyone yelling at once as they surged like a wave toward the G.B, their faces upturned and demanding, their eyes blazing with such defiance it thrilled me to the core. There was no submission in their demeanour, no fear of the ones who had controlled us for so long. Only determination to be heard, and a desire for the truth.

A civilian man leapt onto the side of our podium, middle aged but still wiry, he used the platform to yell over the others, waving his free arm frantically until the noise began to die down, and everyone turned to him expectantly.

"Why are these soldiers here without a court and jury?" the man demanded as his face swung from us to the G.B. "What right do you have to deny them a fair trial?"

"That's right!" someone in the crowd shouted. "We want answers. We want to know more about the evidence that's been leaked to us. Why has this been kept from us?"

"Because we leaked it," Avin shouted down to the crowd. "Because you deserved to know what these so called leaders have been hiding in order to control us all."

"Silence!" Maza screeched. Leaning over the railing her face contorted with rage. "How *dare* you invade us like this...like...like Abwarzians. It is you who should answer to us!"

"The audacity of you, woman!" the citizen yelled, his voice heavy with outrage. "You think we answer to you, and not the law? You think you are above the law? A law that demands a fair trial?"

"He's right!" another woman shouted. "My daughter is in the AOP. She's told me about this woman, and how she punished some of the cadets when they defied her. She's taken the law into her own hands. She thinks she can control us all!"

"It's true." a short girl with brown hair I vaguely recognised in passing stepped suddenly to the woman's side. "She locked that girl up because she fell in love with someone that wasn't her match!" I froze as the girl pointed straight at me, my heart in my throat as hundreds of eyes landed simultaneously on me.

"She did more than that," Brazin roared so suddenly the hairs on my arm stood up. "She tried to kill this girl. We found surveillance footage of this officer trying to bury her alive. There is evidence and I have it hidden in a safe place."

There was a collective gasp of horror from the crowd before individual reactions emerged.

"My God, we trusted our children with these people!" one gasped.

"This is where our loyalty lands us? With our children treated like animals?"

"That officer needs to be taken down!" another cried. "Take her down!"

The crowd responded, their roar of fury filling every corner of the room as they shook their fists at her.

"Take her down. TAKE HER DOWN!!!!!"

Like a surging wave, the people pushed toward the podium, pressing in as the judges' faces filled with terror. Maza blanched, swaying a little as she gripped the rail so hard the bone in her knuckles gleamed white under her tightly stretched flesh.

"Take her down!" the crowd roared. "Take them all down!" As the people banged their fists against the podium it began to shudder, then sway alarmingly. The G.B held onto the railing as they tried to exit the rows, but the force of the shaking grew stronger, and I cringed as one man toppled headlong over a row of seats to the front of the box, his body hitting the edge with a loud bang. Just as some of the other judges

178

reached the exit at the top of the podium, civilians were there to greet them. In no time, the judges found themselves on their knees with their arms pinioned behind their backs.

"You can't do this!" Maza screeched shrilly over the chaos, as the rest of the podium groaned and began to lean forward. Maza looked over at me, her features twisted with both fear and fury. Raising both hands from the railing she dove into the box and crash tackled the eldest member of the Governing Body. They disappeared for a moment as they fell out of sight, scuffling behind the metal barrier they had thought had kept them separate and safe from us. There was a brief lull before Maza sprang up, clutching some sort of device in the air like she'd won a trophy. The man did not rise as Maza used her other hand to point her finger at me like a dagger.

"YOU!" She screeched over the chaos. "You are an abomination! You have tainted our world, and we must have control. I must cleanse us of any threat...starting with you." I knew the device would trigger my collar to poison me. I'd seen this old trick before. My hands flew up, clutching the cold metal as my blood ran colder and I calculated the time I had to pull the device from her hands. But it was too late. Her body leant against the railing for balance, her bloody eyes blazing triumphantly as her finger came down toward the button.

BANG!!! The people shoved hard against the podium, their hands uniting to rock the podium sideways. Maza lost her balance immediately, fear flashing over her features as she pitched forward over the railing. Hurtling toward the crowd she let out a blood curdling scream before her body slammed against the side of the podium, one foot miraculously hooked on the railing.

"Take her down!" The crowd screamed, their hands outstretched toward her as she dangled precariously. "Take her DOWN!" Maza's face was white with fear as she tried and failed to lift herself up, the furious chanting of the crowd making her efforts more frantic.

"They'll kill her!" Avin cried, as he leapt onto the edge of our box. "Come on!" We have to stop them!" I stared numbly at him, then at Maza, my heart beating in time to their chanting. A huge part of me wanted her to fall, the part that wanted revenge for everything she'd done. I could just let it happen, and watch as the crowd tore her apart. I could clear myself of blame, because I was only a spectator. But I knew my conscience would never be cleared if I allowed or encouraged the violence within our race to reignite and consume us all. The people had resorted to anger so quickly it frightened me. It didn't matter how much we said we wanted peace and freedom, it was apparent we still didn't know how to achieve it without more violence. There had to be some level of control, or war would never end, not in our world, or the next.

BANG! The crowd rammed the podium once more. Maza gasped and let go of the device as she flailed, her fingers clawing yet slipping on the smooth sides of the judges' box. One of the civilians snatched it from the air, then held it gingerly in front of him, not sure what to do with it.

"Give it to me." Brazin bellowed to the man. "It activates these collars."

The man obeyed, throwing the device at Brazin, who raised one last hand to catch it. Brazin peered at it, his eyebrows momentarily drawing together in concentration before he grunted in satisfaction, made a fist, and simply punched it. The device shattered into fragments, and instantly the collars sprang open, falling from our necks as we simultaneously sighed with relief.

BANG! Maza finally fell, and as the crowd stretched out their hands to catch her, a terrified wail ripped from her lungs as she realised her fate.

My brain ignited, my powers shooting out of me so fast my head spun and I yelled with the effort. They stung, my mind flinching as it remembered how to use the telekinetic part of my brain that I thought was long dead. Using all of my energy to focus I reached with my mind over the crowd and caught Maza mid-air. Her body jerked to a stop, upside down, and just out of reach of the crowds reaching hands. They fell silent, stonily watching her progress as I lifted her higher. I focused on keeping her aloft while I addressed the crowd.

"STOP!" I yelled. "Don't you get it? If you choose to react this way, with violence, then we are no better than her! We are still no better than our ancestors, and certainly no better than our enemies. Where will it ever end?"

"But then, where is the justice?" Someone in the crowd roared back. "These people have lied to us and suppressed us for too long. They must be punished."

"That's right!" the people chanted, "What about justice!" As they shook their fists up at Maza, my resolve nearly weakened, my grip on her momentarily relaxing as my head battled with my heart. Maza lurched a few inches lower, and her instant wail jolted my senses as I regained my focus. She gazed at me in desperation as I lifted her a little higher. The challenge had drained from her eyes as fear for her life overwhelmed her.

"People of Como," I began, my voice shaking with the effort of holding her up, as well as with nerves. "I went to Abwarz, to find my guardian. I learned a lot about them. Their citizens are more oppressed than we are, and their leaders more controlling. But we fought them, and their leaders have been arrested or eliminated."

"Well, we know that much," a disgruntled looking man scoffed loudly. "They don't mind telling us when the truth is in their favour."

"It is the truth," I replied breathlessly as nerves shook through me. "They are not without blame, but neither are we. And just like us, they are longing for change, for a better way, for freedom. Today, in this room, we either prove we can live in that better way, or we prove they were right when they said we needed to be controlled. Which choice will you make today?"

The people looked up at me gravely as the truth of my words sank in. As the tension in the room lessened, I felt Talon's powers tangle with mine mid-air, taking some of the load. I searched for his face in the crowd and found him, carrying Surina's body in his arms as he slowly made his way back toward us. The crowd parted for him as some of the Army of powers emerged through the crowd, approaching Talon with outstretched arms.

"We are healers, let us take her and see what we can do." A young man took her from Talon's arms and disappeared into the crowd. A moment later they were all seen exiting the hall as several AOP soldiers followed him. I didn't know how many of them it might take to save her, or if it was even possible. But I prayed to the universe that it was as her lifeless body disappeared from view.

"They have told you we wanted a rebellion. But that's not the truth. All we want is the right to choose our futures and our partners. No more and no less. Not violence, power, or control. Just our free will. There is no need for a fight. That's what we stand for and that is what we are asking, for all of us." To demonstrate, I pulled Maza down toward Brazin's podium, Talon helping as he realised what I wanted. The look of disgust on Brazin's face as she was deposited beside him was priceless. Maza cowered beside him as he glowered down at her, and I stifled the sudden urge to laugh as she tried to shrink away from him inside the tiny box.

"Genetics have played a part in creating a better world," I went on, "but we want the option of love matches for those who choose it, and for the partnering age to be extended or abolished. Our generation is no longer content to have these matters decided for us."

"It's true," a blonde woman with too many worry lines around her face called out from amongst the crowd, "My child is of age and she is beside herself with anxiety and stress. Is this really what we want for our children? Our population is largely recovered. We have to question why this law continues to be necessary."

"She's right. It's outdated," another civilian cried as people began to nod their heads.

"But who will lead us?" someone in the crowd shouted. "It cannot be the G.B anymore.

"Will you lead us?" A woman pointed at me, her face so full of expectation, my stomach rolled in retaliation.

"No, no. Our leaders have not always let us down, "I replied carefully as I raised my eyes to the G.B. "They have worked hard to create a safe and sustainable world for us. If they are willing to change some of our laws, I see no reason some of them can't continue to lead us." I looked at Maza very purposefully to emphasise the 'some' part, and the crowd growled in approval. I felt a small twinge of pity as Maza cowered under everyone's stare. It was hard to believe she was ever capable of looking so pathetic. Her once immaculate hair was pulled in all directions, and her beady red eyes were darting and nervous as she avoided my gaze.

"A voting system once worked on Earth, "Avin spoke up over my left shoulder. "Perhaps we can look into this method again to rebuild a fairer system, with our leaders help?"

We all looked to the Governing Body, reading their expressions. Some would stay and be open to change, but others would be quickly overthrown. That much was obvious from the looks on their faces. The elder Governor was doing a great impression of a statue. His whole body was rigid, his features carved into disbelief. But the people responded favourably, their faces filled with new hope and assurance.

"There's one more thing you need to know," I called out as people began to talk amongst themselves. "The general population of Abwarz have asked for our help in learning to conserve water, so they no longer need to borrow from other worlds."

"It's true," Avin chimed in suddenly "Our peacekeepers and soldiers are there as we speak and can attest to this. They are helping them to re-establish order now that their leaders have been overthrown or executed. They want our help to cultivate their world and attempt to increase their own water supplies and farming. We can work with them, not against them. We can help them. Then there is no need for any more war."

Silence stretched out across the room in response, my heart in my throat as I searched my people's eyes for any flicker of hope. I saw their hesitation and understood it. It was such a struggle to believe something that went against the lies they'd been fed for so long.

To my right, Jonaz pressed his lips together, and began to whistle a long low tune. A shiver rocked down my spine as the people caught on, the responding sound of unified whistling bursting out of them in a crescendo of harmony so deafening and determined it crashed over us all, as powerful as a wave. As the possibility of new beginnings washed over us all, wild joy filled my heart so full it overflowed as my own lips pursed to join in unison with my peoples cry of support.

"We want these soldiers pardoned." The man still clinging to the podium glared up at Maza before he leapt to the ground and strode out into the crowd where he could see the GB, still detained on the next level. "They are just kids who had more guts than us to stand up for what's fair and enlighten us all. So let them go, they've earned it."

"Well, erm, I guess we could discuss the possibility that their misconduct was a crime of passion…" the older Governor mumbled, looking helplessly at his colleagues who were no help at all in their shocked state.

"Yes. Maybe they are too young to serve. The pressure got to them perhaps," another GB mused as she twiddled nervously with the tassels of her robe.

"They are asking for mercy." My voice was tight with emotion as I looked hard at each member of the GB. "I begged the Abwarzians for mercy when they were murdering my guardian." I stopped for a moment as grief choked the words in my throat. Jonaz took my hand quietly in his, his fingers locking through mine and giving me strength. "They refused. So it seems to me that mercy might be the only difference between them and us. But that decision is in your hands."

"Pardon them! Pardon them!" the people chanted in unison, the sound so loud it sent a shiver down my spine.

"No!" Maza squawked desperately from her huddled corner. "You can't let them go unpunished or…"

"You have no more voice here." The elder GB turned his fierce gaze on Maza. "It is you who needs to stand trial, for abuse of power and that collar that is a crime against humanity."

"What?" The blood drained from Maza's face, her shock reducing her squeak to a high-pitched wail. "You'll never get away with this! How dare you… don't touch meeeeeeee."

"Where's your dignity woman? Get it together." Looking happier than I'd ever seen him, Brazin pinned Maza's arms behind her back, her furious struggling no match for his sheer size, let alone determination. Giving her a little shove, she toppled straight off the podium into the waiting hands of the Comian Officers.

Handcuffing her, her undignified shrieking as she was carried away, was met with the jeers and boos of the crowd as she struggled and kicked futilely. Her glare was poisonous as she looked over her shoulder to screech her final threat.

"This isn't over… I promise you!" she bellowed before she was lifted off her feet and carried by four officers from the hall.

"Oh dear. Isn't that what all the villains say?" I grinned as I turned to Jonaz.

Jonaz snorted with mirth before his expression sobered. "Do you hear that?" He smiled widely as he reached out and smoothed a strand of my forever-tangled hair off my face. "That's the sound of hope."

The cloak of hopelessness that had weighed down my heart for so long lifted off me, falling away as my spirit soared high above the crowd. Feeling reborn, and stronger than ever before, I gazed into the eyes of the man I had chosen to love. "And with hope, we have a future."

Chapter Eighteen

The partnering ceremony was held a moon later. On a calm clear day, in the cool of the evening, the distant suns sank slowly, casting a pearlescent glow over the distant marshy plains. Soft twinkling lights wove through the rambling creepers covering the walls of the courtyard, while trickling water flowed harmoniously from several water features throughout the courtyard. The sound mingled with the soft chink of crystal as we raised our glasses to the brilliant evening sky.

"To Mekai and Sazika," the celebrant led the salute. "May your partnership be harmonious in union, and abundant in offspring!"

"Erm… I think they still need to work on the wording," I muttered as I witnessed Sazika's cheeks match the colour of her hair.

"Shoosh you, don't ruin the moment." Jonaz winked at me before he downed his flute of sparkling relaxation fluid in one gulp. "This is what they want. That's all that matters."

I sipped my drink slowly, savouring the relaxing sensation melting slowly through my muscles as I observed the newly partnered couple. Sazika had styled her flaming red hair in loose curls down her back, while ropes of heirloom Earth water pearls had been woven through the crown of her hair. Her cream dress was simple but lovely, with long sleeves and a low waist, then falling to her gold sandaled feet in soft pleats. She looked gorgeous, but it was her features that dazzled me the most and left me with no doubts over her choice. She loved Mekai. It was evident from the light in her eyes, and the glow in her expression.

"Just look at Mekai's face," Mira Reen sighed to my right. "A perfect example of why I still hold hope for our partnering laws, amended or not. You can't say they haven't matched these two perfectly."

I rolled my eyes, as I turned to grin at Mira. "Oh, so you've set the date for your own matching ceremony then?'

"Don't be silly.'' Mira tore her eyes away from the newlyweds to scowl at me, immediately ruining the effect of her softer hairstyle and striking deep purple gown. "Now they've relaxed the partnering laws, I see no harm in taking time to get used to each other."

"Get used to each other?" I raised an eyebrow, trying not to smirk. "That's romance, right there."

A wicked gleam filled Mira's dark narrowed eyes as she raised one finger and pointed it in my direction.

"Now, now ladies," Kina reprimanded us primly as she moved her dark blue clad skinny figure smoothly between us. "The only power that should be witnessed here today, is the power of love."

"Excuse me whilst I go and vomit." Mira stalked away with such a disgusted expression I began to giggle, and snorted relaxation fluid right up my nose.

"Classy," Jonaz chuckled as I spluttered. Before I could respond Talon approached, notably absent of his match.

"How's Surina?" I asked, getting straight to the point. The last I'd heard, she was still in a coma.

"She's recovering," Talon replied softly, "but slowly. She has to learn to walk again. And swallow…talk…"

"Wow," Jonaz answered. "It must be hard for you, watching her going through this. We will visit her on the new moon."

"She doesn't want to see you, or me for that matter. "Talon shrugged apologetically. "She applied to annul our match, and I signed the petition. Like we told you, we never wanted to be together. Now she's released from our obligation, I hope she can just concentrate on getting better."

As I struggled with what to say to Talon, a large presence appeared in my peripheral vision, and I looked up with relief to see Brazin looming over us, looking uncomfortably awkward in the Armies black ceremonial uniform.

"Wow, Brazin, you scrub up okay. The medal adds a nice touch." I tried not to smirk as Brazin actually blushed for the first time I'd ever witnessed. He'd received the medal as a citizen's award for keeping our fugitive party safe from Maza. What a turn around. From traitor to hero, because the people had spoken. My own medal was sitting in a drawer at home because I wasn't quite sure what to do with it. It felt silly to display it when I didn't even know how I felt about it.

"What's the progress with Maza's trial?" Jonaz asked Brazin while I used my powers to whisk three fresh vials of relaxation liquor from a passing wait staff's tray. No sooner had I floated them over, Brazin grabbed his out of the air and downed the vial in one large gulp.

"They need you to come in again, to add a few details to your statements." Brazin dropped his voice as he glanced around us. "She's fabricating quite a case against you, but there's no cause for concern. She abused her position, and they have at least three charges against her for abuse of power."

Jonaz took my hand quietly in his as I breathed deeply and squeezed his fingers. The liquor had not relaxed me quite enough to erase the anxiety I felt whenever Maza's name was raised. I dreaded the coming case, even though it was certain she'd be found guilty. They had pardoned my crimes based on believing they were a direct result of Maza's abuse, and other witness accounts, including many of the soldiers at the Army base who testified that Maza had gone too far with her own agenda. From locking me up at the Army camp, to the attempted murder, which still needed to be proved. At the end of the day, I just did not want to see her face again, unless it was behind a thick window of protective glass. Only the thought of that steeled my resolve to get through the trial.

"Hey." Brazin slapped a dinner plate sized hand onto my shoulder as he glared down at me affectionately. "Don't you worry, kid. I won't let that woman see the suns again for a very long time. I won't let her touch you. Not under my watch."

"Brazin. I..." My eyes watered suddenly, a mutual surge of affection choking up my words. "I can't ever thank you enough for everything you have done for me and my friends..."

"Okay kid, no need to thank me." Brazin grunted, but he squeezed my shoulder and grinned. "I'll leave you be to enjoy the night. But just remember you're all still soldiers with a reputation to uphold. So go easy on the drinks and stay classy. Don't let me down."

"Yes, Sir!" Jonaz and I chortled as Brazin spun and strode off into the crowd.

"Twell?" A familiar yet hesitant voice uttered my name. I spun around, my mouth dropping open in shocked recognition.

"Meela! Dash? What are you doing here?" My first impulse was to launch myself into my oldest friend's arms, but I checked myself at the last moment, startled by the changes in both of their appearances. Meela had aged. Much more than the moons that had passed between us. Her once round face had thinned out, making her huge wide eyes look even larger as she stared at me soberly. Her grey hair was no longer in a topknot, the way she had nearly always worn it at school, instead she'd cropped it to chin level, and tucked it behind her ears. She smiled at me finally, a tentative ghost of a smile that didn't quite reach her eyes. When I turned to look at Dash, I thought I knew why. The last time I'd seen him, he'd been an enthusiastic new cadet, finally fulfilling his dream of being a soldier of Como. We'd argued about his ambitions so many times over the last several moons of our schooling. I'd never wanted to be in the army, and Dash had been openly jealous when I'd been conscripted. But now, his haunted gaze conveyed his jealousy was long gone, replaced by the grim reality of the horrors of war. His hair was shorn off, revealing a jagged scar over his left eyebrow, while angry scars tracked down both of his forearms.

"Twellodrama." His old teasing grin made him more recognisable. "Can I have your autograph? You're famous now, you know."

"Oh Dash, stop, it's not funny," Meela said uncertainly, looking at me to gauge my reaction.

"Group hug!" I demanded, throwing myself at the both of them. Meela gasped, her features flickering through a range of emotions before she settled on relief. A small sob caught in her throat as she buried her face in my shoulder. I held her tighter as Dash awkwardly patted us both on the back.

"Er...there there..." Dash muttered as I laughed and broke away.

"How did you guys know we were here?" I finally asked as Jonaz wrapped an arm around my shoulder.

"Because I invited them," Sazika said from behind me. I turned as she and Mekai entered our little huddle, their faces beaming with satisfaction. "Now it's a partnering ceremony slash high school reunion." Mira had returned, and her scowl had morphed into a genuine smile as she greeted Meela and Dash with the traditional palm to cheek gesture.

"It's really good to see you guys," Mira said sincerely. "Dash, did you fight on Abwarz?"

"Yes, in the second fleet sent." Dash nodded. "We went to their smaller cities to extract their old leaders and implement the new peace treaty."

"How did they receive you?" Jonaz asked. "Isn't there still several divisions there now?"

"The smaller towns seemed willing to comply," Dash replied solemnly. "They were so malnourished, it didn't take much to convince them a treaty was in their best interests. But the bigger towns seemed less trusting. All of their leaders are being contained whilst we attempt to work with them."

"But what if they refuse?" I frowned. "We can't force them to believe us, or submit…"

"Well, that's where Avin and Stelli are right now," Talon replied. "Peacekeeping."

I was silent for a moment, as the mention of Avin's name caused a strange pang in my heart. I missed him. I missed many things about him. I hoped he was okay up there, so far away from his friends. I didn't have much faith Stelli would be capable of watching his back though, since she'd never been much of a fighter. In fact, I was pretty certain she was beginning to focus more on his front. I'd seen the way she'd begun to look at him before they'd left, and it was as gooey eyed as the way she'd once looked at Jonaz. I wanted him to be loved, I secretly thought she was a much better match for him. Not because of genetics, but because of their natures. At any rate, they both deserved to be happy.

"But what are they doing exactly?" Meela asked as innocently as any regular civilian still would. "Do they still need to keep the peace up there?"

"They are using their powers to re-educate some of the more resistive citizens, without harming them." Mira shrugged. "It's necessary, to keep things in order."

"Oh. If you don't include brainwashing as harming them." I felt my heart sinking as I looked at my friends in dismay. "We're still forcing them to bend to our will. We still haven't evolved, as long as one of us is still controlling the other."

"Oh, please. Who cares if we are." Mira sniffed. "After all, the point of having a war is to win."

Uncomfortable silence overcame us all for a moment, threatening to ruin the mood of the occasion. It was clear we would not all agree, and I knew that many challenges would lie ahead when it came to navigating a new order. But now was not the time for such battles. For one day, I wanted to feel like any other girl, celebrating her friend's big day.

"Well, there we don't agree." I shook my head, pushing the darker thoughts away. "But right now, is not the time for such debates. Are we going to dance soon or what?"

"Yes, please!" Sazika's face lit up with new excitement. Mekai nodded to the band, who took up their instruments in response. "Just one rule, Mekai, no flying in this dance…you've drank too much relaxation fluid and you might drop me…"

"I would never!" Mekai retorted amongst the laughter and jeering erupting around him. But he was smiling as he led her to the middle of the dance floor. The guests circled the floor, and a hush fell before we pursed our lips and began to whistle a few long notes in unison, the traditional congratulations before the music could begin. The band began to weave a melody that was both beautiful and haunting. Mekai took Sazika in his arms and moved her in time to the beat. They moved in graceful rhythm, and then slowly rose off the floor, Mekai holding her tightly until they were waltzing in the air.

"Mekai! You promised…" Sazika's shriek turned into a giggle and a shake of her head as she put her feet on his and rested her head on his shoulder. Lost in each other as the music swelled, the band changed key, signalling the guests could now join the dance.

"Finally!" Jonaz seized my waist in his hands, turning me toward him in one easy manoeuvre as he winked at me. "I've never had the chance to show you what an incredibly amazing dancer I am."

191

"So modest." I grinned as I fell into his arms and allowed him to lead me amongst the guests. I gasped as he whirled me out of his arms, then back in, spinning me smoothly in time to the music, his body moving against mine so naturally it was like we'd done this forever. I felt lighter than air as my soul filled with exhilaration. Jonaz looked so handsome in his white shirt and light coloured pants, his dark hair curling slightly around his ears as he spun me in a full circle with ease. Blood flushed my cheeks as he smiled at me, filling my heart with warmth and light.

A movement caught my eyes as I whirled around. My vision was still pretty blurry most days, and I was now short sighted where I'd previously had perfect vision. But there was no mistaking the dark presence leaning against the far wall of the courtyard, close to the back exit.

My head whipped around, and as Jonaz spun me again and I stared straight into the eyes of Shanna Vane. The music seemed to pause, along with my heartbeat as Shanna's icy gaze froze me in time. It seemed like I had an eternity to take in her altered appearance. Her legs were no longer flesh and bone, replaced by metal and electronics as she balanced her weight on a walking stick in each tight fist. Her head had been shaved, making the angles of her features sharper, and the narrowing of her eyes made her look meaner as her lips curled in mocking disdain. In one moment, one look, I knew why she was here and what she had come to say. Jonaz wrapped his arms around me from behind, oblivious to her existence, or how stiff I'd become as he rocked me in time to the music. I'd never been a good lip reader, but I didn't miss a single word as she mouthed her promise to me.

"This is just the beginning. With or without you."

Before I could react, or pull away, the direction of the dance changed, the music picking up-tempo as Jonaz pulled me into his arms, and spun me again so I lost sight of her. I paused for a moment, in the middle of the dance floor as I scanned the room to see where she'd gone. But she was nowhere to be found. She'd delivered her message. She knew that was enough. The rebellion was bigger than me now, and out of my control. Where I was happy to compromise in exchange for peace, I knew now that others would not accept any more laws from the

G.B. They wanted a new order, with new leaders. I knew without a doubt Shanna intended to be one of those leaders.

The music changed, slowed as I shook my head and Jonaz pulled me into a slow embrace. Tomorrow would bring its own worries. Maybe war would never end. But today I had peace, and all the people I loved around me, and for now that was more than enough.

"You're beautiful," Jonaz whispered. Holding both of my hands, he pushed me away from him to look at me, his eyes glowing with feelings that made me shiver. My pale gold gown was woven with darker golden thread that matched the flecks of gold in Jonaz's rich warm eyes. My hair, finally tangle free, fell in soft waves down my back, the way Jonaz loved it best.

As he pulled me close again, he wove one hand through my hair and pulled my face to his. His kiss captured me prisoner, washing over me far more effectively than any relaxation drink as my bones seemed to melt. I clung onto him tightly, afraid I'd fall as the spell of our love mesmerised me more completely than any hypnotic power. When he finally released me, I gasped for air before I realised our friends were jeering and whistling around us.

"Oh, for the planet's sake," Mira groaned, rolling her eyes for the thousandth time. "There's a time and a place…"

"Geez, you two are just as bad as ever." Dash grinned as he slapped Jonaz on the back. Meela giggled behind her hand in a way that reminded me of our school days.

Sazika shot Mekai such an anxious look he burst into fresh laughter. PDA was not her thing, nor usually mine.

"Get matched, then get a room and spare us all." Mekai winked. Jonaz only shook his head while I blushed as red as Sazikas's hair.

"He has a point." Jonaz grinned, "The cave was never the right time or place."

"Hold your mogas," I protested, pulling back to study his face, "We've only just annulled our own matches. Don't you want to just enjoy being free for a while?"

"Free to love you?" A flicker of uncertainty faded his smile, as he contemplated my words. "That's freedom, for me."

"I know, Jonaz, me too…and I am never going to leave you again.

I promise." The reassurance in his answering smile curved my own lips as I continued. "But what's the rush? We can decide what else we want to do with our lives now that there are more choices."

"They're finding ways around it though," Jonaz muttered somewhat jadedly, "putting pressure on us to donate our cells or bodies for artificial insemination."

"Or the cloning programme idea they want to vote on." I shuddered, feeling a sudden chill. "Don't even get me started on that doozy."

"It's still a 'voluntary option' though." Jonaz grinned mischievously before mimicking the tone of the latest GB broadcast. "A noble and loyal choice for those who loyally and willingly support our worlds' genetic endeavours for perfection and evolution."

"Mmmm, yeah. Not manipulative at all." I smirked. "But as we are so disloyal and selfish, we'll have plenty of time to explore our new lives, and more time to explore each other…"

The music moved into a faster tune and everyone began to dance around us. But Jonaz held me tight and still, his steady gaze removing the rest of the world as a slow smile grew on his lips.

"You're right." His deep warm eyes twinkled with the challenge as he moved us to a rhythm only we knew. "I think in the old world, they used to do this thing called dating. So what would you like to do on your first date, Twell Anar?"

"Well, for a start, I like long walks in the wetlands."

THE END

About the Author

Kate O'Leary, has loved reading and writing ever since she was young enough to try and get through the back of her cupboard into Narnia, or through her mirror into Wonderland! In high school, she entertained her homeroom reading out chapters of her first novel 'Miranda' about a teenage girls adventures with her horse Rusty. After school Kate studied Children's Literature, and her first drafts of Twell were awarded in writing competitions. Kate's writing interest is firmly embedded in dystopian fantasy, being continually fascinated with the future direction of our world and the concepts of free will and moral vs. lawful obligations. Twell's adventures will continue to explore these ideas in the Como Chronicles Trilogy.

Kate lives in the beautiful Adelaide Hills of Australia, surrounded by rolling hills and wineries and horses, as well as some good rocks to climb when she feels like scaring herself!

Twellanar@gmail.com
https://www.facebook.com/TwellComoChronicles?ref=tn_tnmn
http://twellcomochronicles.webs.com
https://twitter.com/twell2012

Other Books by Kate O'Leary

Twell, Book 1 of the Como Chronicles
Twell and the Rebellion, Book 2 of the Como Chronicles